The Earl Who Played With Fire

A MUSES OF MAYFAIR NOVEL

Sara Ramsey

The Earl Who Played With Fire is a work of fiction. Names, characters, places and incidences are the products of the author's imagination or are used fictitiously. Any resemblance to actual events, locales, or persons, living or dead, is entirely coincidental. The Publisher does not have any control over and does not assume responsibility for author or third-party websites or their content.

ISBN (epub): 978-1-938312-07-6
ISBN (paperback): 978-1-938312-03-8

For my sister

CHAPTER ONE

London, March 1813

Miss Prudence Etchingham was expected to admire the paintings. Instead, she covertly admired the man standing across the room. His back was to her. She preferred to see his face, but this angle had its own charms. His shoulders were broad, capable of carrying something heavier than the burdens of an earldom. His dark hair could have been wild if he weren't quite so proper. The tails of his coat obscured his backside, but they accentuated his well-toned legs.

Not that Prudence should have noticed his legs. She shouldn't have noticed anything about him. But after years of secret study, she knew every curve of his smile, every line on his face.

And when she let herself daydream — as she often did — she could pretend that he had given her his love, not just his charity.

"Fascinating exhibit, don't you think?" her friend Ellie said.

Mr. John Soane's townhouse had some of the best artifacts in London, and he regularly allowed others to attend public viewings of his collection. Prudence turned to her friend and strove for an innocent expression. "It is vastly intriguing."

The marchioness laughed and lowered her voice. "I may be married now, but I haven't lost all my observational powers. When do you plan to tell Salford of your feelings?"

Prudence glanced back at Alex — the Earl of Salford, if she was being proper. There were enough people between them to dampen Ellie's voice, but not enough to block the view. "If he wants me, he knows where to find me."

She had lived in his house for months. Her mother, Lady Harcastle, had attempted to arrange a marriage for Prudence the previous summer, but the engagement had died before it was announced. If Alex's mother hadn't offered Prudence a position as her companion out of pity, Prudence's care would have been foisted off on a cousin instead.

Her mother didn't have the money for another Season, particularly when Prudence was such a bad investment. She only had enough funds left to move between relatives and snipe at Prudence for her failures.

Ellie leaned in to whisper in her ear. "Men can be quite stupid. It took Nick a decade to come to his senses and come home to me. If you can help Salford to realize his feelings sooner, it's better for both of you."

Prudence shook her head. "Nick knew he loved you. He merely had to act upon it. Lord Salford has made no such overture."

"Men," Ellie pronounced. "I think he is besotted with you."

Prudence glanced toward Alex again. This time, she caught him watching her instead of the paintings.

She knew why myths and Biblical tales featured so many fools who looked back and died because of it. She'd never been able to ignore the temptation of looking at him. But today, his gaze killed her. He stood under a skylight, seemingly lit up just for her. She would always remember him like that, half-turned toward her, his body poised halfway between seeking her out and stepping back into the shadows.

Her breath caught. She met his eyes. She always met his eyes, hoping to see something there that would give her an answer.

The beam of sunlight was blotted out by an errant cloud. His eyes dimmed. Prudence dropped hers, not needing to watch as he turned back to the paintings.

She had to stop looking, stop searching for the heart he would likely never give her. She focused resolutely on Ellie. "If he is so besotted, he can tell me. I've better things to do with my time than wait for him."

Ellie was gracious enough — or perceptive enough — not to ask what those things were.

Or perhaps she would have asked, if given time, but they were interrupted before Ellie could continue her campaign. "Lady Folkestone," the newcomer said, bowing over Ellie's hand. "I thought we had lost you to that uncultured man you married. You must stop in to my shop and select a wedding present."

Ellie laughed. Her new husband, the Marquess of Folkestone, was a wealthy trader who had unexpectedly inherited the title. "I'm not lost. Our honeymoon didn't end until a week ago. Still, you should be careful not to insult my husband to his face or he might run you out of business."

"I trust you'll disarm him," Ostringer said.

It was odd banter — but then, Ellie knew everyone in the ton and half the people outside it, and she seemed to share some private joke with all of them. Her smile was supremely satisfied. "No need to disarm him," she said. "The ton will never believe it, but marriage suits us."

Prudence felt a little kick of jealousy — just enough to hate herself for it. Her three closest friends had married wealthy, titled men in the past year. All of them had been love matches.

She was still enough of her old self to be ashamed of how jealous she was. But her new self had bigger problems.

And one of those problems stood in front of her, pretending to be a stranger. Ellie turned to Prudence. "Miss Etchingham, may I present to you Mr. Ostringer? He owns an antiquities shop of some renown."

Prudence held out her hand as though she and Ostringer had never met. "How do you do, Mr. Ostringer?"

"Charmed, Miss Etchingham," he said, bowing over it and betraying nothing.

"My dear friend has a passion for antiquities," Ellie said to the shopkeeper.

Ostringer lifted first one eyebrow, then the other, as though this fact surprised him. It nearly made her laugh even after all these months. Perhaps the gesture amused her because his brows were so prodigious. They rioted under his equally riotous iron grey hair. He was tall, slightly heavyset, but still agile. He must have been nearing sixty years of age, but beyond his hair and the web of lines around his eyes, there were few signs of decay.

"How unusual," he said. "I thought lovely young ladies such as yourself would be more interested in dressmakers than antiquities purveyors."

His statement was innocuous. She responded in kind. "Young ladies are becoming remarkably daring in the modern age, Mr. Ostringer. An interest in antiquities isn't unusual."

Ladies were permitted to have a casual interest in antiquities, particularly as it pertained to decorating their homes. No one liked it if they attempted to make a scholarly career of it, though. Mr. Ostringer smiled. "I thank you for the modern age. If you will pardon my unseemly mention of business matters, my shop does better when the fairer sex embraces yet another decorating scheme."

"The fairer sex and the Prince Regent," Ellie said drily.

Ostringer laughed. "His Royal Highness would be a better ruler if he spent less time redesigning his palaces, but he's doing quite a good job for me."

"Surely you're more civic-minded than that," Prudence teased.

"Don't mistake me, Miss Etchingham. I want the best for Britain. But if the best happens to sell more antiquities…"

He shrugged. His smile was pleasant, but there was something sharp about Ostringer's face that his laughter and wild eyebrows couldn't hide. Prudence suspected he could be quite ruthless. But he had not yet been ruthless with her.

Ellie laughed, but whatever comment she might have made about Ostringer was lost when her husband joined them. "My lord," Ellie said to the marquess. "May I present to you Mr. Ostringer? He keeps an antiquities shop in Mayfair."

Another man might have had heart palpitations at the thought of his wife associating with a shopkeeper, but Nick was either a better man than most, or he had come to terms with Ellie's odd social circles. He shook Ostringer's hand. "Pleased to meet you, Ostringer. I believe I can hold you responsible for half the contents of my home."

Ostringer nodded. "I would be pleased to provide more, should your wife choose to redecorate again."

Nick wrapped his arm around Ellie's waist — not particularly proper, but then, neither of them were particularly proper. "I'm sure she will someday. But I plan to keep her too entertained to think about it for at least a decade."

Ellie blushed. She rarely blushed. With her red hair, it was quite the sight.

Prudence felt another stab of jealousy. Ellie and Nick were newly wed, and the love between them still burned hot enough to scorch innocent bystanders. She looked back at Alex, driven by an instinct that overruled all common sense. But he wasn't where he'd been before. He must have left the room without her noting it.

And without inviting her along.

She'd missed whatever Ellie's reply had been, but Nick laughed — something low and magical, as though he'd forgotten that they had an audience. "Will you come to the staircase with me?" he asked Ellie. "I have something I wish to show you."

Prudence very much doubted that Nick cared for most of the art in Soane's house — he just wanted Ellie to himself. But Ellie nodded and turned to Prudence. "Do you mind if I leave you for a moment?" Ellie asked. "Not that you need my chaperonage at an event such as this."

Prudence waved her away. "If you had told me a year ago that the infamous Lady Folkestone would chaperone me, I would have vowed to eat my hat. I'm sure I won't get into any mischief worse than what you would push me into."

Ellie's sly smile said she would happily push Prudence into mischief if given half a chance. But she said her farewells as though nothing was amiss. That left Prudence with Ostringer, who thankfully still pretended he didn't know her. "Have you seen Mr. Soane's pottery collection, Miss Etchingham?" he asked.

She shook her head. "Lady Folkestone insisted on viewing the paintings while the light was still good."

Mr. Soane had installed clever skylights and windows, just as he had when designing the Bank of London, so the entire collection was more visible and vibrant than anything one usually saw in a private home. Ostringer pressed his point. "You seem to be the type of young lady who prefers objects to paintings. Would you care to accompany me?"

She glanced around the room. There was no one left whom she knew, but that didn't mean gossip wouldn't spread if someone overheard the wrong thing. "This is not a good time for a discussion," she said, lowering her voice.

Ostringer shook his head. "I am well aware, Miss Etchingham. No discussion is required. But there is something I wish to show you."

It was unusual of her to leave a room with a man she claimed not to know, but it was daylight and they were in a public space. Her reputation would be safe enough.

She allowed him to escort her into the hall. Soane's collections were quickly outgrowing his available space, even though he had just finished combining his original townhouse with the one next door. The hall had several shelves of objects crammed into every inch of wall space. A few people were exploring the curios and artifacts displayed there, but Prudence knew them only by sight from nine years of parties and excursions. None of them would remark on her presence.

"What do you wish to show me?" she asked Ostringer.

He gestured to one of the shelves. "There is a most unusual object in Soane's collection. A rare piece of pottery, if I'm not mistaken."

She peered in the direction he had pointed. She saw what he meant immediately, but she took her time, schooling her features so that they would give nothing away. "Very rare, Mr. Ostringer. You have a good eye for what may interest me."

"I sold it to him a week ago. I am not surprised that it took pride of place in this cabinet. It is very well made, after all."

Prudence knew how well-made it was. It had been buried in Lady Salford's garden for a month. It now looked weathered, but it had easily survived the freeze and thaw of London in February. Her arm hadn't survived it so easily; digging into the frozen turf had been a challenge that left her muscles sore for days.

She straightened her spine. "Mr. Soane has excellent taste. But I am surprised he acquired this."

"The artist is very talented."

She didn't like his use of present tense. "I would have thought this piece more likely to appeal to a dilettante instead of a scholar."

That was the agreement they had made — that he would only sell her pieces to amateurs, people who would never realize that they had bought a forgery. Ostringer shrugged. "Soane felt he had to have it. Who am I to deny him when he's so sure of the provenance?"

She was sure she was blushing, and equally sure that Soane's blasted skylights would betray her. "Have you sold any similar objects to scholars of Mr. Soane's standing?"

Ostringer pretended to think for a moment. "The Duke of Thorington has bought several pieces recently. You may also recognize an urn that Mr. Thomas Hope purchased, should you attend one of the exhibitions at his house. But you will have to look elsewhere if you want something similar — I find myself quite out of stock."

She couldn't help herself. "Out of stock?" she asked.

"Completely." His smile wasn't ruthless this time — it was conspiratorial. "If you'll allow me to bore you with business talk again, I can share that the profit approached five hundred pounds."

Five hundred pounds. "I should congratulate you on your good fortune," she said.

She was dizzy with it. Her share would be three hundred —
enough to set herself up in a little house somewhere for a year, if she
was careful with her spending and didn't try to keep a carriage or a
horse.

He inclined his head. "I'm of course eager to make more profit."

"Perhaps you could sell scarabs?" she suggested. "I know they're
not as fashionable as they once were, but they are very easy to store."

She knew they were easy to store. She had several of them hidden in jars of tea under her bed, developing the proper patina. But
Ostringer sighed. "Scarab beetles are all well and good. But they aren't
quite…audacious enough."

"Do you wish to be audacious?"

Prudence was careful to keep their conversation hypothetical. He
responded in kind, but not as kindly as she expected. "Scarabs will
bring a profit, but not as much as one might wish. If I could have my
way, I would demand something worth far more than that."

She wasn't sure she liked the word "demand," but the idea of
making more money thrilled her. She had been preparing smaller forgeries for months — ever since she had begun to realize that she would
likely never marry and would need to find a way to feed herself. She
had started by repainting bits of pottery or stones to match the older
styles. They were easy to do on her own in the endless hours when she
should have been darning socks or sitting as an ornament at Alex's
mother's at-homes. But as she had reinvested her first profits into paying artisans to craft more ambitious pieces, her dreams had grown.

She could make enough to be independent. She could even make
enough to support her mother, if she felt like clasping that viper to her
breast.

But she had yet to make a major piece, one that would bring a significant sum of money. And that would take far more effort. She shook her head as she looked at him. "Audacity sounds intriguing, Mr. Ostringer. But it is also a bigger risk."

Ostringer smiled. "The men who can afford a bigger risk are usually not as intelligent as they think they are. I've sold more pieces than I can count to men who thought they knew what they were doing."

His smile wasn't very kind. In fact, it was rather wolfish. Had she grabbed a wolf by the tail when she had made her bargain with him?

She wouldn't worry about it yet — but it might be wise not to put all of her eggs in Mr. Ostringer's rather questionable basket. She nodded as though she wasn't considering anything but what she might make for him. "Perhaps I will stop by in a few weeks to see your collection. I would like to see what you may sell next."

A shadow fell on them, making her glad that their conversation had been circumspect. "Miss Etchingham," Alex said.

Why did his voice make her shiver? "My lord," she said, turning to him. "May I present to you Mr. Ostringer? He is an antiquities collector."

"I know who he is," Alex said.

His voice snapped. Ostringer didn't blink. "My dear Lord Salford. How do you do?"

Alex didn't respond. He turned to Prudence, ignoring Ostringer completely. "Would you care to accompany me to the library, Miss Etchingham? There is something I wish to show you."

She let him take her arm because she always let him take her arm. Even though it was madness, even though it hurt, she wanted to feel the warmth of his touch — to pretend that it meant something. These moments when they walked together were as close as she could get to him. She never turned him away even when her heart was aching.

But she had too much pride to let him run entirely roughshod over her. "You shouldn't have been rude to Mr. Ostringer," she said as he escorted her from the room. "I know he is a merchant, but I didn't think you were so priggish about such things."

"I'm not a prig," Alex said. "But I do not like to see you associating with charlatans."

"I had never met him before today," she lied. "He seemed pleasant."

"Pleasant for a charlatan. Still, you wouldn't approve of his methods."

Her touch was perfectly proper on his arm, but no bystander would guess that all her attention was focused on her fingertips. "What methods would I not approve of?"

"He is a fraud, Miss Etchingham. Most of what he sells is genuine, but there's always some piece or another that isn't what he claims it is."

"Perhaps he doesn't know?" she asked.

Alex shook his head as they navigated around the people and objects in their path. He was solicitous, slowing down to make allowance for her dress, and she leaned on him just a bit more than she needed to. "Ostringer knows what he's about," Alex said. "I don't mind the usual tricks dealers play — it is up to the buyer to ascertain provenance, after all. But the rumor is that he was a private secretary before he descended into the trade. He must have had some schooling. I don't approve of frauds who know what they are about."

"That hardly signifies for me," she said, smiling as though fraud was the furthest thing from her mind. And it very nearly was — she was too wrapped up in Alex to care much about Ostringer. "I don't have the funds to buy anything from him, real or no."

"I will buy you whatever you need. But please don't associate with Ostringer."

Prudence frowned. "I do not know him. Why would you care whether I associate with him or not?"

"Intuition, I suppose," he said, after a moment of silence. "I feel honor-bound to protect you, Miss Etchingham. All I want is for you to stay safe."

He looked down at her as he said it. She tried to read him — tried to understand his tone.

"I am quite safe here," she said. "You're with me."

His arm tightened under her hand, pulling her just the slightest bit closer. That smoldering look she sometimes caught him with was back in his eyes. "I cannot always be with you. But I want you to be safe without me."

"Why must I be safe without you?"

The question cut too close to the bone. She dropped her eyes as silence pooled around them. He paused for the longest time, long enough for her to answer her own question in any number of ways.

His answer, when it finally came, wasn't the one she wanted. "I'm the best protection you've got at the moment. Allow me to indulge in my protective instincts."

"I am not your responsibility," she said.

It was a test. She looked up. Their eyes met, held.

She should have known better. His gaze slowly cooled. He stepped back, not enough to drop her arm, but enough to make his point. If she hadn't seen that smoldering look earlier, she would have guessed that he was neutral, slightly concerned, but mostly unaffected. As though she was any dependent.

As though she would never mean anything to him beyond duty.

"If you would allow me to stand in for your brothers, I would do so gladly," he said.

The sentiment should have touched her. Instead, it destroyed her.

"How charming of you," she said, trying for banter instead of heartbreak.

He inclined his head. "It isn't meant to be charming. I merely wish to see you have all the happiness you deserve."

He escorted her into the library then. There was a sculpture of some vague renown, but Prudence didn't listen closely to his description. It was clear that he had taken her there to protect her from Ostringer — but his protection came from duty, not love.

Alex would never love her. Even if he would come to, she could no longer wait for him. She could no longer sit in his house, eat his food, use his carriages, and all the rest while waiting endlessly for him to notice her.

She just needed one more object. One more big, valuable forgery that could buy her freedom.

Miss Prudence Etchingham had never been characterized as audacious before. But if she had to choose between audacity and poverty…

She looked up at Alex. His gaze was fixed on the statue, so intently that he was either obsessed with it or was purposefully ignoring her.

She had to let him go. And she would do it now, before she wasted any more of her life on a fantasy.

CHAPTER TWO

Alex Staunton, the Earl of Salford, wasn't quite a candidate for Bedlam yet. But a casual observer wouldn't be faulted for thinking it.

The house was quiet this late at night — perfect for a final glass of whisky beside the dying fire in his study. He tossed another log onto the fire, then picked up the whisky decanter from a shelf full of libations. He poured a finger of liquor and downed it in one go.

It burned as whisky should, but it tasted sour on his tongue. After all these accursed years, he knew he could drink the entire decanter if he wished without feeling anything at all. He didn't bother. Instead, he grabbed the decanter, opened the French doors that led into the garden, stepped outside, and poured it all onto the cobbled path.

The fumes rose up to greet him. He stepped back from the rapidly expanding puddle to avoid ruining his boots. As the stream of whisky turned into a trickle, he heard the familiar sound of metal clinking against crystal, then thudding to the stones.

There was just enough light from the open door that he was able to find the key without too much effort. He picked it up and went inside, closing the door and leaving the empty decanter next to the dirty glass. The butler would refill it without comment in the morning. If the servants wondered why Alex rarely drank, then sometimes drained an entire bottle, they would never question him.

He wiped his hand, then the key, on his handkerchief. Then he opened his bottom desk drawer and pulled out the lockbox hidden under a mass of papers. He sat, scowled at the box for a moment, and turned the key in the lock.

The dagger within was hammered bronze that had somehow never dulled with age. The hilt felt familiar in his hand — muscle memory from years ago, when he used to hold it every night. He could draw the Egyptian characters etched on the blade with his eyes closed.

He traced the blade across the faded scar on his left palm. The scar had knit itself together years before, but it had never disappeared. Even when the dagger was safely locked in his desk, Alex carried the reminder of it on his skin.

He hadn't held the weapon in at least six months. Keeping the key in a bottle of whisky had helped to break him of his tendency to obsess over it — now, it took effort to unlock the box, just enough that he could usually ignore it. He'd been happier, these last years, ignoring it.

But Prudence had set him dreaming again.

Alex closed the box and set it aside, leaving the dagger centered in front of him. A paper had come with the dagger, but he never looked at it anymore — it would crumble if he unfolded and refolded it many more times. And anyway, he could recite the text from memory, both in the Greek it was written in and the English he'd translated it into.

Speak your wish and cut your palm.

So simple. Simple enough to laugh at. Simple enough to make a wish, thinking it all a grand joke.

But he should have paid more attention to the second line. *You will have your wish until the power is broken.*

The scribe who had written the note should have been more bloody precise about the consequences.

He drew the tip of the knife across his palm again. He could never have Prudence. His rational mind knew it. His wish had become a curse. He was no closer to breaking it than he had been a decade earlier, when he'd awoken to discover that his wish had been granted. And, truth be told, when he wasn't obsessing over a cure, his life was pleasant.

More than pleasant, when he ignored what he couldn't have. He had wished, stupidly, that nothing would interfere with his stud-ies. And his life was now perfectly, permanently arranged to give him what he had wished for. He never fell ill. He couldn't get drunk. He never suffered gout, or indigestion, or any other indignities that aging earls were supposed to suffer. When he felt the urge to fuck someone, he could find a high-class courtesan or charming widow without the slightest effort.

Of course, if he loved one of them enough to be distracted, she might choke to death on a chicken bone or poison herself with con-taminated jam. That tended to dampen his ardor.

Still, these last few months of enduring Prudence's presence in his house — the way he would see her unexpectedly and feel his heart leap, the chance to see her at dinner, the smile he sometimes surprised her into giving him — had stirred his old desire for a cure. He'd kept that desire in check, for her sake rather than his. If he allowed her to distract him from his studies, she would die. But still…

If he could read the damn words on the dagger, he might know how to break the curse's power.

He opened another drawer and pulled out a sheaf of papers. He'd tried to decipher the Egyptian before, using a rubbing he'd made of the Rosetta Stone. But he, like everyone else, had so far failed to discover how the Greek and Egyptian letters on the Rosetta Stone might match.

Perhaps he should try one last time. Before he was too old to care. Before Prudence found someone else.

He had just picked up the dagger again when the study door opened. No one ever disturbed him at this hour. He looked up. Prudence stood in the doorway, framed like an offering.

She paused, uncertain, but certainly not a dream. Alex was cursed, but he wasn't a madman. His eyes took in every detail. Her dress was unremarkable; she refused to let him buy her anything, even though he'd have bought her anything she desired. But the body it covered — those lush, mouth-watering breasts that he would never touch — didn't need silk or satin to draw him in. Her chestnut hair gleamed in the firelight, still pulled up in a chignon but otherwise uncovered.

He couldn't let himself think of her hair. He drove the dagger point-first into the polished wood of his desk. "Is there something I can help you with, Miss Etchingham?" he asked.

Prudence's eyes widened. "You're looking rather dangerous tonight, my lord. Are you off to fight the Americans at dawn?"

Alex forced a laugh. "Not worth the effort. But I shall if they've caused you a moment's distress."

Her lips twitched. Alex had always been able to make her laugh. Even tonight she seemed able to be amused despite whatever was on her mind. Something had to be on her mind — she found him in his study occasionally, but never at night.

"I didn't mean to interrupt you," she said, stepping back toward the hall. "I shall leave you to your studies."

He gestured to the chairs in front of his desk. "Please, join me. It's no interruption."

He regretted it as soon as he said it. Not because he didn't want her to join him — because he wanted her too much. Would she fall down the stairs in the morning because he'd asked her to stay?

Her eyes scanned his face. She shook her head. "It is late, my lord. I had thought to borrow a book, but I shall wait until tomorrow."

"What do you need?" he asked, standing up and coming around the desk. He should have stood as soon as she had entered, but he had been so addle-brained that he had forgotten propriety.

"I need nothing that cannot wait," Prudence said. "Good evening, my lord."

She turned to the door. He reached her before she exited. "Stay," he said behind her, placing a hand on her shoulder. "We haven't talked in an age. I would be happy to discuss any book in my collection with you."

They hadn't talked in an age because he had avoided her in an effort to spare them both. But if she wanted to talk about books…that was close to studying, wasn't it? The curse wouldn't care if he talked about history with her, as long as he didn't give in to his baser instincts.

She looked at his hand, but from behind he couldn't read the expression on her face. He felt her tremble, though — a reaction he let himself ignore when she suddenly turned and smiled, sweet and wistful. "Very well," she said. "Conversation may help me to fall asleep."

He pulled his hand away and clasped it over his heart instead. "You wound me, Miss Etchingham. Am I that much of a bore?"

"You know you are, my lord. But I can survive it."

Her smile was lovely as she teased him. She wasn't the stuff of legend. She wasn't the proclaimed beauty of her season. But her wide, ex-

pressive brown eyes, her even more expressive mouth — the irrepress-
ible vitality of *life* as she gazed at him — drew him in. Her eyes held a
secret promise that he wanted her to share with him — a strength of
purpose that almost seemed enough to break his curse.

He gestured her toward the chairs again, shutting the door behind her. "What would you care to discuss, then, if my topics bore
you? Ribbons? Whatever horrid novels you and my sister are reading?"

She pretended to deliberate. "Ribbons. Such a fascinating subject, don't you think?"

Her voice was light, but she gave a sidelong glance at the closed
door. He had never closed them in alone together. But it was late, and
no one would disturb them.

And he wanted to pretend that he could have her. Fool that he
was, he would take what he could get.

"Indeed, quite fascinating." He sat across from her, as though
everything was normal. "Do you prefer satin or velvet?"

She tilted her head, considering. "I find satin to be prettier, but it
is difficult to hold my hair in place with something so slick."

He'd never seen her hair down. It suddenly felt like a tragedy. "Is
your hair quite unruly? I'd never have guessed it of you."

"Do you think me so proper that I couldn't have curly hair?" she
asked.

Dangerous question. He gave the dangerous answer. "No. You
could be quite unruly, I'm sure."

She looked down at her hands. "You know I cannot be."

"I vow you could be," he said. "You just need the opportunity."

"Unlikely, my lord."

Her voice was suddenly quelling — not at all the sort of emotion
he was used to from her. "You could, I'm sure of it," he said.

"I'll grant you that I could be unruly," she said. "But the opportunity is unlikely. How long do you think I could live on others' charity if I misbehaved?"

"You could live on my charity as long as you like."

He meant it as a reassurance, but he knew as soon as he said it that he was in trouble. Her eyes flashed. "Is that what you think I want? A comfortable life with your money?"

She stood. Out of habit, he stood with her. "Of course not. I didn't mean it as an insult."

Prudence flushed. "Do not concern yourself with my feelings, my lord."

She stepped toward the door again. He couldn't let her leave like that. Even if he could never allow himself to have her, he didn't wish to hurt her. He didn't touch her this time — didn't trust himself to touch her. But he moved to block her.

"Allow me to be concerned, Miss Etchingham," he said. "And allow me to apologize. I didn't mean to distress you."

"Was that the apology?" she asked.

The words were sharp, but her voice had softened. He didn't rest on his laurels, though. "No. I am sorry, Miss Etchingham. Please, stay. I vow I'll have more care with my words."

She considered — considered something more than whether to stay, it seemed, given the way her gaze roved over his face. Her thoughts were indecipherable. But he sensed the moment when she had made her decision. He felt it in the air as she squared her shoulders. She looked straight into his eyes. His heart skipped just a bit.

"Very well. I shall stay. But if you expect me to be unruly, I shall require sherry."

CHAPTER THREE

She shouldn't have stayed. She hadn't expected him to be in his study; it was almost two in the morning, after all, and she had thought he would be in bed.

She wasn't there to see him. She was there to look through his engravings, seeking inspiration for whatever she might forge next. But, fool that she was, she was happy to see him.

And he seemed happy to see her. It was another mark in the column that said he might love her.

Stupid girl. She should have drowned herself in the sherry rather than drinking it.

But she let him pour her a glass and turn the conversation to safer waters. They didn't last long on ribbons. Instead, they discussed Mr. Soane's exhibits. That led naturally into a discussion of Grecian art and the latest public sentiments over Lord Elgin's actions in bringing part of the Parthenon to Britain.

Her heart was beginning to warm — and not from the sherry, even though he had poured her another. He looked at her with that special gleam in his eyes. He barely touched his brandy. Was he so taken with her that he forgot to drink?

It was after she'd made a rather risqué joke about Elgin's divorce, after he had laughed like he was utterly charmed, that she decided that this was her opportunity. He had wanted her to be unruly. Surely that meant something?

She pointed at his brandy snifter. "Will you share with me, my lord?"

He swirled his full glass. "You wouldn't like it."

She lifted her chin. She didn't know how to flirt, but she was game to try. "Who is to say I wouldn't?"

"I say you wouldn't," he said. But he retrieved the brandy decanter. "Are you sure?"

"Sure I wish to be unruly?" She reached for the decanter herself. "If you don't wish to aid me in my sin, you may leave."

She said it imperiously, as though it were her house. He laughed. "Not until I see you drink this. If you'll take a suggestion, you may wish to sip it first."

Prudence poured two fingers into her glass and swirled it like a connoisseur. She sniffed it, delicately, and shuddered.

"You can still change your mind," he said, reaching for her glass.

She turned slightly to keep it away from him. "In for a penny, in for a pound."

She sipped.

Then she coughed.

He tried to take the glass from her, but she glared at him even as she covered her mouth with her other hand. "No," she said, when the burn would let her talk. "I may never drink brandy again. I want to know how it feels."

She ignored the flash in his eyes, too sure that it was pity. She sipped again. It burned again, but this time she was ready for it. The burn was friendly enough — the warmth of a hearth, not hellfire.

As daring adventures went, this wasn't much of one. But when she met his eyes over the rim of her glass, it felt like she had dared everything. He smiled, a bit crookedly, as though he was deep in a dream.

She grinned back at him. "I think I could develop a taste for this," she said.

He was what she had developed a taste for, not the brandy. But Alex didn't know her secret heart. "Thank the gods you can't," he said. "I've changed my mind. If you were unruly, you would be a menace."

He was teasing her. She laughed and sipped her brandy again. "Perhaps I'm meant to be unruly. My hair does curl, you know."

She suddenly felt the urge to pull out her hairpins. But she wasn't drunk enough to take that step, even as his eyes narrowed with sudden intent. "I'm sure it fits your nature, Prudence."

He never called her that. Suddenly, she wasn't sure what she wanted. She wanted him to say the words she'd dreamed of, to pull her into his arms and do everything she'd seen in every illicit engraving she'd ever sought out.

But she also wanted to stay safe, in her dream world, suspended between what she wanted and what he had never said. Because if he didn't want her...

She set her glass on the table. "I should go to bed, my lord. I must attend your mother in the morning."

Lady Salford didn't really need her. It made the charity grate a little more, even though Prudence should have been grateful to have so little to do. But Alex scowled. "You don't have to work to live here. I meant what I said earlier, even if I was hamfisted about it. I want you to be happy here."

She stood. "I am happy."

Perhaps he heard something in her voice that she hadn't meant to give away. He stood, but he didn't bow to her. He clasped her hand instead. "I hope you are."

With another, it might have been brotherly. Perhaps he meant it to be brotherly. But she couldn't keep her heart from leaping — couldn't keep herself from looking into his eyes. She searched for the emotion she wanted him to feel for her.

But as she searched, she saw the warm light in his eyes turn to wariness.

"Alex," she whispered, thoughtlessly trying to draw him back into her dream.

He dropped her hand like it had burned him.

Something broke within her. She hadn't realized, until that moment, how very much she'd placed her hopes in him. She'd thought that she had been pragmatic — that she had accepted that an earl would never offer for one like her.

She hadn't known how deeply her heart was engaged until he stepped away. "It is late, Miss Etchingham."

Miss Etchingham. He'd called her Prudence before. But his voice was firm. He wouldn't call her that again.

She nodded dumbly. "Thank you for the drink, my lord."

He bowed. She felt small and rumpled next to his perfect posture and impeccable dress. "You are welcome to explore my books if you still wish. I believe I shall go to my club."

He didn't wait for her to leave. He left before she could, striding away from her like a man escaping disaster. Did he think she would have trapped him into marrying her if he had stayed?

At least he gave her the courtesy of closing the door behind himself.

She swayed on her feet. Perhaps it was the brandy that left her unsteady, but she knew herself better than that.

He didn't love her.

She had come to his study looking for an artifact. She hadn't expected an irrevocable answer to the question she'd harbored.

She hadn't cried in months. Even now, she didn't cry. She just stood, still swaying, and wrapped her arms around herself as though they could compensate for the embrace he hadn't given her.

He didn't love her.

The dagger he'd held when she entered should have been an omen. He couldn't have hurt her more if he'd driven it into her chest instead. He had run from her as though he knew exactly what she was — a poor not-even-relation, dependent on his charity, who might be expected to fall in love with any eligible man and should be pitied for it.

"Bloody bounder," Prudence muttered to herself. It didn't sound particularly threatening, not in his empty study, not when her voice trembled. But it made her feel just the tiniest bit better.

Until she remembered that she would have to see him again in the morning. And the morning after that. And every day after, without hope or end, until she miraculously found a husband or Lady Salford turned her out.

Neither was likely to ever happen.

Alex could go to his club — the sodding Society of Antiquaries that would never accept a mere female like her as a member — whenever he wished. But Prudence was trapped there, a glorified servant even though no one would call her that to her face. She didn't have the funds to go anywhere else. She had friends who might take her in, but she had nothing to offer them in return.

He didn't love her. That fact had etched itself into her heart so suddenly, so brutally, that it had nearly become an unbridgeable ravine. And she was trapped on the other side now, never able to go back to that more innocent place where she could dream that he loved her as much as she loved him.

She should return to her room. But her bed, the bed he paid for but would never share, would not comfort her. She looked around his study instead. She had come there on a mission, after all.

And his implicit rejection of her had confirmed what she needed to do. She had to forge something — something impressive, something that would bring her enough money to fund her escape. She couldn't bear the thought of staying in his house even a moment longer than she had to. Even if she was stupid for loving him, she could be smart enough to find a way out.

Her eyes settled on the dagger he'd embedded in his desk. Her heart may have broken, but her mind still had room to be curious. She walked over to it. She noticed other punctures in the wood around the dagger, all approximately the same size and shape. She'd never seen the dagger in his collection before, but he must have had it for some time — long enough to stab the desk with it more than once.

She traced a finger down the blade to where it ended in the wood. There were Egyptian characters inscribed in the bronze. If the dagger was an original, it was better preserved than any weapon she'd seen from ages past.

If she were more bloodthirsty, she would wait for him to come home, then murder him with his own dagger. But she was no Lady Macbeth, and death seemed like such a stupid punishment for breaking her heart. If she wanted to punish Alex, there were better ways.

Her heart began to expand from the familiar territory of grief to claim a vast new territory of anger. She ignored it for the moment, as she usually did. The papers strewn on Alex's desk all had hiero-glyphs on them — the untranslated, and some thought untranslat-able, language of ancient Egypt. Some doubted that it was a language at all, although Prudence thought the characters were too regular to be mere decoration. The Rosetta Stone, when it had been found in Egypt in 1799, had promised to be the key, but after fourteen years it still hadn't been solved.

Alex seemed to be making an attempt, though. There was a set of sheets with rubbings of the Rosetta Stone — he must have bribed the British Museum to let him copy it. Another set of sheets had identical rows of hieroglyphs across the top of each page and his notes across the bottom. Most of his writing was scratched out, seemingly in anger, but it was easy to see where that set had come from. The rubbings were in the shape of a dagger.

The same dagger he'd savagely stabbed into his desk.

She stared down at it, considering. Her heart was threatening to rebel — it wanted tears, and rage, and possibly something to break. She knew those feelings for what they were.

She was grieving for him. Or, more likely, for the life she might have had with him — for the dreams she'd indulged in. Prudence was intimately familiar with the ebbs and flows of grief.

But it wasn't just grief. It was anger, and shame, and self-loathing, and the knowledge that she was chained to Alex's house by circum-stance even though her heart might not be able to bear it.

He didn't love her.

But Prudence would find a way to survive. The Etchingham men weren't good at survival, but the Etchingham women were champions at it.

She pulled the dagger out of the wood. Then she rummaged through his desk until she found a fresh sheet of paper and a pencil. She made a rubbing of the hieroglyphs, putting too much force into the gesture and shaming herself with how much her immoral plot soothed her.

Then she carefully nudged the dagger back into the wedge he'd made for it and folded the paper into fourths. A new Rosetta Stone would bring a fortune. And if no one ever translated the original, they'd never know that hers was fake.

If her conscience rebelled, she would quell it. She should have been a better person — would have been a better person, if life hadn't driven her to this.

But it was either do something drastic, or spend the rest of her life dependent on the charity of others. And if she had to depend on *Alex's* charity, letting him clothe her and feed her and keep her on the shelf while he someday brought a wife home to rule over her…

She would rather go to hell for her sins than live through that.

CHAPTER FOUR

Six weeks later...

"Who are the most eligible bachelors in the ton this season, Prue?" Amelia, the Countess of Carnach, asked as she poured the tea.

"We only convened a moment ago," Prudence said, stifling her sigh like a good charity case. "May I trouble you to hold the Inquisition at bay until we've taken a bit of refreshment?"

There were only four ladies in attendance, including Prudence and Amelia. They were all part of an artistic society that they had dubbed the Muses of Mayfair, and the ostensible purpose of this gathering was to discuss their latest projects — Amelia's novels, Madeleine's dramas, Ellie's paintings, and Prudence's histories.

But as her friends had begun to pair off with their chosen mates, the conversations had shifted to focus more on their relationships than their interests. Today was no different — her friends were more eager to discuss Prudence's marital prospects than their art. Madeleine, the Duchess of Rothwell, joined the fray. "Aunt Augusta's ball is tomorrow. It is the perfect opportunity for you to examine this year's crop."

Madeleine's Aunt Augusta was Alex's mother and Prudence's employer. Alex would attend, of course. Prudence would be expected to dance with him, if he thought to take pity on her and offer. She pretended it didn't matter. "What if I don't wish to harvest anyone?"

Madeleine shrugged. "I didn't intend to harvest Ferguson — in fact, I rather think he harvested me — but I'm glad of it now. I hope you find a similar match."

"Similar to Ferguson?" Prudence asked, wrinkling her nose. "No, but I thank you for the sentiment."

Ellie, the Marchioness of Folkestone, laughed as Madeleine feigned a wounded air. "My dear brother does not fit everyone's tastes," Ellie said. "Madeleine seems to like him, though, so we'll leave it at that. But I trust that Prudence can find her own match without meddling from us."

Prudence shot Ellie a grateful look. Ellie was the only one of the three who had guessed where Prudence's heart lay — currently in a crushed, bleeding lump under Alex's foot.

Ellie's sympathetic smile was undercut by Amelia's usual determination. "Unfortunately, I cannot assist in person," Amelia said, as though her assistance was something Prudence would miss. "My confinement is too far along for a ballroom. But please promise you'll tell me everything that happens?"

Amelia and her husband Malcolm were living with Alex and Lady Salford while their London townhouse was being remade to suit Malcolm's political ambitions. They had returned to London from Scotland in March, rather unexpectedly since Amelia was now nearly six months along, and had promptly taken up a suite of rooms in Salford House.

Prudence was glad to have her friend back. She had recovered from the rift they'd experienced after Amelia's marriage — Amelia had married the man Prudence's mother had tried to arrange for her, and

Prudence had been hurt even though she hadn't wanted him. And she should have been glad that Lady Salford was so wrapped up in the birth of her first grandchild to need anything from Prudence. But in those awful weeks after realizing that Alex would never love her, Prudence would have liked some chores — digging a ditch from the garden to the Thames might have been a start. Or putting new paving stones down the length of Piccadilly...

"Prue?" Amelia prompted. "Everything."

"You can write a better party scene than what I shall observe," Prudence said.

"Why are you so reluctant?" Madeleine asked, frowning. "Of all of us, you always had the best time at balls and breakfasts and the like."

"I am a year younger than you. Perhaps my age has caught up to me."

"There are still many weeks left of the Season," Ellie said, trying again to divert the conversation. "There is time enough for Prudence to find a match without our input."

"I may not want a match," Prudence said.

Her voice sounded mulish. She looked into her teacup. She shouldn't have said it. It wasn't their problem. And there was nothing less appealing than a charity case complaining about her situation.

But it was growing harder to pretend that she was satisfied with her lot, especially when she was making secret plans to escape it. She loved her friends, but she couldn't tell them everything. She would rather cut out her tongue with a grapefruit spoon than talk about her failed love with women who only knew success.

At least they didn't laugh off her disenchantment. Madeleine sighed. "I know it must be difficult, Prue. How can we help?"

Prudence smiled as she looked up, putting on the happiest face she was still capable of making. "There's nothing to help with, I vow. I'm merely having a case of the blue devils. I'm sure I shall be happier before the ball begins."

Her happiest face must have looked sadder than she realized. Madeleine and Amelia suddenly looked as concerned as Ellie had. "There are any number of eligible men," Amelia said. "I'm sure if you make an effort, you'll find one who suits you."

"If I make an effort?" Prudence asked.

Ellie must have heard the edge in Prudence's voice. "There's no need to make an effort," she said, with a sidelong glance at Amelia. Amelia flushed a bit, as though she'd just realized how her words might be taken.

"No, please tell me, what effort should I make?" Prudence asked. "I've yet to stumble across a duke in an alleyway, or an earl in a library, or a former lover in a darkened studio. Perhaps I should spend tomorrow night looking for men in the shadows of the ballroom?"

Her voice broke off into an uncomfortable silence. All three of her friends had found love in unconventional settings. And she could have had that story, too. If Alex had loved her, her grand love story might have started with an illicit encounter in a darkened study. They didn't know what had happened — she couldn't bear to tell them. But *she* knew, and the knowledge ate at her.

Her jealousy was getting worse. She wasn't just wistful about what she didn't have — she was horridly, unbecomingly jealous. Her friends all had grand love matches, with sufficient titles and wealth to do whatever they wished. And not for the first time, she wondered about their futures.

How long would they remain friends with her if her situation continued to be so far beneath theirs?

If they thought it, they didn't say it. Amelia poured Prudence another cup of tea, as though she was afraid she'd say the wrong thing but wanted to do something to offer comfort. Madeleine moved to sit next to her on the settee. "It may not happen for you tomorrow, Prue," she said. "But it *will* happen."

"It may not," Prudence said, shrugging as though this were a philosophical conversation rather than one that threatened to expose her broken heart. "And perhaps I don't want it to. It wasn't so long ago that all of you seemed more content with your art than you ever thought to be with a man. Perhaps that's still true for me."

Amelia rejoined the conversation, never able to stay silent for long. "With the right man, you may still have your artistic pursuits. But as the one of us who I thought would be least likely to marry, I must say it's worth doing, if you find the perfect match."

Prudence sighed. "Unfortunately, perfect matches are not flinging themselves out of the woodwork at me. Have you seen the men who are available and would be satisfied marrying the daughter of a mere baron? One who has no income and no particular beauty?"

"You are lovely," Madeleine said firmly.

"But my poverty remains," Prudence said.

They were silent at that. Perhaps they knew that none of them could convince her — while Madeleine and Amelia had married much later than was fashionable, they had had dowries that compensated for their advanced ages. Granted, Ferguson and Malcolm cared nothing for their dowries, but they were unbelievably lucky to have found love matches with men who didn't need to care about all the usual qualifications.

"It's a shame that marriage is the only choice," Ellie said. "Perhaps you should marry a rich man and wait for him to die. It's not the worst that can happen."

Ellie had been widowed three days after her first wedding — but for all the lightness in her voice, Prudence knew that Ellie would never wish that fate on her friends. Prudence shook her head. "I have to put marriage out of my mind — it isn't going to happen, unless I want to settle for a missionary. Can you imagine me trying to convert natives in a jungle somewhere?"

"The cannibals would love you even if the missionary didn't," Amelia said.

Prudence laughed despite herself. "I don't like heat, so no missionaries. I thought of trying to become a governess, but I do not like other people's children. I would be a milliner, but I don't wish to waste my eyesight making hats for silly women."

Ellie snorted. "You would be a horrid milliner, my dear. You don't even like hats."

"I know. But it's almost genteel enough, isn't it?"

"True." Ellie tapped her fingers on her chair, considering. "But you would probably stab some poor lady in the eye with a hatpin if you heard how inane their conversations are."

"Is there something you can do with your historical treatises?" Amelia asked. "My novels sell well enough that I could have supported myself if Malcolm hadn't married me."

Prudence shook her head. "Treatises don't have the same appeal as your Gothic romances. None of the historical societies will grant me a stipend — they would expect me to turn up in person, and the ones I correspond with don't know I am a woman. The Duke of Thorington is searching for a private secretary for an expedition to Egypt, which would perfectly suit my interests, but I know he will only take a man. So what does that leave me?"

"*Thorington?*" Madeleine said. "He's even worse than Ferguson used to be, from what I've heard. You'd be ruined if you went to the East End with him, let alone Egypt."

Madeleine was forthright about her husband's former reputation. And she was right — Thorington's was worse. "It matters naught," Prudence said. "I sent him my credentials using my masculine pseudonym, but he never responded."

Their gasps were so in unison that they might have been a matched group of Furies. "You corresponded with Thorington?" Amelia said. "I know you've dreamed of visiting Egypt, but at the price of your reputation?"

Even Ellie — the most scandalous woman of her acquaintance — looked stunned. Prudence shifted uncomfortably. "I wrote as Mr. Chandlord, as usual. And he has never met me as Miss Etchingham before — he would never think to link the two. But it was almost a jest anyway. Do you know how much I dream of all of those horrid men at the Society of Antiquaries realizing that a mere female is just as capable of serious study as they are?"

That sentiment softened their horror just a bit. They knew how long it had grated on Prudence's patience that she could only carry on correspondence by pretending to be a man and routing her letters through a pub in Soho Square. Amelia and Madeleine had both pursued their artistic visions using false names. Of anyone in London, they would understand the risks she took.

They understood enough that she should have told them about her forgeries from the start. They wouldn't judge her for it — in fact, they might urge her on. But if she told them, they would try to rescue her rather than encouraging her. And their well-meaning charity would eventually destroy her pride.

She saw a bit of that in their reaction to her latest statement. "Promise me you will take rooms with me and Ferguson before you come to any of those ends you mentioned," Madeleine said. "Rothwell House could billet an army without feeling crowded. You may stay with us as long as you like."

"Or you may stay with me and Malcolm, once our townhouse is ready. Unless your dislike of other people's children extends to this one," Amelia said, patting her rounded belly.

Prudence laughed. "You know I cannot say anything to that without sounding ungrateful."

Amelia smiled. "Yes. So you must accept to avoid wounding my feelings."

Prudence shook her head. "Thank you. But I shall find a way."

Footsteps sounded in the hall. Madeleine craned around to look through the doorway, then sighed. "It's only Alex," she said, disappointed. "I hoped Ferguson had come to retrieve me."

"If it were Ferguson, he would be more likely to want my husband," Amelia said. "I vow the two of them are plotting to take over the Government — they spend enough time together to do it."

Alex stepped through the door a moment later. Even though she'd steeled herself against him, Prudence's heart still skipped. He looked perfect, the best combination of tousled hair and chiseled cheekbones, a Grecian fantasy come to life.

But he hadn't come to life for her. Alex met her eyes, only briefly, as though he couldn't stand to look at her. He knew she didn't belong.

She knew she was being irrational, that that wasn't how he viewed her. But she couldn't stop the self-loathing litany. Her heart beat faster as though it could outrun the shame. Her new dress — one of several she'd bought with the proceeds of her first forgeries, in one of those weak moments when she thought she might be able to win Alex back — suddenly burned against her skin. His gaze slid over her figure, but was it admiration? Clinical observation of one of his possessions? Did he even notice that she wore something new?

"Did you need something, Maddie?" Alex asked, perfectly calm, perfectly oblivious. "I am off to the Society, but I heard my name — I can attend to you first."

Madeleine waved a hand. "So like a man to care more for his club than for us poor females."

He grinned. His nonchalance was yet another dagger to Prudence's heart. "The club is quieter, after all."

"I doubt that," Madeleine said stoutly. "From what Ferguson tells me, the men gossip more than any group of women."

Alex frowned at the mention of Ferguson. It seemed instinctual, just as it was instinctual for Prudence to watch every flash of emotion across his face in hopes of translating motion into knowledge. "Ferguson does, perhaps. But I assure you, the Society of Antiquaries is entirely sober and straitlaced."

"That's a shame," Ellie said. "Surely you have more sin in you than that."

Prudence saw the flicker in his eyes. She swore he glanced at her, so fast that she wouldn't have seen it had she not been watching him intently. "No sins, I vow," Alex said. "Now, if you will excuse me..."

Amelia cut him off. "Will you please pull me out of this chair before you go? I shall have to confine myself to hard benches for the duration if this babe grows any bigger."

Alex laughed. "Such manual labor is beneath me. Earls aren't meant to haul around great burdens."

"Remind me to kick you in the shin for that when I can find my feet again," Amelia said, holding out her hand so that he could lift her up.

He helped her out of the chair with more gentleness than one might expect after the banter between them. Then he ruffled her hair. "If I see Malcolm out in town, I'll send him home to you. I'm sure the threat of a manservant helping you out of your chair will be enough to steal him away from Parliament for an afternoon."

"No need to play the overprotective brother," Amelia said. "I've made my bed, and I'm quite happy with it."

"We can see that," Madeleine said drily. "Shall I help you up to your room so Alex can leave us?"

The three of them left the drawing room. Prudence closed her eyes. Their laughter faded away as they moved toward the main staircase. Amelia and Madeleine would go up, to Amelia's bedchamber. Alex would go down, to the main door and the street, free to walk out of the house unescorted and unencumbered while Prudence stayed behind, trapped and caged like an exotic pet...

The drawing room door clicked shut. When she looked up, Ellie moved away from the door she had just closed. "Well?" Ellie asked.

Prudence made a show of filling her teacup again. "There's nothing to say."

Ellie came to sit next to her on the settee, taking the place Madeleine had vacated. "I thought you might say something to Salford about your feelings for him. Did something happen between the two of you?"

"The less said, the better," she said.

Ellie examined her face. Prudence wondered what the marchioness saw. Ellie was a painter, after all — perhaps that was why she had noticed what no one else had? Was there something to the color of

Prudence's eyes, or the fine lines starting to web around them when they narrowed as Alex looked at her? Some clenching of the jaw that Prudence herself wasn't aware of?

Mercifully, whatever Ellie saw on Prudence's face kept her from continuing her questions. Ellie sighed instead. "Whatever happened, I'm sorry for it."

Gentle sympathy, without insinuation or action required. Prudence's eyes unexpectedly filled with tears. "I'm sorry, too," she whispered.

Sorry that she had risked her heart. Sorry that she, the most romantically-minded of their circle, would never have what they had.

Ellie squeezed her hand. "It changes, you know. What you're feeling now — whatever happened — doesn't last forever."

Prudence nodded. She couldn't trust her voice for a moment, sure that if the words came out, her tears would too.

Hadn't she cried enough tears? Really, she preferred anger to grief.

They sat in silence for a few moments. When Prudence felt her heart slow, felt her breath ease in and out of her lungs without catching on the lump in her throat, she pulled her hand away from Ellie. "There is something you can help me with, if you'll consider it."

Ellie nodded. "Anything. You can stay with me as well, you know — days or months, whatever suits."

"Not that. I've no wish to shift the burden of my care from Lady Salford to you."

"You're not a bur…"

Prudence cut her off. "I have a plan that will keep me from being a burden, if you'll help."

She hadn't known for sure that she was going to ask Ellie for help until that moment, but the fresh pain of Alex's obliviousness was enough to throw her over the edge. She took a breath, then said the lie that would change her fate.

"I found a stone in an antique shop on Curzon Street that they were selling for a pittance of its worth. It cost me all of my pin money, but I think it could set me up comfortably for at least a year or two. Would you help me to sell it?"

"What kind of stone?" Ellie asked.

She described it — the Egyptian writing, the Aramaic below it, and the type of stone itself. Granite, it seemed, although a casual observer would never guess it came from Wales instead of Nubia.

Nor would they guess that the stonemason was alive and well in Westminster, rather than returned to the sand millennia earlier. Or that the very proper Miss Etchingham had designed the text using Alex's dagger as a guide, then paid the man all the remaining proceeds from her first sales to carve it.

Ellie's eyes lit up. "If you've found another Rosetta Stone, you have a fortune on your hands."

Prudence had so far lied glibly and without remorse, but she still felt honor-bound to warn Ellie, just a little bit. "It could be a forgery," she said. "The cost was astonishingly low, after all."

Ellie shrugged. "If you think it is real, then I shall take your word for it. You're the scholar, not me. But why not take it to Alex? He's the most likely buyer in London."

Prudence started to lie again, but Ellie interrupted, already knowing why. "You don't want him to know it's coming from you, do you?"

Prudence nodded. "I would rather sell it anonymously. He might overpay out of pity."

"And pity is such a bad thing?"

"As though you ever let anyone pity you," Prudence said.

"A valid point. But you should seek as much as possible for this, even if pity fuels the sale. An auction might serve, though," Ellie said, tapping her fingers against the upholstered settee as she thought through the implications. "Men can be so competitive when trying to win something rare."

Ellie already had a vision in mind. Prudence didn't add much to the conversation over the next few minutes; it was all Ellie, and how she would arrange a soiree to incite the most competition between the collectors she would invite. Outrageous public displays were Ellie's forté — the marchioness's parties and bacchanals were legendary. She wouldn't need anything from Prudence to make the next phase of the plan a success.

Prudence knew she should feel guilty. And she did feel some guilt for involving Ellie. But her only choices were Ellie or Ostringer — and she wasn't sure she could trust the man as much as she had thought. If everything went wrong, Ellie wouldn't seek to hurt her. She didn't think Ostringer would be quite so selfless.

Not that she was being selfless, either — she should have told Ellie exactly what she was doing. And she couldn't entirely deny that she was seduced by the notion of keeping all of her profits, rather than sharing them with Ostringer. But her guilt was overruled by a wanton mix of elation and relief. After all, if no one ever solved the Rosetta Stone, they would never know that this stone was a forgery. And in a week's time, she would have the money necessary to leave Alex's house. She didn't know where she would go after that. Her funds would go further on the Continent, even if she couldn't go alone. She might take her mother, though — they had discussed going to Italy before, but Lady Harcastle hadn't been ready to abandon England yet. She might, though, especially if there was money to fund the trip.

The money was the main goal, of course. But if Ellie invited everyone on the list she suggested, Prudence would get some measure of revenge against all the men who had ignored her. She had corresponded with dozens of scholars over the years — including Alex — but always pretended to be the reclusive Mr. Chandlord. They would never accept a woman in their ranks. And while they'd never know that a woman had tricked them, Prudence would know.

Selling one of them a forged rock would be eminently satisfying.

She knew that Alex would be the winner. She waited for her conscience to pain her, but it hadn't yet. Today, again, he'd looked at her like he loved her. That hope was crueler than any cut.

She could match him, though. She would give him hope of a translation, hope that would later be crushed.

It wasn't nice. It certainly wasn't moral. And she knew she might someday regret it.

But she didn't regret it today. "Thank you for your help, Ellie."

"You are most welcome." Ellie smiled, one of those satisfied grins that somehow made Prudence love her despite it. "And you never know what may happen. If you leave Alex's house, he may miss you and finally come to his senses."

The comment dampened a bit of Prudence's excitement. She tried to stay focused. What happened with Alex after didn't matter. All that mattered was that she had a means of escape that didn't involve marrying someone awful, moving in with one of her mother's cousins, or taking advantage of her friends.

Of course, she was taking advantage of Ellie. Was it worse that she was taking advantage of her trust instead of her charity?

She didn't answer her own question. She sipped her tea instead, and dreamed of being able to buy her own tea. That dream was too powerful for her conscience to overcome.

CHAPTER FIVE

Later that evening, after enduring yet another dinner in which Prudence avoided his gaze entirely, Alex retreated to his study alone. Something had broken between them after that night in his study weeks earlier. She was brittle with him now. She never smiled at him. Sure, she pretended that everything was fine. She laughed at his jests. She was civil at the breakfast table.

But she never came to his study.

He missed her. Worse, he knew that he had hurt her. He would have apologized, but there was nothing he could say — nothing she would believe. Still, it was better to have her alive and able to scorn him than dead because he'd indulged his need for her.

He sighed and opened a ledger on his desk. Soon enough he would lose himself in his work. He still loved history, after all, despite what it had cost him. And it was now so nearly the only solace he had — his competence and expertise the only bright bit in his otherwise disenchanted life. It also offered the only hope he had. He was no closer to finding a cure than he had been before, but he would keep searching.

When the door opened thirty minutes later, he was so deep in his books that he didn't look up immediately. He felt his heart leap, though, hoping and dreading that it was Prudence.

It was worse than that.

"Salford, toss your books and have a drink with us," Malcolm said as he strode into the study.

Alex frowned at his brother-in-law and the two men behind him. "You are more than welcome to entertain your friends in the saloon without me."

Malcolm MacCabe, the Earl of Carnach, was Amelia's husband — and, lamentably, Alex's houseguest for the next few months. Malcolm ignored Alex's suggestion as he strode to the sideboard and poured himself a whisky. "Can't leave you out of the fun, brother," he said, tipping his glass up in a mock toast.

Malcolm's best friend, Ferguson, the Duke of Rothwell, was the next to reach the decanter. "A quiet evening *en famille* seems like just the thing, doesn't it?" the duke said.

Alex didn't put down his pen. "If you wish to be *en famille*, you should visit the drawing room. I'm sure our female relations would be more appreciative of your company."

Neither man was dissuaded. They sat down instead, entirely uninvited and without waiting for the third member of their party to finish pouring. Nick, the Marquess of Folkestone, was the only one who couldn't claim relations with Alex. He was Ferguson's brother-in-law, though, since he had married Ferguson's sister Ellie a few months earlier. And he at least had the grace to look at Alex as he picked up the decanter. "Do you mind, Salford?" he asked.

"Please, help yourself. You will anyway," Alex said.

Malcolm leaned back in his chair, fully at ease despite the frost in Alex's voice. "The ladies have many talents, but they cannot help with our current mission," he said.

"You should still ask them first," Alex said. "The last time one of you asked me for help, I nearly killed someone."

That reference was meant for Nick, who scowled at the reminder. "I asked in good faith."

Nick had been trying to ferret out a killer in his house, and he had asked for Alex's assistance. However, the outcome had been unexpected. "I said at the time that you would owe me. I should call in the favor and make you all leave."

Ferguson chuckled. "Waste of a favor, if you ask me. And besides, Carnach and I don't owe you a thing."

Alex sighed. If he were a praying man, he would have prayed for patience. Instead, he stood and poured himself a whisky. It wouldn't taste any better than it usually did, nor would it get him drunk — the curse would eliminate that distraction. But he needed to keep up appearances. Once he'd poured, he turned back to them. "Why have you favored me with your presence?"

They all pretended his sarcasm was sincerity. "Your company is so very charming," Ferguson said. "Or at least good enough to give us a fourth for a rubber of whist."

"Go find another, then," Alex said shortly. "I've no time for whist."

He made a show of returning to his desk and shuffling his papers. Malcolm laughed. "Abandon your Puritanism, Salford. We're not the dissolute rakehells you'd make us out to be."

"Salford wasn't a Puritan when he was younger," Ferguson observed. "But then, I *was* a rakehell. Not every man can change for the better as he ages, as I have."

Alex's patience ran thin. "If I take my responsibilities rather more seriously than you do, that's not a moral failing."

He knew he sounded like a prig even as he said it. Ferguson didn't stop, though. "If I'm not responsible enough for your tastes, I'm still better company than you're likely to get tonight. Come to White's with us. I know you usually only turn up there to castigate me for my failings. I'll save you the trouble of finding me and take you along."

Alex had only "castigated" Ferguson at White's once, during Madeleine and Ferguson's secret courtship. But the words weren't what got Alex's hackles up.

It was the tone in Ferguson's voice, and the way he looked at Alex with something verging on pity.

Nick raised his glass in sympathy. "Ferguson and Carnach already collected me tonight, with similar insults about my inability to hold my own with them. Don't leave me to the wolves."

"I thought marriage would have sobered all of you," Alex said.

Ferguson shrugged. "That's why we need you. We shall live vicariously through your rakehell ways, if you can find them under all your layers of propriety."

Alex laughed despite himself. "I've none left."

"Then you should find them." Ferguson seemed utterly serious, suddenly, as though this was the real intention for his visit. "You're not a young man, Salford. If you save it for too late to run amok, you'll just embarrass yourself."

Malcolm nodded sagely — or drunkenly, it wasn't clear. "Nothing worse than an elderly rake."

Alex wasn't elderly. He was only thirty-three. But he *felt* old, sometimes. Odd feeling, of course; his life was exactly what he had asked for at twenty-two, while Ferguson, Malcolm, and Nick were far more settled than he was. But being trapped in his youthful dream was more aging, somehow, than if he had been allowed to change.

Or perhaps he was aging because of the strain of keeping Prudence at arm's length. All this time, he had been aware of the danger she faced from him. He had tried to save her from his curse by staying aloof. The only way to keep the curse from striking her was to keep his own heart disengaged.

But he hadn't anticipated that she would put him in mortal danger as well. Because every time he'd seen her after that horrid night six weeks earlier was another little slice at his skin. No single glance was enough to kill him — but a thousand such glances might do it.

He had done the right thing by pushing her away. He had to believe that. If he didn't believe it…well, in that case, he couldn't live with himself any more than he could live with her.

He'd lapsed into brooding, as usual. And as usual, Ferguson couldn't take a hint and leave him be. "Salford, you're turning into a corpse. It's my sworn duty as your cousin to take you to a club and get you foxed."

"Cousin-in-law," Alex corrected. "Take Nick out and get him foxed instead. He's your brother-in-law — surely you owe him more attention than you do me."

"We shall get him foxed as well. But you are our primary target. And if you won't come with us, we're not above kidnapping you."

Alex rolled his eyes. "Is there anything I can do to convince you to leave?"

"No," Ferguson and Malcolm both said simultaneously.

"Then let's do this quickly, shall we?" Alex said, pushing himself away from his desk. "I wager I can drink you under the table and be home before midnight."

*   *   *

They had been fools to take that wager. But then, how could they know that the curse prevented Alex from becoming inebriated? The worst suffering he felt during a night of drinking was the unpleasant taste of whatever he chose to drink. But his drinking companions would all have headaches in the morning — if they were even able to wake up before noon.

"To the ladies, God save us," Malcolm said, slurring his words.

Nick raised his glass. "I can drink to that."

He couldn't quite drink to that. Alex saw him fumble as he set his glass on the table. Another round of claret and the rest of them would be out for the night.

Alex reached for the bottle and offered to pour. Ferguson looked at his steady hands suspiciously. "You're more sober than I. Impossible."

Alex shrugged. "My Puritanism has given me an excellent constitution."

"You should try Puritanism, Ferguson," Nick said, after watching Alex's pouring ability with the childlike curiosity of a drunkard. "Less mess for the servants."

Ferguson frowned at the red stain that had spread around his glass from his own attempts to refill it. "Less mess. But where's the fun in that?"

Alex laughed along with the rest of them. He had pretended to enjoy himself at first, mostly to keep the attention away from himself and on whatever bits of Parliamentary gossip they were sharing with each other. But perhaps by the very act of pretending, he actually *had* enjoyed himself.

Of course, his enjoyment would end soon. The drunker they became, the less he understood why they found everything so amusing.

But if his life had been different — if he hadn't ruined it for himself by wishing for his studies when he was too young to know better — he could have enjoyed many nights like this.

Still, coming out in public meant seeing people he would rather not see. And one of those people came up to their table just as Alex finished pouring the next round.

"Salford," the Duke of Thorington said, sketching a small bow. "Haven't seen you here in an age."

"Thorington," he said, returning the bow with an incline of his head. "You're looking well."

Thorington was the only man in London who knew of Alex's affliction — because he, too, was cursed. They had been Alex and Gavin to each other in Cambridge, and had still been the best of friends when they'd made their wishes together. But new titles and old bitterness had changed all that.

Malcolm, though, was too drunk to notice the ice freezing between the two men. "Your grace," he exclaimed, in a too-loud voice that somehow melted into the din of the club. "Thought you'd be playing somewhere deeper than this. Join us, will you? We need a troop of reinforcements in our campaign to get Salford foxed, but you'll do for a start."

"You may need a battalion," Thorington said, taking the chair Malcolm had offered. "But I'll strive to best him."

There was more to his words than that. Did the others notice the glance Thorington gave Alex — the speculation in his green eyes, or the hint of challenge in his chin?

They couldn't have noticed. Malcolm was too busy trying to signal a footman for another glass. Ferguson was still watching Alex's hands, looking for a tremor he wouldn't find. And Nick was attempting to stack playing cards together into a house — a fool's effort, since either his fingers or the jostling of the table would fail him every time he tried a second level.

That left Thorington and Alex to circle around each other warily, a battle waged in plain sight. "How goes your collecting?" Alex asked, after Thorington was settled into the chair a footman had brought him.

"Prodigiously. But there are always new items to be acquired."

"And have you found anything worth acquiring?"

The duke shrugged. To the casual observer, he seemed noncommittal. But Alex knew Thorington far too well to be fooled. He was impeccably dressed, his dark hair perfectly cut, but he was no gentleman. There was menace there, something ugly and taunting. "We don't share, do we? A shame. If we worked together, we would get farther."

That would be true if they wanted the same thing. But where Alex wanted a way to destroy the curse, Thorington wanted to ensure that the power behind the curse was never broken.

Alex saw the scar on Thorington's palm as he took a glass from a footman. Their scars matched, the only physical reminder of that night so long ago when they had both used the dagger to make their wishes come true. The note that had come with the dagger was the only tangible clue they'd ever had. And it was just too vague to know whether breaking the curse would only affect the one who broke it, or anyone who had ever made a wish.

Thorington had wished for wealth. It was a necessity for him, as the first responsible member of his family in decades. His ancestors had created a dynasty made up entirely of profligate spenders, cast-off mistresses, and bastard progeny who demanded outrageous upkeep.

Alex, whose life had been perfect by contrast, had instead wished for something more scholarly.

They were silly wishes, but then, they had been drunk and cock-sure, men of science having a lark with a bit of superstitious nonsense. And Alex's father had been pressing him to leave Cambridge and take on more responsibilities with the estate — perhaps it was natural for a son to wish that his father would get off his back.

Nothing had happened immediately. It was only the next day that everything changed for both of them. Alex's father had died in the night; he would never interfere again, to Alex's eternal regret. And then Thorington had gotten foxed and found himself trapped into marriage with a rich, unprincipled social climber.

Alex had gone to Gavin a week after his father's funeral. The door of the grand house on Grosvenor Square sported a muffled knocker and a vast mourning wreath, but Alex didn't turn away. The foot-man, wearing black instead of livery, frowned, but escorted him into a drawing room. Gavin had entered minutes later. Already his eyes were harder, but Alex hadn't known then how far his friend could fall.

"Condolences on your loss, Salford," Gavin said, shaking Alex's hand.

Using Alex's title — the title that had been his father's until a week earlier — was the first shot in what would become their private war. "We must find a way to reverse this, Huxley," Alex said.

Gavin, as next in line to the Duke of Thorington, was Earl of Huxley by courtesy. If he wouldn't call Alex by his Christian name, Alex would give him the same formality. But Gavin shook his head. "Did you not hear? I am Thorington now."

To any other man, Alex would have offered condolences. To Gavin, he merely said, "The curse?"

"It got something right after all," Gavin said. "I'm to marry a harpy, and I win so much at cards that I'll likely duel half of London for accusing me of cheating, but at least the old man can no longer bleed me dry."

Alex's head reeled. "What does your family think?"

Thorington shrugged. Later, his shrug would be perfected into a gesture of cool dismissal, but that day he'd still had a heart. "They'll muddle through or come to me when they need something. Same as always."

Alex rose to pace, no longer able to stay still. The room was cold, underheated for the blustery March day. He'd thought the footman rude for not taking his greatcoat, but he was glad to have it. He dug his hands into his pockets and took a breath. "This cannot be real," he said. "It must be a coincidence."

It was a litany he'd repeated to himself since the morning he'd awoken to the sound of his mother's screams. But Thorington denied his sad attempt at comfort. "It's real. You know it is."

"Then we must stop it," Alex said. "The note said our wishes will come true until the power is broken. Who else will die for us?"

Thorington was silent for a long time. Alex could only see his father's coffin in his mind, and the grave Alex's wish had driven him to. But the new duke saw a different fate.

"What's done is done," he said. "All we can do is live with the consequences."

Alex stopped pacing and stared at him. "There must be a way to break the curse. We can find it together."

The dagger had come to them, along with several other artifacts, in a lot sold by a trader who had smuggled them out of Egypt after the British had defeated the French. If the note mentioned breaking the power, then logically there must be a way to break it. But the cure wasn't included in the note.

"That presumes I wish to break it," Thorington said.

"Why wouldn't you?"

The duke gestured around the room. "I can barely afford to heat this house, let alone maintain it. My family runs through everything faster than I can produce it. And I would like to bring my mother back to England in style, even if she may not live long enough to enjoy it."

Alex had forgotten about Thorington's mother. The duchess had gone to Europe in some sort of secret disgrace years before. But his own mother's grief was too fresh to spare much concern for a woman he hadn't seen in years. "The cost is too great. We can find…"

Thorington cut him off. "We won't. Search if you like. Or wish for something better than what you wished for. But I won't allow you to break the curse if I have any ability to prevent it."

Those words had severed their friendship, completely and irrevocably. Alex had left, furious, and determined to find the cure. Over the years, Alex's determination had only grown — especially when he realized he could never marry for fear of the curse killing any woman he grew too fond of.

But Thorington's determination had grown too, augmented by his dark, ruthless reputation. They'd been polite in public, but in private they tried to outbid each other for anything and everything that might help their opposing causes. And they weren't above spying on each other to look for clues that the other might have found a crucial object.

But this was White's, not an antiquities shop. Alex could feign nonchalance. He lifted his glass. "To the hunt."

"The hunt," Thorington repeated, sipping his wine.

"What are you hunting?" Malcolm asked.

"Never say you're thinking of settling down," Ferguson said.

Alex shook his head. "Of course not."

"On that, we are agreed," Thorington said. There was an old flash of humor in his eyes, just enough that Alex felt a twinge of regret over the divergent paths their lives had taken.

But the humor was odd, since Thorington's wife had died less than six months earlier. "I take it you are not looking for a new duchess?" Alex asked.

"No, although lately I've thought it might be better to find one than have one foisted on me," Thorington said. "But she will have to be more frugal than the last one."

His eyes, as they met Alex's over the rim of his glass, spoke volumes. He'd been trapped into marrying his first wife, likely by the curse deciding that he needed an heiress. But the woman had spent increasingly vast sums on clothes and jewels — had the curse finally decided she was more of a debt than an asset?

"Condolences on your loss," Alex said.

Thorington finished his wine and reached for the bottle. "It's a shame you haven't married yet, Salford. I'm sure you could do better than I did."

It was an insult, since Thorington knew Alex couldn't marry. "Thank you for your concern, but I've no wish to do so."

Thorington smirked at the mention of a wish, but the other men didn't notice it. "You should think about marriage, Salford," Nick said, not looking up from his cards. "It may surprise you how good it can be."

Ferguson nodded. "For once my esteemed brother-in-law speaks the truth. Marry Miss Etchingham, if you don't want to waste time courting someone. I'm sure she'd take you."

"She didn't want me," Malcolm said, sounding almost affronted. "Not that I mind. But she can be a cold one."

Alex glared at him. "The lady deserves more than you, just as she doesn't deserve your insults."

Ferguson tapped his fingers on the table. "Kind of you to defend her. You could do worse, you know."

"If she isn't a harpy and won't run through your money, she sounds like a paragon to me," Thorington said.

Alex didn't like the sudden gleam in Thorington's eyes — as though he had heard of some new object for his collection. He couldn't risk giving Thorington any more reason to think of Prudence. "I've no interest there. Too busy with my studies to waste time with a bride."

"Scholars," Ferguson said in disgust.

Malcolm snorted. "You read more than any scholar I know, Duke."

"No need to insult me by using my title, MacCabe," Ferguson said, drunk enough to be distracted away from his attack on Alex's marital state. "I'll call you out for it."

"If you call me out, who will I use as my second?" Malcolm complained.

"Last time I seconded for you, you nearly shot me instead of your foe," Ferguson said. "I might as well fight you in a duel so I have a chance to shoot you instead."

Malcolm laughed and finished off his glass. When he set it down, he dragged a bit of the cloth across the table, knocking over Nick's cards. The marquess cursed, then looked up and joined the conversation as though he'd never left it. "Talking of scholars, are we? That reminds me, Salford — my wife asked me to pass a message to you."

Alex suspected that any message Ellie wanted to pass to him wasn't one that he wanted Thorington to hear. But there was no way to stop Nick from speaking. He was already digging into his jacket.

"She said to give this to you straight away," he said, handing Alex a crumpled piece of paper that had been folded over and sealed with wax. "Don't tell her I forgot or I'll gut you."

"Less than three months into your marriage and she's got you delivering messages to another man?" Malcolm asked. "You're already sunk, my friend."

Nick smiled and went back to his house of cards. "Ellie can speak to whomever she wants. Makes no difference to me."

There was a wealth of trust in his voice — not the carelessness of a man who neither loved his wife nor cared who she was with, but the certainty of one who knew that she could spend time with a hundred men and never be tempted away from him.

Alex almost hated him for it. How had *Nick*, of all people — a man who had come back from India with the hungry look of someone intent on revenge — found that, when Alex wanted it and couldn't have it?

He tamped down his unseemly jealousy and slid a finger under the sealing wax. When he opened the paper, another piece slipped out of it and into his lap. But Ellie's bold handwriting drew his attention first.

Salford - A friend has asked me to sell a most unusual stone. I have enclosed a partial rubbing of the piece to whet your curiosity. Please do be in touch to confirm your interest. We shall auction it a week from tonight. Yours, etc., Lady Elinor Folkestone

Ellie knew Alex's tastes. She preferred paintings to ancient artifacts, so they rarely moved to acquire the same pieces. Still, she was well aware of what had value on the market and what didn't. Just the fact that she described something as "unusual" piqued his interest.

But when he picked up the second scrap of paper and turned it right side up, his heart stopped.

The hieroglyphs across the top were a perfect match to the ones on his dagger. He could see the symbols even when he closed his eyes — a gathering of carved lines that might save him if he could only learn how to read them. Those symbols were on whatever rock Ellie was selling. And below it, half a line of what appeared to be Aramaic, just enough to show him the promise of the stone without giving him access to more of it.

Alex exhaled a breath he hadn't realized he'd held. Ellie thought he would be interested because it was another version of a Rosetta Stone — another possibility to translate the Egyptian language. The Rosetta Stone was such a find that it had been specifically included in the negotiations between the victorious British and the defeated French at Alexandria in 1801; the French had very nearly smuggled it out of Egypt illegally before a clever soldier retrieved it.

The Rosetta Stone was far larger than this piece. The stone Ellie was selling wouldn't be as useful for translation purposes, although any fragment could help. But for Alex, this was even more precious.

If the Aramaic matched the Egyptian, it would tell him what the dagger said even if he never learned how to translate the symbols themselves.

He was already racing toward the thought of what he could do if he broke the curse. He could have Prudence, if she would have him after how he'd treated her. He could have *this* life, the life he would have grown into if he had not frozen himself into the life he'd wanted at twenty-two.

He looked up. The others had gone back to their drinking. Within the hour, they would either go to their beds or rally for one final bout of carousing, if he read their flushed cheeks and glassy eyes correctly.

But Thorington's eyes weren't glassy. And they never missed anything. "So she told you as well."

Alex nodded. "Lady Folkestone knows every man who would bid on this. She'll have told all of us by tomorrow, I'm sure."

"Then I shall have to outbid you," Thorington said, taking a long draught of his claret.

"You can't." Alex could spend as much as he wanted to on the object. Until he broke it, the curse would find a way to replenish his finances so that he wouldn't have to waste valuable study time on managing his estate. As long as he had the money in hand to pay for the object, he could bid as high as he wished.

Thorington's shrug was noncommittal. "Perhaps. Or perhaps you don't know as much as you think about my affairs."

Thorington had wealth, but from what Alex knew of Thorington's business, most of it was tied up in his lands or in trusts for his family. A purchase from a lady like Ellie would be treated like a debt of honor — it would have to be paid immediately, unlike shopkeepers who might go months or years without being reimbursed.

Alex would gather all the resources he had to bid on the rock. He couldn't allow Thorington to win it.

"To the hunt," he said to Thorington again.

Thorington's teeth gleamed. "I wish you all the fortune you deserve."

CHAPTER SIX

On the surface, everything at Lady Salford's ball the following night was perfect. Prudence wore a new, gauzy evening dress of purple silk that was wildly expensive compared to her gowns from seasons long past. She had already danced with six men, none of whom had stepped on her toes. And she had yet to see her mother.

Perfect — if one ignored the fact that her lies had paid for her dress, that her friends had cut those men out of the flock for her like sheepdogs, and that her mother would inevitably find her.

Her last dance partner had left her on the edge of the ballroom with a glass of lemonade. She watched the couples swirling through the steps of a country dance. Ellie had yet to say a word about the auction. It was quite possible that everyone had seen through her forgery and there would be no bidders.

If she wanted to escape and have a home of her own, that left marriage as her only option. Not that anyone had offered it, of course. With the wars Britain had fought over the last decades, there were no longer enough men for every woman who wanted one. Those men who still lived could do much better than her, if money and lineage were all they cared for.

She straightened her shoulders. She didn't want any of them, either. Most were crashing bores or controlling prigs.

And then there was Alex. "Bloody bounders," she muttered into her glass.

"What did you say?" her mother said from behind her.

Damn. She schooled her features before turning around. "Mother," she said, kissing her briefly on the cheek. "How do you do?"

Her mother frowned. Prudence winced. Even with everything that had come between them, she should have said something better than that. But if Lady Harcastle was hurt that Prudence would say "how do you do" after not seeing her in weeks, she didn't say it. "Daughter," she said, returning the kiss. "You look well."

Her eyes slid to Prudence's dress — a dress she couldn't afford to give her. While Prudence was dressed in the very latest fashion, Lady Harcastle's dress was a black bombazine from their mourning period four years earlier. They had still had money for dresses then, in those bleak, awful weeks between receiving the news from Talavera and when Prudence's father had died from the strain of losing his sons in battle.

Prudence flushed, but she couldn't say where she'd gotten the dress. She lied instead, a skill she was becoming adept at. "Thank you. Lady Salford has been most generous these past months."

It could have been true; Lady Salford was always offering to buy her dresses. Her mother believed it. "I am glad. I thought she might be giving you too many tasks since you haven't had time to visit or write."

Prudence deserved that little hit. But even though she felt guilty, something had snapped after that awful night in Alex's study. Something bigger than her heart. It was as though her whole life had broken apart — as though everything she'd found important before was no longer important, as though the Miss Etchingham the ton knew was dead and buried.

Prudence wanted to be someone else. Someone who got what she wanted. Someone who *lived*, rather than dreamed.

But when she saw her mother, the life she wanted crumbled in the face of the life she should settle for.

"I am sorry I haven't written," Prudence said. "Very busy, of course."

"Of course." Her mother looked straight into her eyes as though trying to read her inner thoughts. Lady Harcastle wasn't quite a mirror for Prudence — time and grief had hardened the lines around her eyes, and her brown hair was fading to white. But Prudence could see how her own face might look if she spent the next few decades making the best of things.

"Are you sure you're well?" her mother asked. "You look peaked. Perhaps we should sit?"

Prudence found herself in a chair along the wall before she could say no. Not that she could say no. Her mother's force of will was indomitable. They were slightly away from everyone else, with her mother holding her hand, before Prudence could protest.

She finally found her voice, but she couldn't tell her mother to leave. "Are you comfortable with your cousin, Mother?"

Lady Harcastle nodded. "Eliza was very kind to take me in again. But it would be pleasant to have my own house, with room enough for you."

"You do not need to worry about me," Prudence said.

"I cannot help it, you know. You're my daughter. And you're all I have left."

Her mother's hand on hers suddenly felt like a dead weight, bearing her down into a vast subterranean lake of grief. "I'm sorry, Mother.

But I..."

"I know you are better off here," her mother said, ignoring her. "You deserve everything Augusta has given you — everything I cannot give you. But I miss you."

Prudence looked away. "I wish..."

Her mother interrupted again. "There's little point in wishes, I know. And I shouldn't have pushed you to marry Carnach last summer, or behaved so badly when you did not. But it doesn't take money to visit each other, does it? Or to have Salford frank your letters to me? I'm sure he would do it if you asked."

"Salford has done en..."

"Have you thought to try to marry him?" Lady Harcastle asked, her voice dropping. "I vow Augusta had it in mind when she asked you to move in with her."

Prudence closed her eyes. "I'm sure Salford can do better than me, Mother."

Why was *that* the sentence her mother allowed her to finish? She felt the assessment in her mother's silence, and wasn't surprised when the woman sighed. But the answer shocked her. "I don't think he can. You are pretty, well-behaved, and your unfashionable interest in history is actually a benefit to him. I'll grant you, the money is a problem..."

For once, it was Prudence who interrupted. "What do you know of my interest in history?"

Lady Harcastle snorted. "It wasn't your brothers who were marking up the history texts in our library when you were younger. They were smart, honorable young men — but interested in history they were not. If they had been, they would have known better than to buy commissions."

It was the first time she'd ever heard her mother make something like a jest about George and Andrew's fates — or say something that might have been a criticism. "How did you discover my markings?" she asked. "I thought none of you used the library."

Lady Harcastle looked down to where their hands were still intertwined. "In a different life, I might have been a bluestocking myself. But my father insisted on finding a better match than a mere scholar. And Lord Harcastle didn't enjoy reading..."

She cut herself off. Prudence leaned forward. "Did Father stop you from reading?" she asked.

"No, of course not," her mother said. "He was a good man, albeit a bit dull. But my duty was to him, not my own interests. You'll discover the same when you marry."

Prudence had never heard her mother criticize her father. She was so surprised that she accidentally said exactly what she was thinking. "I don't think I wish to marry."

Her mother just laughed, the same indulgent laugh she used to give when Prudence, as a child, had been so sure she'd someday be a princess. "You'll do your duty in the end. You're my daughter. You are too well-bred to be selfish forever."

And like that, the brief moment of rapport vanished. Prudence had been angry at her mother before — more and more often in recent years, as she grew impatient, then guilty, then impatient again over how long it had taken her mother to recover from Andrew and George's deaths.

But this was the first time Prudence had hated her.

Her salvation came from an unexpected quarter. She hadn't seen even a glimpse of him in the crowded ballroom, but suddenly Alex stood before her. "Miss Etchingham. May I have the pleasure of your company for this dance?" he asked.

He was perfectly dressed, as usual, with a dark evening suit and a silver waistcoat. His smile was friendly, but his eyes were somehow inscrutable. It wasn't a description she often used for him — after so many years of watching him, she knew nearly every expression he was capable of. But tonight, she couldn't read him.

"I'm sure you have other guests who would appreciate your attentions," she said. "No sense wasting time on me."

Finally, his façade cracked. She didn't see what she wanted to see — didn't see lust, or love, or any other emotion that she longed for. Instead, she saw concern. "My mother would no doubt like to see me dance with every woman here. But I, for one, would like a bit of comfortable conversation."

They hadn't had a single comfortable conversation since that night in his study weeks earlier. But his eyes flickered to Lady Harcastle, who seemed intent on every word they said to each other.

If Prudence had to choose between dancing with Alex and letting slip to her mother that there was any difficulty between them, Prudence knew which evil she should take. She held out her hand. "Of course, my lord. If you'll excuse me, Mother?"

Lady Harcastle let her go. "Enjoy yourself, my dear. I hope to see you again soon."

Again, the guilt. Prudence nodded, noncommittal, and let Alex lead her away. His grip on her was firm, almost commanding. But his voice was soft. "Are you feeling well, Miss Etchingham?"

"Is there a reason for the sudden concern for my health?"

She couldn't stop the venom from seeping into her voice. But he didn't drop her hand. "I have always been concerned for your health, regardless of what you might choose to believe."

She would rather believe that he had never cared anything for her at all. It might have been easier to recover if he had loathed her, rather than merely loved her as a friend. She couldn't say it, though. "I thank you for your concern, my lord. I am feeling quite well."

He pulled her into his arms as they reached the floor. A waltz had started — just her luck, that he would choose a waltz.

"I know you better than that," he said shortly. "As though I could leave you to your mother's tender mercies. What did she say this time?"

"The usual nonsense about how I must marry to save us."

"I thought she was comfortable living with her cousin? She could move here with you if she isn't — I have no objection."

Prudence shook her head. "My mother and yours are friends, but can you imagine them spending every day together?"

Alex shuddered in an exaggerated way that wrung a laugh from her. "You are right, of course. But you don't need to accept whatever marriage she might arrange for you."

Prudence's instinct was to read something into that — to let herself believe that he meant for her to wait for him. But she knew she was lying to herself. "She already tried one arranged marriage. I'm sure she won't waste her time trying again."

"Carnach wasn't a good match for you," Alex said. "That doesn't mean there won't be another."

"He was the best offer I was likely to ever receive. An earl with a suitable fortune? I should have done everything in my power to win him."

"You didn't want him," he retorted. "I was there, if you recall. It was obvious your affections weren't attached."

His eyes were dark as he said this. She held his gaze for a moment. As they swayed through the room together, it felt like the rest of the world had fallen away — that the connection between them could set them free of everyone else.

"Of course my affections weren't attached," she said quietly. She couldn't lie about that, not when she was looking him straight in the eye. "But marriage isn't about affection, is it? I would have a house of my own now if I'd accepted him."

Alex looked away. He was silent for a full turn around the dance floor — long enough for her brain to obsess over why he was talking about marriage with her, when she wanted to discuss any topic but that with him. "I understand why you would want a house," he finally said. "The economics of the marital state are more important for most people of our class than the emotions of it. But you deserve affection, too. And you certainly deserve better than Carnach."

She didn't let herself mull over that statement. She couldn't look below it, for fear of reading too much into it. She tried for a teasing tone instead. "You forced your sister to marry him — do you really hold him in such low esteem? That's not very brotherly."

His eyes flashed. "They love each other. It was obvious from the moment they saw each other that the spark was there. Just as it was equally obvious that you would never love him. Did you never think that I pushed them together to save *you* from him?"

Her eyes widened. His widened too — so quickly that she knew he had never planned to confess. His lips flattened into a thin line, trying to trap the words that had already escaped.

But it was too late. "What do you mean by that?" she asked.

Her voice trembled. If he heard it, he didn't acknowledge it. His hand, at the small of her back, turned into a fist. It pressed into her spine like a warning. The hard knuckle of his thumb grazed against her backbone as though both ridges of bone were weapons and only one of them could win.

But if his touch menaced, his voice was light enough to make her doubt it. "Call it instinct. Your brothers cannot protect you, so I took it upon myself."

She hadn't needed protection. She and Malcolm might never have loved each other, but he wasn't the type to beat or starve her. He was good in other ways, of course — or at least Amelia believed him to be. But when Prudence had seen Malcolm for the first time, all she had thought was how she wished he were Alex instead.

Still, she should have married Malcolm. That plan had died when she and Alex had caught Malcolm with Amelia instead. She had always thought that Alex had demanded their marriage out of some overprotective brotherly piety. The four of them could have chosen to sweep that ill-timed kiss under the rug without the ton ever finding out.

But did he really force the issue because it would save Prudence?

And if he had saved her, what was he saving her from...or for?

She couldn't ask. She couldn't bear to hear the answer — sure that it wasn't what she wanted. Instead, she grinned as though they had been discussing anything but her failure on the marriage mart. The grin may have wobbled, but it was the best effort she could make. "I suppose I should thank you for intervening. But if a duke offers for me, don't rescue me."

His laugh sounded startled. "You don't want a duke. They are universally dreadful. Look at Ferguson."

He gestured toward the side of the room. Madeleine's husband stood there, watching them dance as he twirled his quizzing glass between his fingers. He gave a little wave when he saw them looking at him, but he didn't bother to hide the scheming look on his face.

She shook her head. "I'll grant you that dukes are mostly dreadful. But Madeleine could have found a worse duke. At least he isn't eighty and gouty."

"Of course. But can you imagine living with him?"

She shuddered, just as he had done earlier. "Heaven forbid. But earls aren't any better. The whole lot of you are too arrogant for words."

"Perhaps because we are so vastly superior to the rest of you," he said, tilting his chin up and looking down his nose at her.

She laughed. "God save us all. I should run off and marry a missionary after all."

"Would you really do that?" Alex asked.

The concern was back in his voice. She didn't want to hear it — didn't want anything serious between them, when laughter made it easier to pretend that nothing was wrong. "Of course not, my lord. Remember, I require a house, not a tent."

He grinned. "Stay mercenary, Prudence."

He'd used her Christian name. She couldn't help but stiffen in his arms. He pressed his lips shut again, then inclined his head. "My apologies, Miss Etchingham. Sometimes I forget myself."

She shrugged. The dance was ending. It was inevitable that they would crash back to earth, that reality would invade. "No apology necessary, my lord. I am living by grace of your charity, after all. I suppose you may call me whatever you wish."

"I wish you didn't see this as charity," he said.

She looked away from him. "There's little point in wishes."

Her words matched her mother's, but that was a fact that would bother her later — now, she was too consumed by Alex. His thumb grazed her spine again. She felt his gaze on her, but she refused to look at him. She had already ruined their banter — she didn't want to extend the conversation.

But he didn't take the hint. "I know. Wishes are dangerous things. But you…"

He trailed off. Her mind immediately started to fill in the rest of his thought. But she was too poor. Too old. Too far on the shelf.

The music stopped. The chatter around them crescendoed. She had to look at him as he bowed to her, and it was as she came up from her curtsey that he drove the dagger home.

"You deserve to be happy, Prudence. Miss Etchingham. And I vow I will find a way to make it so."

CHAPTER SEVEN

She wasn't sure how she had washed up on the side of the ballroom like a bit of flotsam tossed from the crowd. Alex must have escorted her out of the dancers, but she was too stunned by his final statement to remember it.

He wanted her to be happy. But what did that mean? Was he on the verge of offering for her? Or did he plan for something else?

She took a breath and prayed for calm. She couldn't let her face betray her now, not after all these years of never putting a single foot astray in public. She lived in Alex's house, after all; if anyone suspected he had taken advantage of her, she would be ruined before anyone thought to ask her the truth of it.

But breathing didn't help. The music, the people, the jeweled colors of their gowns and waistcoats, the overly sweet odor of flowers and perfumes trying to disguise sweat and coal smoke — it all pressed against her, a mad profusion of sensory detail battering against her as though she was an intruder at the gate. She thought she might be sick.

Her rebellious stomach must not have shown on her face. Ellie strolled up a few moments later. If she noticed anything amiss, she didn't say it. "Will you take a turn about the ballroom with me?" she asked.

"Of course," Prudence said, mostly because she couldn't think of a reason not to. "I must say I am surprised that you haven't found another man to force to dance with me."

Ellie shook her head as they began to walk the perimeter between the chairs and the dancers. "That was mostly Madeleine's doing. But no one had to be forced. You are a lovely woman, Prudence."

Prudence shrugged. "Was there something you wished to discuss?"

Ellie looked around, then lowered her voice. "Your find is already attracting significant interest. If you had the funds for it, your eye could likely rival Alex's when it comes to collecting."

"I thank you, but I don't care to build my own hoard of dust-covered objects."

If she wanted a hoard, she had the skills to create one for herself. She didn't know if Ellie would laugh or berate her if she saw the pottery shards in various states of completion in one of Lady Salford's disused attics. But she didn't mention any of it.

And she might never need to sell them, if Ellie was correct. "You shall have the money to do whatever you wish in a week," Ellie said cheerfully. "Within reason, of course. But I predict it will bring more than enough for your immediate needs."

"I'm sure it's too soon to know that," Prudence said, trying to stay neutral in the midst of the sudden war between her greed and her conscience.

Ellie very nearly looked offended. "Don't doubt that I know how to sell this. A few messages to the proper individuals last night and the entire world knew of it. Alex is currently the top bidder, as expected, but there are others who have come to me with offers."

"I thought you wouldn't auction it until next week at the earliest."

"I won't. But there is no harm in escalating the opening offer in advance. I want you to win an outrageous sum."

She was gratified to hear that, of course — more than gratified. But if the auction attracted so much interest, the chances that she would be caught increased. "Surely it isn't worth an outrageous sum. I would be happy to settle for something reasonable."

"Nonsense. Settling for something reasonable is always the worst course of action."

Prudence eyed Ellie's profile. Was her friend still talking of auctions? Or did she have something else in mind?

A man stepped into their path, neatly stopping their forward progress. "Lady Folkestone," he said, bowing to Ellie. "Would you do me the honor of introducing me to your friend?"

Ellie arched a brow. "I never thought to see you here, your grace. I had heard that you and our esteemed host are no longer close."

The man — a duke, based on Ellie's address to him — smiled. "Lord Salford does not love me, it's true. But his brother-in-law was good enough to invite me last night. I could hardly turn down the invitation."

Malcolm had invited someone Alex didn't like to attend a ball at Salford House? Prudence would have laughed if she didn't suspect, suddenly, who he must be.

Ellie's next words confirmed it. "Miss Etchingham, may I present to you his grace the Duke of Thorington? Thorington, this is my dear friend, Miss Etchingham. Be kind to her," Ellie added — a reminder that wasn't usually necessary in the ton.

But then, Thorington was not usually presented to unmarried ladies. Prudence was level-headed enough to curtsey to him, even as she wondered what he wanted.

He bowed. "Miss Etchingham. I am very pleased to make your acquaintance."

"I appreciate the nicety," Prudence said.

Thorington was perhaps the wrong man to be insouciant with. But after being silenced by her mother, then stunned by Alex, her tongue was in open rebellion. And something about his grim eyes made her want to spike his guns.

The duke smiled. It wasn't a friendly smile, though. There was something too hard in the set of his mouth for genuine humor — as though his politeness was a thin veneer over something much darker.

"I hope you shall appreciate another nicety and give me the pleasure of this dance."

It wasn't a question. He already held his hand out to her. She looked at Ellie, who shrugged delicately. "The duke won't bite. At least, I don't believe I've heard any rumors of him biting anyone."

"There is always a first time," Thorington said. "But it shan't be tonight."

Prudence was utterly out of her depth. She had never been much of a flirt. But Thorington raised a brow and wiggled his hand in her direction.

She placed her hand in his. It felt like being captured by the enemy. He swept her onto the floor and into another waltz — really, Lady Salford's musicians were too fond of the blasted waltz.

Why would the duke want to dance with her? Why was he even there? He hadn't been seen at an event with unwed ladies present in over a decade — not since he had been found in a compromising situation with one of the richest heiresses of the day.

He'd married the girl, but by all accounts the marriage hadn't been happy. And she'd died less than six months earlier. It was early for him to be looking for another wife, especially if his advert for a secretary had been accurate about his plans to travel to Egypt.

He didn't leave her guessing about his intentions. "I regret to inform you, Miss Etchingham, that I cannot hire you."

He said it with complete nonchalance, as though he was informing her about the weather. He caught her off guard, enough so that she was sure her face gave her away. She tried to recover. "I beg your pardon, your grace?"

"My secretary must be a man, of course," he said. "But your letter intrigued me."

"I do not know what you are talking about," she said.

He tsked. "It's poor form to lie. Or so I've been told. But if you insist on my proof, I'll give it. I discovered that my dear correspondent Chandlord's letters were routed through a pub in Soho Square and retrieved there by one of Salford's footmen. You can understand why I might investigate further."

"Who is Chandlord?" she asked, brazening it out. "I am appalled that you would think a gently bred lady capable of writing to you."

"Gently bred ladies have surprised me before," he said. "But that's neither here nor there. It wasn't Salford; he knows all the men Chandlord corresponds with and wouldn't need a pseudonym. At the time the letters started, I assumed it was either the Duchess of Rothwell or the Countess of Carnach, since they were still unmarried and living with Salford. But then I learned of your friendship with them. I realize you likely thought that I had never noticed you — a fair assumption, given your humble antecedents in comparison to my own. But you are the obvious solution to my puzzle."

He had very nearly insulted her. Her father had been a baron, after all, not a chimney sweep. But if what he said was true, how had he known who she was?

He didn't give her a chance to ask. He continued as though it hadn't occurred to him to let her talk. "Again, this is all neither here nor there. I do wish I could hire you. Your letters were quite impressive, even before I guessed you were a woman. Possibly the only highlight of my days."

She was probably supposed to take that as a compliment, but it just reminded her of all the other times she'd heard that women weren't qualified for her chosen area of study. "I should apologize for drawing your interest, then," she said, letting the chill in her heart seep into her voice. "My letter about your secretarial position was a lark. I've no need of your patronage."

"A shame. I was prepared to offer you another position, if it would suit you."

She waited a few turns of the waltz before responding…sure he was baiting her, but too curious to let that remark pass unanswered. "What position would you offer, your grace?"

Thorington smiled — that cold, calculating smile again, the one that didn't reach his eyes. "Would you care to be a duchess?"

*   *   *

Alex had escaped the ballroom as soon as he left Prudence. His mother would notice his absence and be disappointed. She had three children, but with Amelia indisposed and Sebastian not in town, Alex was the only one she could demand attendance from.

Still, he would rather face her disappointment in the morning than Prudence's disappointment tonight.

He shouldn't have said what he had said about her failed engagement to Carnach. He knew it as soon as the words had slipped from his mouth. It was all true, though — when he had gone with her and Amelia to Scotland the previous year and seen that Prudence really would marry another man purely for the sake of a comfortable life, his temper had overruled his sense.

He had told himself that stopping her marriage was the right choice. Prudence deserved someone who would love her, not just the most convenient option. As it turned out, though, he had lied to himself when he thought he could accept the possibility of her finding love elsewhere.

But for the first time, he had a real chance to win her. He opened his desk drawer and pulled out the paper Ellie had sent him. He'd already verified that the symbols were identical, wasting another bottle of whisky to open the dagger's box the night before. It was impossible that this was a coincidence.

The Aramaic below it had taken him twenty minutes to translate. The words were tantalizing, but incomplete. The only line Ellie had included said, in ancient block letters, "Cleopatra, Queen of Egypt."

What did Cleopatra have to do with the dagger? He had thought it was older than that. But then, perhaps the dagger was made first and the inscription came later.

It didn't matter. Once he had the stone, he would have the answer. And if he broke the curse, he could have Prudence.

Which meant he had to win the auction, no matter the cost.

He flipped open his estate ledger. He had ten thousand pounds that he could make available at once. He might be able to release another five thousand without much effort. Surely fifteen thousand pounds was more than enough — Elgin had spent seventy thousand acquiring the marbles from the Parthenon, all of which were more impressive and well documented than a single Egyptian stone. One would have to be mad to spend fifteen thousand pounds on a single rock.

But was it mad to spend fifteen thousand pounds on a new life?

He was tallying up what he might be able to sell when the door opened. Amelia stopped in the center of the doorframe, a book in one hand and a surprised expression on her face. "I thought you would be at the ball," she said.

He returned the paper and the ledger to his desk drawer. "I was. But I wanted a bit of quiet."

"And a brandy, I'd wager," she said, entering and shutting the door without waiting for him to invite her. "Do you mind if I join you? I cannot sleep with the music coming up through my floorboards and the babe kicking in time to it."

He offered her a chair. "It would serve you and Malcolm right if you gave birth to a child who loves to dance. I can think of no better punishment for parents who like books and politics."

She wrinkled her nose at him. "For what do I deserve such punishment?"

He abandoned his desk and sat on the settee across from her. "Perhaps you don't. But I would be amused regardless."

"Evil brother," she complained. Then her smile turned sly, something that she attempted to disguise as innocent concern. "Have you given thought to your own offspring? I think you deserve a son who is mad for hunting and boxing."

His heart jerked. His voice stayed firmly casual. "No sons for me yet. I've plenty to do trying to earn enough to keep you from eating me out of an estate."

Amelia threw a cushion at him. Then she demanded it back so that she could prop herself up with it. "Teasing aside, Alex, you should give a thought to it. I'm sure Mother has told you often enough, but someone needs to carry on the line. And we can both guess that Sebastian isn't likely the one to do it."

Alex shrugged. "All in good time, Mellie."

It was past time for him to marry, though. He should have married years ago. This should have been his ball, hosted by his wife, with his children trying to evade their nursemaid so that they could peek down at the dancers through the slats in the main staircase. At twenty-two, he had never imagined that he might want that life, the life his father had seemed so trapped in...

But now all he wanted was the life his father had had. The same life Alex's wish had cut short. The guilt over his father's death no longer consumed him as it once had; either the curse had numbed it to keep it from distracting him, as seemed likely, or time truly did heal all wounds. But he could still remember how his father had been satisfied with his family, his estate, and his evenings at his club — a life Alex would wish for now, if it meant he could have Prudence at his side.

Amelia didn't know any of that. She just saw what everyone else assumed — that he was a confirmed bachelor evading his responsibilities. She frowned, her hand stroking her belly as though her annoyance had irritated her child. "I never thought I would say this, since I never wanted to marry. And I don't know why you seem to feel the same way. But I think it's time for you to reconsider. I would be so glad if you found the same happiness that Madeleine and I have found."

"I doubt I could be so lucky as to find someone as special as Ferguson or Malcolm," Alex said drily.

Amelia wasn't deflected by Alex's jest. "You know you could. And you know that she's sitting right under your nose."

Any remaining humor Alex felt toward the situation immediately died. He feigned ignorance. "I will consider your advice."

Alex knew how to cut someone off at the knees when a conversation was no longer to his liking. But Amelia couldn't be dissuaded that easily. "Honestly, Alex, I don't understand. You are titled, wealthy, young, and better-looking than most earls of our acquaintance. You could have any lady in the ton if you made just the slightest bit of effort. And if you want someone with whom you could have an intelligent conversation, you could do much worse than Pru..."

He cut her off. "I shall not discuss Miss Etchingham with you."

She was startled. He usually humored her. He loved her, after all, and she had idolized him when they were children.

But a man had his limits. And Alex's limits included discussing the woman he wanted to love with his sister.

She opened her mouth, then shut it again.

"Wise choice," he said.

He couldn't resist taunting her just a bit. It was an instinct born of thirty years of sibling squabbles between them, one he couldn't deny even when it baited her into speaking again. She scowled at him. "Madeleine and I should find a way to force you into marrying someone. You forced both of us. It would be a deserving fate if we returned the favor."

He felt a flash of unease at that. His sister and cousin were smart enough, and devious enough, to find a way to accomplish it.

But his unease dissolved into irritation when the door opened again. Ferguson entered, uninvited as usual. "I hate to interrupt this charming *tête-à-tête* between my two least-favorite Stauntons," he drawled. "But my wife requests Salford's presence in the ballroom."

Amelia did not take his words kindly. "Hardly fair to say we're your least favorite when you barely know Sebastian."

"When he stays in London more than a few months at a time, I shall revise my opinion," Ferguson said. "But you can always try harder now to gain my favor."

She sniffed. "My poor cousin should have held out for someone better than you."

The enmity between Ferguson and Amelia had been very real a year ago. Now, Alex suspected it was mostly a jest. Ferguson played along with their usual argument. "Madeleine could not have found another better than me. Unless she'd chosen to marry Thorington, I suppose. His duchy is less prestigious, but his wealth is rumored to be greater."

"If Thorington had offered for her, I would have skewered him," Alex said. "I am relieved that he was still married while Madeleine and Amelia were out."

"And Miss Etchingham?" Ferguson asked. "She's quite undefended in the ballroom. Madeleine thought you might be interested in returning to protect her virtue."

Alex wouldn't rise to the bait that all of his relatives seemed determined to throw at him. "She's safe, I'm sure. And besides, Thorington would never attend such a tame affair, even if I'd invited him."

Ferguson examined his cuffs and made a minute adjustment to the edge of his shirtsleeves beneath his jacket. "Did you not hear Malcolm invite him last night? The duke is in your ballroom. Dancing a waltz with Miss Etchingham, if my eyes didn't mistake me."

Amelia gasped, half horrified, half delighted. But Alex didn't hear whatever she said to Ferguson — something about Trojan horses infiltrating the gates. All the sounds around him disappeared, blocked out by the image of Prudence in Thorington's arms...of Thorington ruining her to hurt Alex.

He stood abruptly. "I shall attend to Madeleine. Feel free to stay here as long as you like. In fact, I insist upon it."

Ferguson shook his head. "Allow me to escort you back — wouldn't want to miss whatever you do. I shall enjoy your temper more when I see it directed at someone other than me."

Alex ignored him. Ferguson could trail behind him if he wished. Or he could stay and tease Amelia over the fact that she would miss the fun. Or he could go to the devil.

All that mattered was whether Prudence was safe. And if Thorington tried to harm her, he would kill the man.

CHAPTER EIGHT

"I beg your pardon?" Prudence asked.

Thorington sighed. "Shall I rephrase? I thought you were intelligent enough to grasp my meaning, but I shall make allowances for your sex. Will you do me the extraordinary honor of becoming my wife?"

She was too stunned to respond, either to the dripping sarcasm he'd paired with "extraordinary" or to the question he had asked. Thorington sighed again, more dramatically. "If questions are too much for you, I shall try again. Marry me, Miss Etchingham."

Her brain, normally imperturbable, couldn't think of a single reason why he would request such a thing. "Why on earth should I do that?"

"Because I asked you to. You could do much worse than me, but I am also sure you cannot do better."

Thorington hadn't missed a step of the waltz as he said this, but Prudence, stunned to the point of dizziness, could barely stay on her feet. "I need to sit," she said.

"No," he said. "And stop gaping at me as though your world is coming to an end. If you show distress with me, the old tabbies sitting along the wall will have your reputation in shreds before you have a chance to catch your breath."

"Is that why you asked me now?" she asked, still so shocked that she could only think to ask the most recent question, not the most important one. "Did you want to stop me from reacting as I wish?"

"How do you wish to react?" he asked.

She barely knew the man, and he was a duke besides, but Prudence's shock overcame her circumspection. "I wish to pour a pitcher of water over your head and tell you not to be a fool."

Thorington laughed — something that sounded almost genuine, or as genuine as she thought him capable of being. "I already like you more than I liked my last wife. Salford will regret losing your wit."

Alex wouldn't regret anything if she married Thorington. She frowned. "Are you asking for my hand just to upset Lord Salford?"

"I won't deny that stealing you away from him appeals to me."

"I shan't marry you for your petty revenge," Prudence said.

"Then marry me for yours. Won't you enjoy being a rich duchess instead of his poor dependent?"

On another night her mercenary heart might have been seduced. She ignored the temptation. "You can marry whomever you like. I won't stoop to argue with your claim that I cannot do better than you. But I am sure you can do better than me."

Thorington inclined his head. "Of course I can. But I require a wife who is neither silly nor shrewish — harder to find than one might expect, Miss Etchingham. And I require one now, before any of the matchmaking mamas find a way to trick me into compromising their darlings."

Prudence had heard all the rumors about his first wife, but she'd put little credence to the notion that he had been trapped into it. His eyes, though, told a different story. They were hard and cold again, with the steely determination of a man who has been through hell before and plans to avoid another sojourn there.

However, Prudence didn't have to be the woman he used to save himself. "I thank you for the offer, your grace. But I regret to say that I don't think we would suit."

It was a polite brush-off. She found it surprisingly easy to say considering that she had never had cause to turn down a proposal of marriage before.

But all her smoothness of speech was wasted on Thorington. "I understand you wish to consider your options. Send word when you've decided to accept and we may agree on a date. Sooner would be better, but I understand if you need a few weeks to prepare your trousseau. Send the bills for your wardrobe to me — unless you want to bleed Salford a bit before you go."

She narrowed her eyes at him. "Did you not hear me say that we won't suit?"

"You said you don't *think* we would suit. I encourage you to take the time you need to reconsider."

"I will not change my mind," she snapped, losing patience entirely.

He shrugged. "I usually get what I want, my dear. Better for you to know that now."

The man was mad. Infuriatingly so. But if she walked away in the middle of their dance, it would draw far more attention than if she stayed. And if anyone started gossiping about her and Thorington…

She might as well choose her wedding gown. Or her coffin. Only the latter sounded appealing.

So she finished the waltz with him, although she stubbornly refused to answer any of his conversational gambits. When the music stopped, she expected him to return her to Ellie, or at least to the edge of the floor.

But there was no need for that. Alex appeared at her elbow before they'd taken more than five steps.

"Are you feeling well, Miss Etchingham?" he asked. It seemed to be the only question he was capable of asking her. Her temper was piqued by it, but he continued before she could answer. "I am sorry that you were disturbed by our uninvited guest."

"I was invited," Thorington said over Prudence's attempt at speech. "You may run off and ask your friend Carnach about my invitation while I take Miss Etchingham in to supper."

Alex took her other arm. "Miss Etchingham promised that I could take her in to supper," he lied. "You may run off and ask your friend Carnach to join you instead."

She started to protest, but Alex glared at her as though to warn her of something. Thorington didn't let go. "Carnach wouldn't want to intrude on my dinner with Miss Etchingham."

Ferguson strolled up then. "Perhaps Miss Etchingham would rather dine with me."

"You should dine with your duchess," Prudence said.

She tugged on her arms, but neither Alex nor Thorington let her go. Ferguson raised his quizzing glass. "But you are the woman everyone is fighting over. I want to follow the latest fashion."

"Go to the devil, Ferguson" Alex said.

Prudence gasped. Thorington tried to pull her closer to him. "Not in front of the lady."

She was going to scream. She could feel it bubbling up inside her, threatening ruin if she let it out. She struggled more obviously, extricating her arms from theirs with a wholly ungraceful wriggle of limbs.

It was just awkward enough that they stopped arguing and gave her a chance to speak. "I shan't dine with any of you."

Alex and Thorington both turned on her, hemming her in. "Miss Etchingham," Alex said, low and urgent. "Come with me."

Thorington was just as insistent. "Allow me to escort you, my dear."

"'My dear'?" Alex asked, rounding on his former friend. "Watch your tongue, Thorington. Miss Etchingham is not for you."

"Is she not?" Thorington asked, raising an eyebrow. "I think she will be mine, once she accepts my offer. And in any event, she's your mother's companion, not yours. Unless you have an interest here that you've kept secret?"

It was a dangerous question — not merely because it was another stab to Prudence's heart, but because her reputation would be destroyed if anyone thought that Alex had taken her to bed while she lived in his house. From the reckless, angry light in Alex's eyes, she wouldn't like his answer.

And she was *tired* of everyone speaking over her. So she did the only thing she could think to do — the only thing she'd wanted to do all night.

"Once you've decided how I should behave, please send me a note," she said, catching them off guard with the edge to her voice. "Until then, I shall pursue my entertainments elsewhere."

She lifted her chin and offered her hand to Ferguson. "If you'll give me the honor, I would appreciate your escort away from here."

"Gladly," Ferguson said.

He was mad enough to wink at her. She was sure Alex would have throttled him if he could do it without swinging from a noose for it.

But she didn't care. She couldn't stay with either Alex or Thorington another moment. If she had to choose between Ferguson's meddling and listening to Alex and Thorington argue over her like she was a silly, incapable female — for once, she made the choice she wanted to make.

And if either of them decided to follow her…she might be willing to risk ruin by kicking them in the shins.

*   *   *

Even if he were capable of getting drunk, there wasn't enough alcohol in the world to take the edge off Alex's temper. He'd waited for hours in his study, brooding over a pot of tea like a sad abstainer, knowing that he couldn't be caught going to her. He was mad enough, and angry enough, that the thought tempted him — if he was caught with her, they would be forced to marry. Better that than losing her to Thorington.

But he couldn't offer for her yet. It was still too likely that the curse would never be broken.

He knew he should wait for morning. But morning was for rational conversation. There was nothing rational he could say to Prudence about why she shouldn't marry Thorington, unless Alex told her about the curse or offered for her himself.

She would think him demented if he said he was cursed. She would also think him demented if he said she should abandon a duke to remain his dependent.

He should leave it alone and let her do whatever she pleased. At least she was alive to do it; if she interfered in his studies, she might die for it. Or something might happen that would effectively remove her from his life. The last housemaid who had broken one of his artifacts had run off to Canada the next day — had she ever come to her senses and wondered how in the hell she had found herself in Newfoundland? Would Prudence similarly find herself on a ship to some foreign land, not quite knowing why she'd decided to leave him?

He should leave it alone.

But Prudence was a wound that never healed, one that he couldn't ignore. And if he needed another excuse, he couldn't let her marry Thorington — his curse might kill her just as easily as Alex's would. As the clock in the hall chimed three in the morning, Alex stood and threw his teacup into the fireplace. It would have been more satisfying if it was a wineglass, but he took what pleasure he could find.

Then he took one of the lighted candles, snuffed the rest, and strode boldly out of his study and up the stairs. He didn't bother to sneak down the hall. Sneaking always attracted more attention than forthright, direct action. But he wasn't foolish enough to knock. He turned the handle instead, then pushed the door open as silently as he was able.

Prudence's room was dark. The banked fire didn't give enough light for him to make out anything beyond the bed and a vague outline of the body sleeping there. His candle flame shuddered as he exhaled. When the light was strong again, he moved into the room and closed the door behind him.

Suddenly, he didn't know what he was doing there. He couldn't tell her about the curse; he couldn't tell her why she couldn't marry Thorington.

But he had to do something to convince her to wait for him. He needed a week — long enough to know whether Ellie's rock could break his curse. If he stayed cold, calculated, disengaged — could he convince her to wait for him without tempting his curse into taking action against her?

He set the candle on her bedside table, then sat on the edge of her bed. "Prudence," he whispered. "Wake up."

She mumbled something in her sleep. If he didn't know she was too proper for it, he might have thought she said, "Bloody bounder."

He touched her forehead, brushing a bit of hair away from her face. "Prudence," he said, louder this time.

She shifted, blinked, blinked again. Her hand moved up to flick his away as though he were a gnat — then stilled abruptly as she touched him.

She sat up faster than should have been possible for someone who was so deeply asleep. Her head cracked against the headboard. "Easy," he said. "I..."

She didn't let him finish. She pulled back her fist and punched him in the mouth.

CHAPTER NINE

She had never heard him yelp before. As she woke up, the scientific part of her came alive to tick a mark against that observation.

"What in the bloody hell was that for?" Alex demanded, keeping his voice low as he pressed his hand against his lip.

The emotional part of her came alive wanting to punch him again, harder, and while she was awake enough to clearly remember doing it. "Have you gone mad?" she asked, somehow whispering it rather than shrieking it. "Why are you here?"

She tried to pull the covers up around her. But Alex was sitting on them and didn't seem inclined to move. She crossed her arms over her breasts, suddenly flushing. This was as close as any man had ever come to seeing her undressed.

When she had dreamed of a moment like this, she had imagined her hair down and her plain cotton nightrail replaced with something bolder. She had imagined Alex kissing her awake, whispering sweet words about how he couldn't wait any longer.

She had not imagined that she would punch him. But then, she had given up hoping that Alex would ever come to her. Now that he had, she didn't know what to do with him.

She wasn't supposed to want him anymore. So why was her

breath short and her face hot?

"I came to talk, not to ravish you," Alex said. "Although if you are considering Thorington's proposal, you should make yourself accustomed to unwanted ravishment."

She balled her hand into a fist. "I shall hit you again if you don't leave immediately."

He held up his hands. "No need. I didn't come to insult you, either."

"You are not succeeding."

He laughed. A bit of tension escaped with that laugh, letting her see a glimpse of the old Alex — the happier one, the one who had been comfortable with her before that awful night in his study.

"No, I'm not succeeding," he replied. "I thank you for the reminder. Will you allow me to try again?"

She pointed at the door. "Perhaps you will find more success in the morning."

Alex shook his head. "This conversation is better suited for the dead of night."

"Then you should return tomorrow night. We're closer to dawn than midnight."

Why was she trying to put him off? Two months earlier, she would have died, blissfully complete, if she had awoken to find Alex in her bed.

Tonight, she wanted to hit him over the head with a chamberpot.

Alex stayed, unmoved by her coldness. "You cannot marry Thorington."

"You came to my room to discuss *Thorington*?"

His shoulders stiffened. "I care about your well-being, Miss Etchingham."

"So you continue to say," she said. "And yet you're here, risking both our reputations. Whether I wish to become a duchess is really none of your concern."

He didn't say anything for the longest time. She couldn't see his eyes very well — the candle was behind him, edging his brown hair with bits of burnished gold and obscuring the expression on his face. Zeus might have looked like this, preparing to dazzle, then ravish, some innocent maiden.

Alex couldn't possibly be there to ravish her. And yet she sensed the moment when he made some decision about her — about them — that she couldn't quite comprehend.

He loosened his cravat. "You cannot marry Thorington, Prudence."

Her Christian name didn't comfort her. She edged away from him. He didn't love her — he had made it so shatteringly clear. Which meant he was there for one thing.

"Are you drunk?" she asked suddenly.

He snorted. "If only I were. But no."

"I wish you were," she said. She knew he was a gentleman, but the odd intent in his voice, the very fact that he'd come to her in the dead of night when he didn't love her, made her doubt him. "I don't think I shall be able to forgive you if you take advantage of me while you're in your sober mind."

He had fully untied his cravat, but his hand froze before he could pull it away from his neck. "Do you truly think I would do that?"

"Isn't that what men do?" she asked. "Take pleasure wherever they can find it?"

Alex frowned. "That's not why I'm here. Surely you know I value you more than that."

"So you *would* take pleasure if you didn't value me?"

He scowled. "Don't turn my words against me. I came to apologize for not listening to you in the ballroom. Thorington had me too enraged to give a thought to your opinion on the matter. Will you be quiet long enough to let me apologize?"

She almost laughed — claiming that as his reason for visiting seemed utterly absurd. A proper apology wouldn't be given by a man who seemed intent on stripping his clothes off. She tried for a sharper tongue, one that might warn him away. "You proved capable of talking over me in the ballroom tonight. I'm sure you can find a way to do it again somewhere other than my bed."

Alex dropped his cravat to the floor and untied the string holding his shirt closed. He'd never done that in front of her. She saw a scrap of throat that she'd never seen before and suddenly wished that her room was full of daylight instead of darkness.

But then he would have seen how she was blushing…how her hands were trembling as they still braced against the mattress. Better that she was protected by the darkness, even if she was no longer sure she wanted to be safe.

She'd been so distracted that she lost the thread of their conversation. But Alex was still capable of picking it up. "I am sorry if you felt silenced. But I only had your best interests at heart."

"That is still not an apology," she said. "Not for anything that has come before, nor for tonight. If I need you to keep my 'best interests' in mind, I shall tell you. If you deign to let me speak, of course."

It was an audacious thing to say, and not at all the sort of opinion a charity case should express to the man who provided for her. But then, that man shouldn't be taking off his jacket.

Alex stood and shrugged out of his coat as though it was entirely normal for him to undress himself in front of her. "If you have something to say, please, say it," he said. "My apology can wait."

He was in his shirtsleeves. His braces still held up his trousers, but he slung those off his shoulders and let them hang against his thighs.

What was he doing?

She hadn't realized she was holding her breath until the burning in her lungs demanded air. She sucked in a breath, then let it go in a rush of sound. "I've nothing to say. What are you doing?"

"I had planned to apologize, then discuss your engagement as rational adults. But since the lady doesn't want words, I shall try a different approach."

His grin turned devilish. It was one of those secret grins that he used to give her, when something happened at some boring society gathering that he knew would amuse her.

It was one of those grins that had made her believe he might someday love her.

She took advantage of his standing pose to pull the covers tighter around her chest. "Shall I ring for a footman to take you to Bedlam?"

"Not when I've finally come to my senses. You looked beautiful tonight, you know. The purple color suited you."

"It was puce," she said.

She was already cursing how stupid she sounded when he laughed. "Puce, purple, plum, berry — call it whatever you like. I thought you looked perfect in it. I should have said so right when I awoke you, but I forgot in the aftermath of your vicious assault on my person."

He sat on the edge of the bed again. His voice was so light, but there was a deeper intention lurking in the curve of his lips, in the way his hand rested casually on her knee.

"I am sorry I hit you," she said.

"I doubt that. Did you enjoy it, hitting me?"

His other hand came to rest on hers, curling around the fist she'd made unconsciously. "Yes," she whispered.

She didn't like herself very much in that moment. When had she become so horrid? What had happened to her heart, that she would take such vicious pleasure in knowing she had caused him pain?

She didn't want to be bitter.

She didn't want to be her mother.

That thought was enough to toss an entire vat of cold water over her head, but Alex didn't know that her thoughts had taken her in such a dark direction. He caressed her fingers until she opened her fist. "You may hit me again if it would help," he said.

She shook her head. "Don't torture me, Alex. Please. If you ever cared for me at all…just let me go."

He didn't answer her for the longest time. He turned her hand in his, stroking her palm with his thumb as though it were his own. His knee still pressed against her thigh, his breath still mingled with hers. So close — and yet, he would never give her what she wanted from him.

"I can't, Prudence." His voice, when he finally spoke, was almost hoarse, as though he'd argued with himself for so long that he no longer had the sound left to give her an answer. "I can't let you go."

Then he gathered her up into his arms and kissed her.

* * *

He should have kissed her months earlier. Years earlier. She was sweet and warm, with the soft curves he'd dreamed of kept from him by only the thinnest layer of white lawn. She gasped as he claimed her lips, but it wasn't a protest — it was welcoming wonder, a heady combination that threatened his tenuous control. He needed to be slow, steady, unaffected...

She hesitated. She wasn't quite enthralled yet. But she didn't pull away.

And then, unexpectedly, her hand came up to his cheek. Her thumb grazed his cheekbone, then skimmed lower, until her fingers wrapped sweetly around his neck. She was artless but unafraid.

The combination was explosive.

He buried his fingers in her hair, unraveling the plaits of her sleep-ready braid until her hair fell in rivulets of curls down her back. He let his other hand come up to her torso, skimming over the heart-stopping curve between her breast and hip. He wanted to see her, to see everything, to strip her bare and explore the hidden territory he'd denied himself for so long.

He didn't. He had to stay disengaged. And anyway, she didn't seem to want him to abandon her mouth. She opened for him, finally, and he pulled her closer. They fit perfectly, fused together, wrapped around each other. Her hand around his neck was no longer sweet — it was demanding, keeping him in the kiss with all the intensity he wished he could give her.

He should let her go. But he couldn't — not if she wanted him there. Not if there was a chance that every night could be like this. Not if there was a chance that he could find the cure and have *this* life, not the life that condemned him to his study instead of her bed.

He shut down that thought. He told himself that she was any other woman, any quick bit of pleasure the curse allowed him to take. He let his fingers go where they wanted, claiming her breast, reveling in how she filled his palm. She made a soft sound in his mouth. Her other hand dropped to his knee, bracing herself against him even as she arched into him. He was already hard for her, but her hand so close to his manhood and her breast so soft to his touch were going to kill him.

It had been madness to undress himself. He would have to stop. He wouldn't ruin her, not when he didn't know for sure that he could keep her. Surely this was enough to make her think again about Thorington's proposal.

"Alex," she whispered as he pulled away.

Her eyes opened. She looked dazed, but she scanned his face. He loved and hated her for how well she knew him. He sensed the moment when she knew his intention, an instant before her body reacted. Her hands slid off his body, an army stopped mid-pillage and forced into a retreat. She pulled her knees up to her chest and wrapped her arms around them.

"You should go to bed," she said. "Please."

So polite, even as he broke her heart. "It isn't you, Prudence. But I can't ruin you."

She shot him a glare. "A shame you didn't remember that while you were removing your clothes. It will be tedious to watch you dress again."

He touched her shoulder. She shrugged him off. "Prudence, listen to me. I…"

"No," she said. "You cannot do this to me. You cannot…" She stopped abruptly, as though her voice was choking her. But she forced herself to continue. "You cannot keep making me think you love me, then showing me you don't."

He was a devil. She deserved so much more than what he could currently give her. And if he seduced her, then failed to break the curse, tonight was the night that would eventually make her hate him.

Still, he couldn't let her go. Not when his cure was almost at hand. If he could show her, once, that he meant it, perhaps it would stop her from seeking out Thorington. He would have to avoid her after, refocus on his studies with complete diligence until he broke the curse. But he'd avoided thinking of her too much before — he could do it for one more week.

"I want you, Prudence," he said. "And I plan to prove it to you."

CHAPTER TEN

Yes.

He kissed her again. It was commanding, demanding — something that promised pleasure even as he took everything she had.

She should stop him. Her memory knew what would come next. He would raise her hopes, then abandon her.

But her memory was like Cassandra, wailing warnings that her heart and body didn't want to hear. She had loved him, wanted him for so long that this was still a dream coming true, not a nightmare.

"Let me show you," he murmured, brushing his lips across her still-closed lips. "Let me prove it to you."

Why was he doing this? What game was he playing?

Again, the warning of memory was lost to the onslaught of his touch. She parted her lips for him. He took the invitation, claiming her mouth with the sure, steady strokes that she was so quickly growing accustomed to. The feel of him in her mouth — *in her mouth* — was better than she would have guessed from all the illicit engravings she'd seen.

She could have fallen in love with his mouth even if she had never loved him otherwise. She could fall in love with his hands as they caressed up her spine, as they coaxed her arms to fall away from her legs, as they nudged her knees apart. His hands were everywhere, somehow, as though they'd waited a lifetime and couldn't wait another second to know her.

She had already fallen in love with him. Her heart and body conspired to forget everything else. All that mattered was that she loved him and that he currently claimed to love her back.

She exiled her reason to the cold side of her bed and embraced the warmth Alex offered instead. His hand brushed against the sleeve of her nightgown, tugging the fabric down, untying the ribbon that held it closed to free the breast he'd already explored. But the difference between his fingers grazing across cotton and his thumb caressing around her suddenly-bare nipple was shocking, enough so that she gasped against his mouth.

He stopped kissing her. She thought she had done something wrong. But he didn't move away — just moved down, grazing his lips over her jaw, taking a quick jaunt to her ear before sliding lower, down the aching column of her neck, down the suddenly sensitive ridge of her collarbone, down the slope of her skin to the point he'd already teased to hardness.

It wasn't overstating it to say that he was a revelation. She had wanted him before, but it had been an abstract kind of want. They were the dreams of a woman who had some idea of how he might feel, but who didn't have the experience that would turn theory into knowledge.

This was better than any dream she'd had of him. He sucked her into his mouth, biting lightly to draw a moan from her. Her fingers clawed against his shirt, wanting more, needing more...

He pulled her up, pushing both sleeves down until she was bared to the waist. She nearly covered herself with an arm, but he grasped her hands in his as he pressed her back into the mattress.

"I've dreamed of this, Prudence," he whispered across her skin as he kissed the valley between her breasts. "If you knew what I dreamed of, you would run from me."

She closed her eyes, unable to meet the wicked look he gave her for fear it would turn to regret. But his voice didn't stop. "I want to see all of you," he said, brushing a kiss across her other breast, the one that ached from his neglect. "I want to undress you, strip away everything, consign all your clothing to the fire so you could only wear what I provided for you. You deserve bold silk, Prudence, not the grey gowns you came here with."

He paused a moment, swirling his tongue around her nipple in a gesture that took the sting out of words. "I want you to burn for me. I want you unable to sleep without me, the same way I cannot sleep for dreaming of you."

The whispered words turned fervent. She pulled her fingers free of his hands and let them run through his hair, let them press his mouth against her.

"I've always dreamt of you," she whispered.

His mouth demanded again, abandoning words to wring a reaction from her skin instead. He stroked his tongue over her, matching it with his thumb along her other breast to keep it from missing his attentions. And then his hand slid lower, pushing her covers away, tugging at the hem of her nightgown…

It all happened so quickly after that. Or perhaps it happened slowly, endlessly, but her brain couldn't comprehend the impossible story her body tried to tell it. He pulled her nightgown up, shifted her in his arms so that it cleared her waist, and then stripped it off her body. It joined her abandoned reason on the other side of the bed, leaving her completely bare to him. He pulled off his shirt as well, in a fluid motion that was much too fast to allow her to thoroughly comprehend the rippling muscles of his torso.

Her blush was strong enough to keep her warm. But his hands were hotter still, and his mouth could start an inferno. He knelt over her, his leg keeping hers from closing. He leaned down to kiss her again, deeply. Then he bracketed his hands on either side of her shoulders.

"Prudence," he said. "Look at me."

She'd closed her eyes, as though she knew that opening them would pull her out of the dream. But when she looked up at him, the need she saw there was worth the risk. His eyes were dark and intense, his lips hungry.

She caressed a tentative hand over his chest, flattening over one of his nipples, both so similar to and so different from her own. She saw pain in his eyes, suddenly, and wondered if she had hurt him. But he didn't stop her.

"I want you to have more than dreams," he said. "I want you to have everything."

He kissed her again, too soon for a brain that had ground to a stop while trying to comprehend what he had just said. Any power she had to analyze, calculate, understand was destroyed by the onslaught of raw emotion his words had raised.

All she could do was kiss him back.

Eventually, he moved away from her mouth, down her body again, in a rhythm that she was becoming familiar with. But this time, he passed her breasts, going lower, lower still, passing her ribcage, passing her navel...

And then his mouth came down on her, devouring her as though she was the last meal he would ever take.

She moaned. It was a sound that might have embarrassed her, if she were younger or if he were less adept, but there was no longer room for any shame. "Alex," she whispered.

He knew it wasn't a plea to stop — she was giving in to some deep, ancient desire to say his name, to claim him as hers even as his mouth did the same to her. He teased around her clitoris, avoiding it at first, until she somehow needed him there urgently even though he'd yet to touch it.

Was he so good at this because he had more experience than her? Or was it because he *knew* her — knew how to read her body, knew how to listen for the shift in her breath? His mouth closed over that point where her pleasure was concentrated, flicking it with his tongue, giving it just the barest scrape of his teeth.

She writhed under him, needing something she didn't know how to ask for, hoping he knew because she was in the dark now, beyond where her imagination had ever taken her, with only him for a guide. His wicked tongue descended on her again, and it was enough to drive her to the edge. Then his hand came up and found her breast, tracing around her nipple with the same speed as his mouth teased her...

He'd always been so proper with her before. But there was something supremely primal, supremely male as he looked up at her. "Come for me," he murmured, before giving her another intimate kiss. "Let me give you this."

He shifted an arm under her derriere and pulled her up to him. That, and the promise in his voice, was enough to throw her over the cliff. She cried out as her climax wracked her, flinging her arm over her mouth to stifle the scream she hadn't known she had within her. Everything was hot, shuddering, torture and release in the same breath.

Torture and release. It was no wonder she loved him, if this moment was a perfect mirror of everything that had happened before. She loved him, hated him, needed him, dreamed of him — a pain and a completion that fed on itself, the same way her climax stretched on, seemingly endless.

She loved him. Even if he didn't love her.

And she would have to find a way to live with it.

As aftershocks went, that was a bleak one. She came down quickly, pulling her arm away from her mouth. Alex looked smug as he slid back up her body. "Did I please you?" he asked, as one does who expects a certain answer.

"Yes," she said. She couldn't lie to him about that.

But it wasn't the *yes* she wanted to give him.

His grin faded. "Did I hurt you somehow? I thought I was slow enough, but your breasts...I may have carried myself away."

She nearly laughed at that, but she sensed that laughter about this particular situation might injure him. "You didn't hurt me. You were lovely."

Alex frowned. "What is it, then? Something is wrong. Why?"

At least he asked. Mortifying as it was to tell him, at least he hadn't walked away feeling satisfied with himself.

"Why did you do this?" she asked. She had to know. She was stupid for asking, but it was a compulsion. "Was it...was it because of Thorington?"

"*Thorington*?" Alex said. "Were you thinking of him just now?"

He sat up beside her, didn't stop her when she pulled a sheet over her body. He left his shirt off, and she saw the bulge in his trousers — whatever he had come for, he wasn't satisfied.

That knowledge emboldened her. "Of course I wasn't thinking of him. But why did you stop? I know what is supposed to happen next."

She didn't quite have the vocabulary to ask for what she wanted. But if he was ready to keep her, she was ready to let him.

He paused, though, too long for her comfort. Her rational side slunk back over from the cold part of the bed, whispering doubts in her ear.

"Not yet." He was silent another moment. "I want to. God, I want to. But I need a week."

"Why would you need a week?" she asked, bewildered enough that she didn't promptly punch him again. "What purpose could possibly be served by waiting?"

Alex seemed to consider something. She saw the doubt in his eyes as he mulled over whatever he was deciding about.

The doubt won. "Give me a week. I promise I will have an answer for you then."

She didn't want an answer — she wanted a question, the question she wanted to say *yes* to.

"Find me when you have it," she said.

The dismissal in her voice chilled even her. She turned on her side away from him, refusing to meet his eyes, refusing to turn over again when he touched her shoulder. "I will give you an answer, Prue," he vowed. "Just…please, wait for me."

He shifted off the mattress. She heard him gather his things, but she didn't turn to see whether he put his clothing on properly or just shoved it into a bundle under his arm. Then the shadows from the candle moved, the floorboards creaked, the door opened…

And he was gone. She flipped onto her back and stared at the ceiling, willing herself not to scream. She had known that he would lead her astray. She had let it happen, too seduced by the pleasure of his touch to remember the inconstancy of his heart.

This was how all the women in Amelia's favorite novels came to some bad end. Prudence had always scorned them before. Who would choose scandal and disgrace over proper conduct, when proper conduct guaranteed a roof over one's head? If this were a novel, Alex would have ravished her that night and she would have begun a quick, dreadful descent into the brothels.

She was being melodramatic. But she punched her fist against the mattress and wished it was his face instead. Anger warred with the hot tears leaking, unwelcome, from her eyes.

"Bloody bounder," she muttered to herself.

He had asked for a week. If she were a better woman, she would wait meekly for him, the charity case consigned to the shelf while he went about his business.

But in a week, the auction would be over. She would have the funds to start another life. If he didn't want her — if those few gorgeous moments of pleasure were an aberration that he never planned to give her again — she would leave him. Surely there was somewhere in the world where she could forget him.

And if she couldn't forget him...

She punched the mattress again. She'd lost her father, lost her brothers, lost her home, and was very near to losing her place in society. She'd survived it all. She wouldn't lose herself just because Alex Bloody Staunton didn't want her.

Her curiosity, wretched beast that it was, would give him his week. But she couldn't wait any longer for a life she would never have.

CHAPTER ELEVEN

Six days later, Prudence no longer felt like wringing Alex's neck.

The thought had tempted her over the intervening days between that night in her room and Ellie's auction. Alex had mostly avoided her, even though she felt his eyes watching her at dinner every night. He never made mention of the week he'd asked for. Nor did his voice, during the few moments they'd spoken to each other, hold anything more than distant affection.

If she hadn't known better, she would have thought him mad. At least madness would have been an explanation for his actions. And she might not have wanted to strangle him if she'd been able to send him to Bedlam.

But by the evening of the auction, Prudence was no longer angry. She thought she might be sick instead.

"You shall be rich after tonight," Ellie pronounced.

The marchioness adjusted the stone one final time. It was much smaller than the Rosetta Stone, approximately the size of a man's outspread hand. The stonemason had roughened the edges and chipped a few flakes into the text so that it might look weathered, but it was still legible if one knew how to read Aramaic. Ellie had centered it on a piece of red velvet, adding a rich, sumptuous backdrop to the granite. Two footmen stood guard solemnly behind it — a pair of well-matched brunets, scandalously dressed in pleated white linen that was reminiscent of Egyptian drawings.

Prudence was immorally proud of her efforts. But she was no longer sure that she wanted the results. "This is really too much," she said.

"Nonsense. Allow me to indulge my artistic inclinations and say that this tableau is perfect."

The craze for Egyptian furnishings had given way to other decorative schemes, but Ellie must have kept all of her old collection in her attics. She had redecorated her largest drawing room as an Egyptian fantasy, with low couches, large urns, and miles of white gauze. The stone stood in the center, on a pedestal, as though it was already important enough to be the premier attraction in a gallery.

The tableau *was* perfect — if the stone itself wasn't a forgery.

"We shouldn't do this," Prudence said. "What if someone discovers that I am the seller?"

"They won't. I will take the money and give it to you, with no one the wiser. No one questions my dealings. And in any case, I have never canceled a party when the guests have already arrived, and I shan't do it now."

"But what if it isn't real?" Prudence asked. "What if I was wrong about its provenance?"

It was as close as she could come to a confession. Even with the idea of ruin staring her in the face, she didn't want to take the more honorable step and tell Ellie the truth. Ellie might hate her if she knew, and Prudence wasn't ready to lose her friends.

Ellie just laughed. "As I said, if the men are stupid enough to buy it, that is their business."

She waved another footman off in the direction of the musicians. They were seated behind a painted screen in a corner of the adjoining room, which guests might spill into when the main room became too crushed. As soon as they began to play, she nodded at the butler. He threw open the doors to the entrance hall, admitting the din of excited would-be buyers.

Prudence was going to faint. Perhaps if she knocked over the pedestal as she toppled, she could grab the stone and run before anyone realized what she was doing.

Ellie moved away to mingle with her guests. Prudence thought of going to the retiring room and hiding there until it was all over. She moved toward the door, intending to squeeze unnoticed past the entering guests.

But Ostringer stood in the doorway, blocking her path. She was so startled to see him that she froze an instant too long, long enough for his sharp eyes to pick her out of the crowd. He walked toward her, slowly enough not to draw notice, but too quickly for her to escape. "Miss Etchingham," he said, in a low voice that sounded like a judge pronouncing a death sentence. "A pleasure to make your acquaintance again."

"Mr. Ostringer," she said. "If you will excuse me, I was just on my way out."

"Are you not feeling well?" he asked. The question was solicitous, but his tone wasn't. "I had hoped you would have explored the offerings at my shop during these past weeks."

He had sent her several messages through her courier at the pub in Soho Square, each asking whether she had thought of something else to forge. She'd responded to the first few with vague murmurings about scarab beetles and vases — the projects she was working on in case the stone failed to sell. But she had burned the last two notes unanswered.

"The Season is rather demanding," she said. "I'm sure you understand."

He looked past her to the stone standing in the center of the room. "Of course, Miss Etchingham. I assume you've been quite busy helping Lady Folkestone with this little soiree."

"Lady Folkestone manages well enough on her own," Prudence said.

"She is a very intelligent and resourceful woman," Ostringer agreed. "I wish all the ladies I knew were so adept at accomplishing their goals without courting disaster."

She wanted to ask him to state his business in plain English, but there were too many people around them. "I hope that you don't hold me in such low esteem," she said, in a voice made for shallow flirtation.

"I could never hold you in low esteem. I suspect you could be like a daughter to me if I had the opportunity to know you better," he said.

It would have been touching, if it weren't for the hard edge to his voice and the horde of people who might overhear him. "I thank you for the sentiment," she said. "But I should retire now so that I may return before the auction."

His gaze held her in place. "I'm sure you wouldn't want to miss seeing the sale. Men who don't know better might be tempted to spend an extravagant sum on this stone."

"Do you intend to bid?" she asked.

He laughed. "I know better. As should you, Miss Etchingham."

Her hands were cold and clammy in their gloves. "I'm no scholar,

Mr. Ostringer."

She was trying to remind him of their public situation, trying to steer the conversation away from the deep waters she was near to drowning in. He didn't seem to care. "It is for the best. I don't hold with some of the prohibitions against the fairer sex — one of the smartest people I ever knew was a woman. You could rival her. But you don't seem to know the difference between audacity and stupidity."

His voice was still low. No heads turned toward them. But Prudence's stomach dropped into her shoes. "Now is not the time for conversation," she said as quietly as she could.

He shrugged. "Perhaps we will have the opportunity to converse again someday. But if you aren't more careful, I rather doubt it. Good evening, Miss Etchingham."

He left her dumbstruck in the middle of the drawing room. He *knew* the stone was forged. And he knew she was responsible for it.

Would he demand money from her to keep her secret? He hadn't mentioned money at all, though. It was as though his warning was about something else entirely.

She was too confused to parse his words, and her blood was running too hot and cold to allow her to calm her nerves. And anyway, she was surrounded by people — there was no room to consider what he had meant.

She tried to leave for the retiring room again. But again, she was caught before she could melt into the shadows. Madeleine intervened, accompanied by Ferguson's younger sisters, Lady Maria and Lady Catherine. "I am too jealous that you saw the room before Ellie opened the doors," the duchess said as she kissed Prudence's cheek. "Isn't it lovely? But the twins were late, as usual."

Kate and Maria both protested. "We didn't keep you waiting above five minutes," Maria said.

"It was closer to twenty," Madeleine said.

"In our defense, it was Ferguson's fault," Kate interjected. "His lecture this afternoon rivaled the longest ones Father ever gave us."

Prudence didn't want to hear anything about their day, but she would attract far more attention to herself by leaving. "Where is Ferguson?" Prudence asked Madeleine.

"Dining with Malcolm at Aunt Augusta's house," she said. "He asked me to tell Nick to meet them there for a drink when he tires of this 'nonsense.'"

"Perhaps we should consider living with Ellie," Kate said, looking around the room. "She has more than enough room for us. And she wouldn't balk at spending money on entertainment."

The twins had lived with Ferguson and Madeleine since their father had died the previous year, but at two-and-twenty they were beginning to chafe against their brother's rules. Not that he had many. Or any, as far as Prudence knew. Ferguson had been a confirmed rake before marrying Madeleine. He was the last man Prudence thought to see turn into a conservative protector of female virtue.

"What was Ferguson lecturing you about, if you pardon the question?" she asked.

The twins both shifted. "He may have…taken umbrage at our new musical instruments," Kate said.

"It seems he did not know how much a new piano and harp might cost when he gave us permission to buy them," Maria added solemnly.

Rothwell had more than enough money to buy new instruments. "Is that all?" Prudence asked.

The twins were silent. Madeleine snorted. "What they aren't saying is that they also hired a music master along with the instruments. And that the music master is very young, very handsome, and very Italian."

"We must learn from someone," Maria pointed out. "It isn't Master Angiello's fault that he is young."

"Or handsome," Kate added, with a laugh she couldn't quite suppress.

Prudence smiled, but as they continued to prattle about their music master, her quicksand thoughts sucked her back in. She hadn't been as carefree as them in...well, ever.

She took a deep breath. Perhaps it was going to be all right, after she sold the stone. She would have to take care of Ostringer, of course.

And she would have to escape Thorington. She'd burned six of his notes in the past week as well. They had all been attached to a single rose. All had said the same thing, as though he'd had them printed on a press: *Miss Etchingham - do you have an answer yet? Yours, etc., Thorington.*

The man was surely mad. She'd ignored the notes and given the flowers to the maids.

But once she paid off Ostringer, encouraged Thorington to find a better mark, and convinced herself to forget Alex, perhaps she could be the carefree sort of woman she had always longed to be.

She couldn't be carefree yet — not when her night kept getting worse. Alex found them then. It wasn't lost on her that she was the first person he sought when he arrived.

"Madeleine, Lady Catherine, Lady Maria, Miss Etchingham," he said, bowing to each in turn. He didn't linger over her name, nor did he promote her above her order of precedence even though she was older — hopefully dearer? — than the twins. "I hope you shall forgive my intrusion."

Kate spoke before the older ladies could respond. "How charming of you to join us, Lord Salford."

Was Kate *simpering*? Prudence took a glass of champagne from a passing footman and prayed for calm.

If Madeleine noticed anything amiss, she gave no indication of it. "Do you mean to bid on the stone, cousin?"

"Have you ever known me to refrain from such a find?" Alex asked.

"No. But it's just a stone," Madeleine said. "Wouldn't you prefer to save your funds for a statue or painting instead?"

He shook his head. "It isn't just a stone. It holds the key to unlocking everything."

Prudence couldn't bear to hear his assessment of the rock she'd forged. "I'm sure the twins will be bored by the topic if we continue it. Shall we discuss something else?"

"No need," Maria said brightly, ignoring Prudence's dampening intentions. "We find auctions thrilling."

"Have you ever been to an auction?" Prudence asked, with enough skepticism that she was sure her annoyance was obvious.

"No," Maria said. "But anything that secures Lord Salford's interests sounds quite special indeed."

Alex inclined his head. "I do not deserve such flattery, but this particular object holds significant promise."

The twins continued flirting with him, asking him questions about the object, its provenance, and why he cared for it. Prudence barely listened. Her attention was focused instead on everything he *wasn't* saying.

The words themselves were calm, assessing the object as any collector might. But the cadence of his voice was faster. His shoulders were stiff, as though he needed the extra muscular control to keep from leaning forward and showing how eager he was. And while his loose stance was eminently proper, he was absentmindedly stroking his left palm with his right thumb — a gesture Prudence knew.

He was feeling *something* intensely — whether it was worry or excitement, she didn't know.

"I doubt anyone shall decipher the language," she said during a break in the conversation, before the twins flirted with him again. "You'd be better rewarded spending your money on your estate."

The statement came out all wrong, with more judgment and bitterness than she had intended. Alex frowned. "My estate has never suffered because of my collection, Miss Etchingham. Besides, I thought you would understand the appeal of a scholarly pursuit."

If the rock were real, she would be intensely interested in it. "I see the appeal, of course. But we must all become adults. Perhaps you should reconsider your interests."

Something flashed in his eyes. He stroked the palm of his hand again. "I wish I could have such a simple view of the world."

"Better a simple view of the world than a foolish one," she snapped. "At least I am smart enough not to chase a fantasy."

"Better to chase a fantasy than settle for less than you deserve," he retorted.

Their eyes met, and held, for far longer than either of them likely wanted. But Prudence couldn't look away. There was such a depth of feeling in his lovely brown eyes — eyes that made her feel hot and cold all at once. He looked at her like he wanted her to know him, like his soul was a garden he invited her to walk in. And, Heaven help her, she *wanted* to know him.

No. She wanted to forget him. She turned her attention to Madeleine. "Are you ready for your ball tomorrow?"

Madeleine's green eyes were moving back and forth between Alex and Prudence as though she had noticed something about them that had escaped her attention before. Prudence willed her face to be perfectly still, hoping to keep her friend from guessing her secrets.

But the transition had been too abrupt and the duchess was too perceptive. "I shall be glad when it is over and we will have time for a proper conversation," Madeleine said.

Damn. Ellie already knew about Prudence's feelings for Alex, and now Madeleine seemed well on the way to guessing. Could the night be any worse? She hoped that she could plead a headache after the auction and miss the celebratory supper. She no longer felt like gloating.

She felt like throwing everything into a valise and taking the next mail coach out of the city, before the world she'd constructed collapsed around her.

As it happened, though, the night could always be worse. Thorington strolled up, a glass of champagne in one hand and a glass of lemonade in the other. "Here, my dear," he said, thrusting the lemonade at her. "You are looking too fatigued for champagne."

The twins gaped.

Madeleine gaped.

Alex looked like he wanted to punch the duke in the face.

Prudence frowned, but she took the lemonade — she could hardly leave him standing there with it. Especially when she suspected he would force her to take it if he wanted to.

"I thank you, your grace, but there's no need for concern," she said. "May I introduce you to my friends?"

"No," he said. "Will you walk with me?"

Kate and Maria gasped in unison. He bowed to them, but the mockery in the gesture was clear. "Please don't take offense, my dears," he said, using the endearment as indiscriminately with them as he did with her. "But you are safer not knowing me."

They exchanged a look. Prudence saw some scheming intention that reminded her how closely they were related to Ferguson and Ellie. Alex had other matters on his mind. "Miss Etchingham would be safer as well. We all would. I suggest that you find another circle to impose your conversation upon."

"You aren't very safe to be around yourself, Salford, even if you are a dull one. Shouldn't you be holed up in your study?"

Alex didn't twitch, but his eyes turned deadly. "The lady doesn't wish to be acquainted with you, Thorington. Leave us, before I must make a scene."

Alex was right — she didn't want to be acquainted with Thorington. But he'd done it again — answered for her before she could slip a single word into the conversation. He'd asked for a week, but that time was almost up, and with absolutely no indication of what he would do at the end of it.

And Prudence was *done* with others making decisions for her.

"Just a few words with the duke will do, I think," she said, pushing both her lemonade and her champagne into Alex's hands. "Since he asked so prettily."

Alex's eyes said he wanted to do violence to her person, but his hands closed over the glasses instead of her throat. "Don't go on the balcony with him, no matter what he says," Alex warned. "Or out of the room in any direction, for that matter."

"You wound me," Thorington said. He tossed his champagne

down in one go and held the empty glass out imperiously until a foot-man rushed over to retrieve it. "I can ruin the lady in plain sight. I don't need a dark garden to accomplish it."

The twins gasped again. This was surely a better show than any-thing their Italian music master had given them. Madeleine, though, was concerned enough to grab her arm. "Do you want me to escort you?" she asked.

Prudence hadn't told any of her friends about Thorington's pro-posal — she was sure he would abandon it, and it was too absurd for words. But she knew, then, that their engagement was the only topic of conversation the duke would pursue. She shook her head. "I won't leave the room. If his grace tries to abscond with me, send a rescue party."

It was a jest that should have drawn laughter. But her party was entirely silent as they watched her walk away.

Thorington wasted no time. "Have you decided to accept my offer?"

"No, your grace."

Her voice was as flat and final as she was capable of being. The duke was either the most tone-deaf person in England, or he simply did not give a fig for anyone else's plans.

"Do you think you require another day to decide, or another week?" he asked. "My hothouse will run out of roses if you continue to ignore me. More importantly, I should like to be married at St. George's in Hanover Square, and even with three weddings a day the church's schedule fills as the Season draws closer to its end. We shall be married by special license, so there's no need to wait for banns to be read. But the venue is a consideration."

It was not lost on her that she'd abandoned Alex for making a correct assumption about her desires, only to talk to Thorington about plans for a wedding she did not want. "I am not going to marry you," she said through gritted teeth.

"You will," he predicted. "When you see that I have more of everything than Salford has, you will make the only choice you have. Especially when you finally realize that he is never going to offer for you."

"Do you think your title and your wealth are all that I might care for?" she asked. "Did it not occur to you that I might want warmth, and conversation, and someone who asks for my opinion rather than my blind obedience?"

She'd never voiced what she wanted in a husband before, but she knew, instinctually, that the duke wasn't a candidate. But Thorington shrugged. They had stopped next to the pedestal on which her rock sat — the rock he didn't know she was responsible for. He reached out a finger and drew it over the Egyptian characters, then trailed it down to the Aramaic letters below. The footmen behind it stayed impassive. They wouldn't stop the Duke of Thorington unless he tried to steal it. Even then, they might hesitate.

When he spoke, his voice was as cool as the stone and just as indecipherable. "I want those things as well. But I will settle for protecting myself."

Then he turned his green eyes on her. He looked ancient, suddenly, as though he knew more about the human heart than anyone else — as though the knowledge was too much for him. "You will settle too, Miss Etchingham. For protection. And for revenge. Send for me when you know it."

CHAPTER TWELVE

Alex shouldn't have spent a week marshaling his finances. He should have spent it learning Aramaic so that he could have read it on sight. It stood in front of him, the answer to all his prayers, offered up on red velvet like the bloody crown jewels.

But it was just as indecipherable as ever. And the bidding was going higher than he had expected. "Eight thousand pounds," Thomas Hope called out from the back of the room.

Ellie's husband Nick had been dragooned into playing the auctioneer. "Is there an offer for eighty-one hundred?"

Alex raised his hand. Nick acknowledged the bid with a nod. "Does anyone offer eighty-two hundred? I'm sure someone will find it a good value to buy a single rock instead of an entire farm's worth."

His sarcasm elicited a laugh from those who were there merely to enjoy the spectacle. Ellie had invited at least sixty guests, but only a handful had the resources or the desire to buy the stone.

Thorington covered his mouth, yawned, and then raised his hand.

The bids went higher, then higher still. Alex stayed calm, detached, striving to look amused. Mr. Hope eventually dropped out, as did Soane and a representative for Lord Elgin. But Alex and Thorington were still committed to the battle they'd been locked in for a decade.

"Twenty thousand," Alex said.

The crowd gasped. The previous bid had been sixteen. But he wanted to end this. He could go to twenty-five. He didn't think that Thorington could go higher, unless the curse had given him an unusually large influx of hard money in recent weeks.

Thorington looked over at him. There was something in his eyes that reminded him of the old Gavin — something sad, but still determined. If Alex broke the curse, would it give Thorington a chance to become the man he should have been?

Nick turned to Thorington. "Do you wish to bid?"

Thorington flipped open his watch and checked the time. "I grow tired of this. Fifty thousand pounds."

The crowd gasped again, louder this time. But the only gasp he heard was Prudence's. He looked over, even as he knew the gesture might betray him. All the color had leached from her face. Her hands were balled into fists at her side, and she swayed slightly on her feet as though her knees were locked.

He thought it odd, but somehow sweet — she didn't want him to lose.

"Salford?" Nick asked.

He closed her eyes. He'd failed her. He had failed them both.

"I'm out," he said.

"Many congratulations, Thorington," Nick said, smiling as the crowd clapped. "I hope your heirs someday appreciate their good fortune when they inherit this."

The crowd laughed. Some of them whistled. Thorington accepted Nick's ribbing with unusually good grace. Everyone moved to offer him their own congratulations, even those who would usually avoid him. The amount of his bid was simply so audacious that no one could stay away from him.

Some stopped by Alex on their way to Thorington and offered their condolences. But none of them truly cared about what had happened, beyond the titillation they felt at being bystanders to such an event. They would gorge themselves on the supper provided by Ellie's excellent chef, drink all of the wine stocked by her butler, and then spread wild tales about the auction in the morning.

As soon as he could escape, he went to Prudence. She hovered near the far wall, immune to the magnetic pull of Thorington's victory. "Are you feeling well?" he asked quietly.

She looked up at him. There was something in her brown eyes that he hadn't seen before — something like guilt, which made no sense whatsoever. But whatever it was, the vitality he usually saw there was crushed by the darker feelings she labored under.

Had he caused this, by seducing her and then avoiding her? At the time, it had seemed better than losing her to Thorington. But he hadn't won the auction. He had made a bet with her heart, and he had lost.

She didn't know that, though, so her odd sorrow must be about something else. "I have a headache, I think," she said.

Her lie was transparent. He couldn't keep himself from asking the obvious question. "Are you going to marry Thorington?" he asked.

She didn't respond. "Do you think your coachman would take me home? I really am not feeling well."

"I shall escort you, if you wish."

The way she avoided his gaze was answer enough. Her words were more circumspect. "I'm sure I don't wish to interrupt your evening, my lord."

My lord. Not Alex.

It might never be Alex again.

He was angry, suddenly, letting the rage burn through the shock of losing. "I will take you home," he said, his voice turning authoritative. "But will you grant me a favor first?"

"What is the favor?" she asked warily.

"Will you distract Thorington? If I can take a rubbing of the stone before he removes it from the house, it won't matter so much that I lost."

Prudence scowled. "You cannot do that, not with the guards standing there. And I cannot distract Thorington well enough to stop everyone else from noticing you unless I kiss him in front of the whole room. Do you wish for me to do that?"

"Never," Alex said. And he meant it. Even to give himself the chance to marry her, he wasn't sure he could bear seeing Thorington's mouth on hers. "But I must know what that stone says."

"Why does it matter so much to you?" Suddenly she sounded irritable, as though his voice chafed her. "Can you not at least be glad that you didn't waste fifty thousand pounds on a mirage?"

"Why do you think it is a mirage?" he asked. "I know that the Rosetta Stone has not yielded the results we had all hoped, but surely this can help."

She closed her eyes. "Can we discuss this at home? If you insist on a discussion, of course. I would much rather discuss anything else."

Something was wrong. This wasn't the Prudence he knew. The Prudence he knew would be excited by an interesting bit of history, not in denial of its importance. The Prudence he knew would be cheerful, not irritable.

He was going to lose her. Just as he had lost the rock. Just as he had lost his father. Just as he continued to lose everything but his studies. It was the fate he had condemned himself to.

He didn't have to lose her tonight, though. "Let's go home," he said, offering her his arm.

*   *   *

Fifty thousand pounds. Thorington had paid her *fifty thousand pounds*.

As betrayals went, she had been handsomely rewarded. Fifty thousand pounds was better than thirty shekels of silver. But she would surely go to hell for it.

They hadn't discussed the stone on the way back to Salford House. The carriage ride passed in silence, with Alex brooding over his loss and Prudence brooding over her win. But when they walked into the house, Alex placed a hand on her shoulder. "Will you take a drink with me?" he asked. "I know you do not feel well. But I would like to ask a favor."

There was nothing she could say to make him feel better. Unless she told him the truth...unless she told him that he had bid on a chimera, not a prize.

She couldn't think about it. "Not tonight."

"Please," he said.

He never pleaded.

She sighed and held out her hand. He escorted her down the hall to his study. They should have left the door open, as they would be expected to. Tonight, though, he closed it.

"I know I don't have any right to ask this," he said, waving her into a chair as he walked to the decanters. "But I need your help."

She sat, perfectly still and upright on the settee she had always wanted to lounge on. "I doubt there is anything I can do to help you, my lord."

He poured a single glass of sherry, which he handed to her before taking his own seat. Oddly, he chose to share the settee with her rather than sitting behind his desk — an intimacy she would have craved if she didn't know better.

"I need a rubbing of that stone," he said. "You're the only person who can help me get it."

She set her sherry on the table. "I doubt Thorington will give me a copy of the stone even if I ask for it."

"There are other ways. Ellie surely made a full copy. She is more likely to give it to you than she is to me. Or perhaps you can arrange a time to meet Thorington, and I can break into his study while he's out…"

Her horrified laugh cut him off. "You cannot break into Thorington's house."

"I've done it before," he said, shocking her. "I suspect he's searched my study as well. We tend to keep abreast of each other's collections. But I'm not stealing anything. And it doesn't matter to him if I take a rubbing of the stone."

It sounded suspiciously close to how she had rationalized her forgery. He surely knew that Thorington would be livid if Alex tried to copy it. And yet something drove him that was more important than any moral code.

"Why do you care so much?" she asked. "I've never known you to be so obsessed over something."

He looked her over. "I have been obsessed over things other than that rock, Prudence."

Her Christian name was back on his lips. She frowned. "You should leave the rock be. Be glad you didn't waste such an awful sum on it."

"You don't understand," he said. He rubbed his thumb over his scar. "I must know what that stone says. And I will do anything within my power to get it."

He looked haunted, with his skin taut over his cheekbones and the firelight casting shadows over his eyes. And she had done this to him — used an object from his own collection to start the forgery. She wondered, again, what the dagger meant to him.

She could leave him to wallow in his obsession. She could leave him to chase a fantasy. She almost wanted to — he'd done the same to her, coming to her room and then ignoring her.

But in the end, she couldn't be that cruel. "I might be able to procure a copy for you," she said.

"Do you know that one exists?"

There were three copies in her bedroom. She looked away. "Ellie promised me one."

It was odd, how the energy in the room changed. He had seemed despondent before, but now he was flying high, eager, excited. "Shall we go back there? We can cool our heels in her drawing room until the supper is over, if you don't feel like eating."

"Now?" she asked. "Why must you have it tonight?"

He paused. "You're right, of course. We can wait for morning."

"Why are you so desperate to know what the stone says?" she asked. "This isn't just about learning to translate Egyptian, is it?"

His eyes shifted. There was wariness there, suddenly, and a secret he wouldn't divulge. "I have an object in my collection that has the same characters in Egyptian," he said, not mentioning the dagger directly. "You can understand why I might be curious to know what it says."

She could — and yet she couldn't. "So curious that you cannot wait until morning?"

He shrugged, but he wasn't as relaxed as he pretended. "I allowed myself to be carried away."

She debated. The stone wouldn't give him the real message. But she only had two choices.

She could confess that it was a forgery and destroy his opinion of her forever.

Or she could tell him what the stone said and let him believe that it was true.

If she were a better person, she would tell him. She would deliver the news quickly, mercilessly, like a *coup de grace* — severing their friendship and abandoning all hope of ever winning him.

Nobility was to be admired. When she was younger, she would have vowed that honor was more important than anything else.

She didn't care much about nobility anymore. Not when she would lose everything by confessing. "I could tell you what it said," she said slowly. "If that would help."

A flicker of surprise flashed through his eyes. "Did Ellie have someone translate the Aramaic?"

Even though she didn't deserve his respect anymore, the scholarly part of her was annoyed that he doubted her capabilities. "I can read it. Can you not?"

Aramaic wasn't a common language for scholars to learn, but she'd had plenty of time for it while she was in mourning. Alex had likely never thought he would need it. "Obviously I am not as well-learned as you are," he said.

Other men might have sulked over that, but he eyed her with newfound admiration. She twitched. "I have a skill for languages."

"Then tell me — what did the stone say?"

He leaned forward, as though she was about to tell him a story he'd waited a lifetime for. She closed her eyes for the recitation. "Cleopatra, Queen of Egypt, sends you good tidings and wishes you luck on your quest."

It was a bland enough statement. He didn't respond immediately, waiting long enough for her to think he had lost interest. She opened her eyes, but she found fury on his face instead of apathy. "No," he said harshly. "You must have misinterpreted."

She stared at him. "I vow that's what it says."

"No," he said again.

He was always saying no to her. "You can see it for yourself in the morning," she said mulishly.

He stood to pace around the room. "Why would it say that?" he muttered, more to himself than to her. "Cleopatra's darker dealings were mostly with the Romans. Why would she have the dagger inscribed in Egyptian? Unless it was meant for a priest?"

Prudence stayed still as stone. Alex would surely realize that it wasn't real.

He hadn't come to that conclusion yet, though. He was still talking to himself, still pacing. "It must be a riddle," he said. "What is the quest?"

She stood up, unable to watch. "I should go to my room."

Alex turned to her. For a moment, he was full of life, full of some fire that was determined to burn through whatever riddle he thought the stone had given him. He didn't look like a scholar; he looked like a warrior preparing for battle.

But then, oddly, he deflated. "It sounds too straightforward to be a riddle."

Even though he looked directly into her eyes as he said it, it seemed that he was a million miles away. She hesitated, then said in a rush, "It doesn't matter, does it? Solving a riddle that old is probably impossible."

The silence turned bleak. "I will never know what it means," he whispered.

He picked up her sherry glass, drained it, and threw it into the fire. The sudden violence shocked her. "Alex," she said. "What is wrong?"

"You should go to bed, Miss Etchingham," he said distantly.

She was so confused. Her guilt still ran high, but he'd given her much more of a mystery than she had expected. "Is there nothing I can help with?"

He was half-turned away from her, so she could see the strain on his face but not the emotion in his eyes. "No. I don't know. I need to think."

Prudence debated again. He had not reacted as she had expected him to. The dagger meant something to him that she didn't understand. But she couldn't ask without giving away her secret.

She felt, oddly, that this was the end. She walked toward the door, still considering her options. Tonight was nearly the end of the week he'd asked her to give him — alone in his study, they could have discussed whatever it was he intended for her. But he hadn't said a word about it. She sensed, in his strange stillness tonight, that he never would.

She reached for the door handle. Despite it all, she couldn't leave without taking a final look at him. She turned back. "Goodnight, Alex," she whispered.

She didn't expect a response. But his pacing had brought him closer than she had realized. He closed the distance between them and grabbed her wrist.

He pulled her away from the door and into his arms. He didn't kiss her. His touch was fierce, but the fierceness of a goodbye, not the passion of a greeting. He just held her, pulling the cap off her hair and brushing his lips across her forehead.

The bloody bounder was the most confusing man she had ever known. Was this love? Hate? The ravings of an unstable mind?

But his arms felt so good. And this moment might be the last good one — one tiny scrap of comfort between the bleak chain of memories stretching behind her and the dark future that awaited her.

So she let him hold her. She let his arms close around her, let his hand stroke her back, let his masculine scent soak into her skin. She let herself pretend that everything would come out all right in the end.

He kissed her forehead again. "I am sorry, Prudence. So, so sorry."

"Why are you sorry?" she asked, pulling back enough to look into his eyes. "Nothing has happened."

Everything was still unspoken between them. But he threw it all into the light. "I am sorry I cannot have you," he said. "Sorry that I have to let you go."

"No," she said, emphatic. "You don't have to let me go." She promptly forgot her better intentions. If he wanted her, she'd let him have her, even with her lie between them.

"I do. I must. I wish you happy, you know. Very happy."

She stroked her hand over his heart. "I wish you happy too, Alex."

His name seemed to pain him. He closed his eyes. "You should find someone who can give you what you deserve, Prudence. You deserve so much. So much more than I can ever give you."

"What are you carrying on about? I want nothing more than what you can give me."

She meant it with all her heart. He looked into her eyes as though willing her to understand something about him. But whatever she was supposed to understand was lost when the door opened. It hit Alex in the shoulder. He stepped back instinctively, pulling her with him, shielding her with his arms.

He should have tossed her across the room.

Ferguson stepped through the doorway. Malcolm was close behind. The duke saw them standing together, then darted his eyes to where her cap lay on the carpet.

His surprise turned to immense satisfaction. Prudence's heart stopped.

"Salford," Ferguson said, his voice positively dripping with delight. "Not so Puritanical after all, are you?"

CHAPTER THIRTEEN

No. It was the only word he seemed capable of thinking tonight. But then, the night kept surprising him in terms of how much worse it could get before the end. He had thought that Thorington's obvious interest in Prudence was bad enough. Then he had lost the auction, which was certainly worse.

Then Prudence had been so vague and noncommittal about whether she planned to marry the duke. Alex hadn't dwelled on it; he was too concerned about the stone to consider it. But if her translation was correct, he didn't see how the stone could possibly hold the answer he needed.

He would have to let her go. That realization had surely been the worst.

The night wouldn't relent, though. Prudence was as startled as Alex was by Ferguson's entrance. She tried to pull away from him. But Alex made the fatal error of tightening his grip on her arm. His instincts screamed to protect her — but he couldn't protect her.

"Ferguson," he said, as calmly as if he had expected to see him. "I trust you can make yourself comfortable elsewhere while I finish a bit of business with Miss Etchingham."

Ferguson wouldn't be fended off that easily. His grin turned feral, a predator about to make a kill. "Interesting bit of business, Salford. What do you think, Malcolm?"

Malcolm shut the door. "I think Salford should send to the archbishop for a special license."

Prudence drew herself up before Alex could speak. "He hasn't touched me," she said. "We're merely friends."

Merely friends. It was all they could ever be. But the frozen, stunned sound in her voice made him want to draw her back into his chest.

Ferguson sighed. "You do not have to make excuses for him, Miss Etchingham. The man was embracing you. Unless you lost your cap due to a rogue gust of interior wind, I'd wager there was some passion involved. Malcolm, do you agree?"

"Looks just as damning as how he found me with Amelia," Malcolm said, in a voice that sounded more smug than judgmental.

"He didn't even see me kissing Madeleine before he took it upon himself to make me marry her," Ferguson added.

Prudence stiffened. Alex knew they were trapped, completely, but he tried anyway. "As Miss Etchingham said, we are friends of long standing acquaintance. It's surely different than your situations."

"Doesn't look different to me," Malcolm said, circling around them to seek out the decanters on the other side of the room.

Ferguson nodded. "Miss Etchingham, since you have no brother to protect your honor, I would be glad to serve that purpose." Then he turned his gaze on Alex. His sharp blue eyes held an equal mix of resolve and unholy glee. "Salford, you must marry the lady and make her reputation good. Or I'll have no choice but to call you out."

The night could definitely be worse.

"I cannot," he said.

Prudence stepped away from him. "Nor can I."

"I didn't imagine that Salford would be the least gentlemanly of all of us when confronted like this," Malcolm said as he came back with a glass for himself and one for Ferguson.

The duke shook his head. "I warned him not to let it go too long before he gave in to sin. He really has made a muck of things, hasn't he?"

Alex held up his hands. "Nothing happened. Miss Etchingham's virtue is entirely secure."

"For someone who didn't entertain our excuses, you seem oddly confident that we will listen to yours," Ferguson said.

Alex knew he was sunk. He had played a strong role in both their marriages — but Ferguson and Malcolm had both been secretly glad to marry Madeleine and Amelia. It was the ladies who had been less sure of their circumstances.

It grated on Alex's conscience that he couldn't step up to his duty like they had. But he would never break his curse. If he married Prudence, and she died because of him...

He shrugged, steeling his heart against what he had to do. "It is your word against mine. If you choose to pursue this publicly in order to force the issue, I will still refuse. Her ruin will be on your conscience. Now, I have business to attend to. You may take my brandy and go elsewhere."

Ferguson frowned — a real frown, not an affectation. "Never thought I'd see the day. You truly intend to ruin her."

Prudence coughed. "Do you think I might have a say in what you are discussing?"

"Do not worry, Miss Etchingham," Ferguson said, in a soothing tone that Alex knew would infuriate her. "We will make sure Salford does what he should for you."

"And if I don't want him to?" Prudence asked.

Malcolm shrugged. "Amelia didn't want me to do my duty either, but she's happy with the result."

"I'm not your wife," Prudence said. She stooped to pick up her cap as she said this. She wrapped it tightly around one fist, looking for a moment like she was preparing for a boxing bout. "As you no doubt remember, since you threw me over for her."

Malcolm had the grace to look abashed. He sipped his brandy, too quickly, and nearly choked on it. When he had finally recovered from his coughing fit, he sighed. "My apologies, Miss Etchingham."

She nodded briskly. "Nor do I wish to be your wife. Or Ferguson's wife. Or, heaven forbid, Salford's wife."

"But he has taken advantage of you," Ferguson pointed out, gentle but undeterred. "I cannot ignore that. He will marry you even if I must hold a saber to his neck while he says the vows."

"You cannot," Prudence said, her voice oddly rushed. "I have already agreed to marry the Duke of Thorington."

If the night turned any worse, Alex might have to shoot himself.

"What?" Alex said.

She didn't look at him. "I thank you for your hospitality, Lord Salford. And I suppose I should thank the rest of you for your concern, although I don't think I shall. I am quite capable of arranging my own life, no matter what any of you men seem to believe."

For once, Ferguson was so shocked that his face showed it. Alex would have enjoyed it more if he wasn't sure he wore a similar expression. When the duke spoke, he sounded confused rather than amused. "Thorington? I know he's a duke, but trust me when I say that most dukes have little to recommend themselves as husbands."

Malcolm frowned. "Are you sure we cannot force Salford to marry you instead? He's a dull stick, but your life would be better for it."

Alex wanted to demand an explanation. He wanted to make her admit that she was marrying Thorington for security, or even revenge, but not for love.

He wanted to force her to stay and marry him instead.

But he couldn't do any of that, not when marrying her would surely kill her. So he merely said, "I trust that the lady is capable of making her own decisions. And I wish her very happy with them."

"I thank you, my lord," she whispered.

Her face, shadowed by the fire, looked haunted, a Fury carved in marble rather than the warm, eager woman he knew. She didn't look at Alex, giving him only her profile.

He wanted more. He wanted to give her more.

But she deserved more than he could allow himself to dream of. And yet he couldn't seem to stop the words. "I am sorry."

"I don't believe I care. I will leave your house tomorrow so that there are no more...inconvenient moments like this."

She was gone before he could think of a response, elbowing through the wall Ferguson and Malcolm had made and fleeing through the door. Would she start packing her things immediately, or would she wait until morning?

Would he survive, each night, knowing that she was in Thorington's bed instead of his?

Malcolm closed the door behind her and turned the key in the lock. Ferguson took off his jacket and began to roll up his shirtsleeves.

"You've interfered enough for one night," Alex said. "No need to start a brawl."

The duke shook his head. "You have disappointed me, Salford."

Alex ignored what Ferguson thought in most circumstances. But then, in most circumstances, Ferguson didn't sound so sincere. "Like Miss Etchingham, I don't believe I care."

Malcolm left his jacket on, but the look in his eyes as he picked up his brandy was dangerous. "A gentleman would care. But just because the lady let you off without consequences doesn't mean we shall."

"So is it to be fisticuffs or a duel?" Alex asked. "Either way, I'm at your service. But it won't change the facts of the matter."

"The fact is that you're a coward," Ferguson said.

It was the kind of word that made men fight and die — the kind of word that slapped Alex across the face and settled into the pit of self-hatred he already nursed in his belly. If he cared for his honor, he would call Ferguson out for it and demand satisfaction for the insult.

But honor didn't matter. Nor did Ferguson's opinion. All that mattered was that Prudence had safely walked away from him...that she would continue to live, that the curse wouldn't perceive her as a threat to his studies.

Ferguson still waited expectantly for Alex to respond to his taunt. Alex just held up his hands, taking a breath to say what he must say. "Very well, I am a coward. I am not the gentleman you expected me to be. Think whatever you want of me — you always have. But don't breathe a word of anything that would harm Miss Etchingham's reputation, or I will kill you both."

He'd shocked them into silence. They both seemed to mull over his words as they would a Parliamentary speech, something to be analyzed, then judged. But their judgment, when it came, wasn't what he expected.

"Do you know why she chose to marry Thorington?" Ferguson asked.

Alex shrugged. "He offered. She must have decided he was better than waiting."

Malcolm sprawled into one of the chairs, abandoning the idea of a fight. "And you intend to let her marry him?"

Alex clenched his fists to avoid rubbing his scar. "It is not my decision."

"So you aren't satisfied with this turn of events," Ferguson said. "But if you aren't, why not seize on our interference as an excuse to marry her yourself?"

"That is what I did when you interfered, Salford," Malcolm pointed out. "And I thank you for it, even if you'll never hear me say it again. I might never have convinced Amelia to marry me without you."

In a different life he would have taken the same action. But in this life, the life he'd cursed himself to bear, he only had two choices: let her go, or convince her to wait for a day that might never come.

"It does not signify," Alex said. "She will marry Thorington. I wish them very happy."

He didn't. And they knew it. But for once in his life, Ferguson stayed silent.

And Alex was left to wonder how he would survive losing her — and whether there was any way he could keep her without destroying her.

CHAPTER FOURTEEN

Later that night, Prudence was still awake, in her nightgown with a robe wrapped around her, sorting through her possessions. She would write to Ellie in the morning and ask to stay with her until she could find another home — or until she married Thorington. Since she couldn't sleep, she might as well start packing.

Why had she lied and told the men that she had decided to marry Thorington? It had been the first excuse that popped into her head when Ferguson made it clear that he would force her to marry Salford. As much as she would rather marry Alex, she couldn't bear to do it if she would know, all her life, that he had been coerced.

But *Thorington*? She should have asked for a firing squad instead.

She carefully pulled one of her cases out from under her bed. She could have stored her baggage in the attics with the family's trunks, but she'd kept this one close at hand. Flipping open the clasp, she raised the lid. There were eight jars of tea nestled within, buffered from each other by lengths of old muslin.

She grabbed her oldest petticoats from her wardrobe and layered them into the case, making sure the jars wouldn't move or break in transit. The scarabs were close to having the right patina, and she didn't want to start over with them. When she was done, she sat back on her heels. Even after the disastrous auction, she was still proud of her efforts. She could forge a new life for herself with her art.

She knew then that she was depraved. She had fallen too far to ever be redeemed if she still considered forging antiquities after swindling the Duke of Thorington out of fifty thousand pounds — and breaking Alex's spirit in the bargain.

The door opened without warning. She dropped the lid on her case before she turned, knowing who it must be. "I'm not sure I ever wish to see you again," she said to Alex.

She'd kept her voice low, but he still glanced up and down the hall. He stepped into the room and shut the door behind him. She stood, not willing to give him the advantage of having her on the floor. But he still loomed over her. His jaw was tense and his eyes were dark, but even though his height had never bothered her before, tonight it added an edge of menace. He could break her if he wished.

"Tell me you're not marrying Thorington," he demanded.

Prudence shook her head and held her ground. "It's no business of yours, Lord Salford."

She emphasized his title. It should have reminded him that this was a conversation they shouldn't have.

He didn't take the reminder. He stepped toward her, until they were only a pace apart.

"This is highly improper," she said.

He snorted. "*This* is improper? After everything that occurred the last time I came to your room?"

She didn't want the memory. She went on the attack. "Do you not like that word? I'll choose another. This is asinine. Or imbecilic, if you prefer. Or ill-considered. Shall I continue, or are you satisfied with those?"

He gestured toward the straightbacked wooden chair that Prudence used when one of Lady Salford's maids arranged her hair. "You should sit, Miss Etchingham. You seem overwrought."

"Overwrought? Why would you think that? I'm as calm as one can be when dreaming of her wedding day."

He flinched. "Please, sit, so that we may discuss this."

She crossed her arms. "Say whatever you've come to say. I trust I can remain standing long enough to see you out."

He stared at her a moment — not with the look of a man who wants a woman, but with the confused, slightly annoyed air of a man who has been stymied. "What's become of you, Prudence?"

"What's become of me?" she repeated. "What's *become* of me?"

She wanted to slap him, or punch him, or kick him — preferably somewhere painful, such as a shin, or perhaps something higher than that. Instead, she took a breath. She could be reasonable for at least a minute — long enough to convince him to leave before her nerves were utterly shredded.

"Nothing's become of me," she said. "And nothing will ever become of me if I stay here. I should thank you for making that so perfectly clear to me. Now, if you would be so kind as to excuse me, I must pack."

He cut her off with an impatient shake of his head. "You could do much better than Thorington. Say you won't marry him."

"Better than Thorington?" She laughed, a brittle little sound that dressed itself up as humor. "He's a duke and he has all his teeth. I cannot do better than that."

"Is that all you care for? A title?"

"And teeth," she reminded him. "I am particularly fond of men who have all their teeth."

"Thorington cannot give you what you deserve, Prudence."

He was back to her Christian name. "What game are you playing?" she asked abruptly.

"Game?"

He truly sounded confused. She dropped her arms from her chest. "You do not love me," she said, patiently, as though schooling a child. "Or anyway, you do not love me enough to marry me, even when both our reputations are at stake. Why does it matter to you what I deserve and whether Thorington is the man who may give it to me?"

She scanned across his face, looking for some meaning hidden in the hollows of his cheeks or the tightness around his mouth. He shoved a hand across his scalp, ruining his stern look as his hair turned wild. "It matters. You matter. More than I can say."

His voice was low, as though he could barely bring himself to say anything aloud. It was a terse, deathbed confession, the last words of a man on the gallows.

For that, she wanted to see his head on a spike. "I matter," she repeated, flat and unemotional. "Lovely. Now leave me be."

He grabbed her shoulders, faster than she could anticipate. Whatever restraint he'd placed on himself shattered. "You *matter*, damn you." His grip branded her, his thumbs grazing her collarbones in a gesture that was both intimate and intimidating. "To me. You always have."

He paused. Their eyes met. The same connection they'd always had reared to life, a fire that a single glance could stoke.

"You always will, Prudence," he said. "You have to believe me."

She inhaled, a shaky breath that had to sneak past her rapidly-constricting heart. She wanted to believe him. Damn her traitorous heart, she *did* believe him.

But there was belief...and then there was action. She mattered to him. But she didn't matter enough. And if she accepted what he offered — which was precisely nothing, save a few pretty words — she would be compelled to continue in her odd, shadowed half-life, residing on the periphery of the life she might have had.

"You say it as though repetition will make it true. But words aren't enough," she said. "I want more than you can give me."

"Is it a dukedom?" he asked, with a bitter edge to his voice.

She shook her head. "It's not his title that appeals. And I know Thorington won't give me a grand passion. But he won't make me fall in love with him, either. Why wouldn't I choose that, instead of hearing one moment that I matter and the next that I don't?"

"You have too much passion for him, Prue. You'll be bored of him within a fortnight."

She shrugged. "I'm bored of this conversation, and yet it continues. I shall survive Thorington as well."

"For a night, perhaps. Or a week. Or a month. But a lifetime? A lifetime of banal conversation at your breakfast table?"

"Thorington is an intelligent man," Prudence said stubbornly. "I'm sure we shall converse perfectly well."

"A lifetime of quick, unpleasant lovemaking? Done solely to make an heir, not to give you pleasure?"

She kept herself from gasping, but she couldn't quite control her blush. "What do you know of Thorington's lovemaking?" she retorted.

Alex somehow choked on a laugh. It turned into a cough, and he dropped a hand away from her shoulder to stifle it. Prudence took the opportunity to slide away from him. She moved to the window, briefly speculating that she might rather jump out of it than continue this discussion.

She knew that Alex wasn't done. And he didn't leave her waiting. As soon as he could speak again, he said, "I've known Thorington for years. And I know his demons. Better than anyone, I'd wager. He's using you to get to me. He won't toss you out when he's done with his revenge, but that doesn't mean he'll take any time to make your life more pleasant."

She shrugged, not looking back even though there was nothing worth seeing through the dark, slender crack in her chamber's curtains. "Again, it's not your concern. But if it comforts you, I care very little for how well Thorington...pleases me." She stammered just a bit on the words, uncharacteristically. "If he gives me a child and enough pin money to keep me in books and parchment, I'll consider it a deal well made."

The better deal would be to take Thorington's money and run away, but she couldn't tell Alex about her secret plan. But she hoped that her supposed desire to marry Thorington would get him to leave her in peace.

Alex's hands closed over her shoulders again. He turned her around. "Prudence," he said softly. "Enough nonsense."

She saw in his eyes, heard in his voice, what he intended to do. "Don't do something you'll regret," she warned, as much to herself as to him.

He shrugged. "My regrets would fill a book. But if I am responsible for you believing that you deserve anything less than the grandest passion..."

He leaned in to kiss her. She anticipated it, wanted it...

And at the last moment, she turned her face away. His lips landed awkwardly on her cheek, perilously close to her eye.

She shoved his chest, pushing him away from her. "Enough non-sense," she said, mimicking his earlier words with a nasty edge to her voice. "If you touch me again, I shall scream. Your mother is less likely to overlook your indiscretions than Ferguson and Malcolm were. And then we will both be in trouble."

"Just promise me you won't marry Thorington," Alex said, urgently, ignoring her threat entirely.

She pointed to the door. "If you won't marry me yourself, you've no right to ask me that."

They hovered on the edge of something…else. Something that, in a dream, might have turned to something sweet. She could almost feel it — almost feel him dropping to his knees, begging her forgiveness. Taking her to bed. Showing her that he was capable of giving her the grand passion her heart had always longed for. The passion she only wanted from him, despite what she said.

Instead, he scrubbed a hand against his mouth, as though to wipe away the kiss she'd denied them. "I can't lose you like this. But I can't keep you."

The words were wrenched from his very soul. She felt herself waver, torn between pragmatic plans and not-quite-dead dreams.

She didn't want to waver. She tried to stand still, to will him away. But the part that still loved him overruled everything else. "Why can't you keep me?" she asked.

He looked down at his hands, tracing the scar in his palm. He was silent a moment, then another. But his words, when they finally came, gave an excuse she never could have expected.

"I'm cursed, Prudence," he said.

She almost laughed. But he looked up before she could react, shocking her as his eyes filled with despair. "And if I marry you, it will surely kill you."

CHAPTER FIFTEEN

His words took a moment to turn from sound into meaning. When they finally did, Prudence wanted to strangle him.

"That is the most idiotic excuse for inaction I have ever heard," she snapped. "Do you really think I'm enough of a simple-minded female to believe such superstitious nonsense?"

Alex winced. "I know you may find it difficult to understand…"

"The only thing I find difficult to understand is how your rational, scientific mind could come up with a Cheltenham tale such as that." Her blood heated as her heart beat faster, fleeing from the memory of the moment when she had thought, again, that he truly loved her. "Tell me another, my lord. Shall you tell me next that you cannot marry me because you're a selkie, destined to return to the sea?"

He held up his hands. "Hear me out, Prudence."

She stepped around him, moving toward her desk. "I've no need for your excuses. If you mean to belittle my intelligence by giving me a fantasy in the place of an apology, I consider our acquaintance at an end."

"You are the most intelligent person I know. Which is why I never told you — I knew you wouldn't believe me."

His words stopped her more effectively than his hands could

have. There was a compliment buried in that statement — an immense one, one that seduced her more than any meaningless flattery about her beauty ever could have. But still, a curse?

She slowly turned back to face him. He was rubbing his thumb across his palm again. She recognized that old gesture and suspected, suddenly, what he thought had cursed him. The dagger she'd found in his study, the amount of money he'd bid for something that might have given its translation, the crushing loss he'd felt when he found out the stone's Aramaic lines weren't what he expected…

She couldn't guess out loud. But she could lead him to it. "What caused this curse?"

"You won't believe it."

"I won't believe you unless you tell me," she pointed out.

He paused and looked down at his hand. Finally, he said, "It was an ancient Egyptian dagger that I bought a decade ago. I made a wish, cut my palm with it, and woke up to find that my wish had come true. And it will continue to give me what I wished for, for the rest of my life. Even if I no longer want it."

"What did you wish for?" she asked.

"That nothing interfere with my historical studies."

His voice sounded self-deprecating. She laughed. "That doesn't sound so terrible."

In fact, it sounded almost sweet. But he shook his head. "I never should have wished it. But I was twenty-two, and Father was making noises about having me take up more duties with the estate rather than continuing my education at Cambridge."

He didn't continue, but he didn't have to. She knew the history of his life nearly as well as she knew her own. "Your father died that year, didn't he?"

"In his sleep, the night I made my wish. And it's my fault."

Prudence bit her lip, considering. "It could have been a coincidence. Men die too young every day. Are you sure you aren't blaming yourself where there is no blame to be had?"

Alex had the look of a man confessing his greatest sin under torture. "It's no coincidence. Nothing has significantly distracted me from my studies since that night. And if anything threatens to distract me, it is always eliminated."

"But you're not studying now," she said.

He shrugged. "It seems to eliminate the major barriers, not the minor bits. I still must sleep, eat, and groom myself. I can go to a party if I feel like attending. I can spend days at a time doing whatever I like. But if someone or something takes too much of my time, the curse removes it from my life. It took 'interference' in a very literal sense."

She moved away and sat on the edge of her bed. There was no point in standing toe to toe with him, not when she had the oddest urge to pull him into her arms and soothe him. "What do you mean, the curse removes it? Has anyone else died besides your father?"

Alex closed his hand into a fist. "There was my first mistress — a freak windstorm blew a tree onto her carriage. Then there was the incompetent land steward who kept asking for more and more of my time to address issues with the estate, until he ate some toadstools that he thought were mushrooms. The second land steward didn't die, but he broke his leg in a bad fall down the stairs of my country house and decided to retire. Thank God I found a good one after that."

Prudence might have laughed if Alex didn't seem so serious. "Those could all be coincidences, you know."

"I could go on — I have a ledger if you care to examine it. I make anonymous tithes to their local churches every year in honor of all of them."

"No need," she said. "I'm sure you think this is true."

"You don't believe me."

It wasn't a question. She shrugged. "You must admit this is a bit fantastical."

He wasn't defeated by her denial — if anything, it spurred him. "I would have said the same ten years ago. I *did* say the same, in fact. My wish was a joke. How could a man of my intellect believe that a cut across the hand could do anything other than bleed? But if you knew how it felt to make that wish, fall asleep, and awaken to find your father dead..."

He lapsed into silence as she considered. Finally, she said, "I still do not see why this would prevent your marriage. Most husbands and wives in our circle hardly see each other beyond dinner and the occasional ball. A wife surely wouldn't interfere with your studies enough to matter."

"Would *you* be satisfied with that?"

His question was too direct. She shook her head.

"Then you know why I cannot marry you. I would want to lose myself in your bed for weeks and let my studies rot. If I trusted my willpower, if I thought I could confine myself to only an hour a day with you — perhaps I would risk it. But I can't help myself with you, Prudence. I wouldn't be able to resist you if you were truly mine. I wouldn't be able to ignore our children, if we had them. And I would inevitably cost you your life."

He believed what he was saying. There was such sincerity — such a wealth of regret — in his voice that Prudence couldn't doubt his beliefs. Even if it was entirely inexplicable and irrational, Alex believed that he was cursed. And that belief kept him from marrying her.

Her heart should have soared at that. She hadn't expected to hear him ever discuss the possibility of marrying her.

But the downward pull of his doubts was too strong. "Is there a way to break the curse?" she asked.

"I have spent a decade searching for it."

That wasn't an answer. "And you thought the stone that Ellie sold would give you the cure?"

He sighed. "It was the closest I've ever come to changing my fate."

Her conscience poked at her. "At least you didn't waste your money on it. You should be glad it was Thorington who threw away a fortune for the rock."

Alex sighed. "I pity whoever Ellie sold it for. Thorington will know as soon as he reads it that it won't help his ends. And the curse will make sure he gets his money back."

"What do you mean by that?"

Alex didn't speak for a moment. A different woman might have suspected that he was preparing a lie, but Prudence knew the quality of that silence. He was deciding how to phrase something unpleasant.

"Thorington and I were friends at Cambridge," he finally said. "He suffers from the curse as well."

Prudence rested her chin in her hand and tapped a finger against her nose — a most unladylike gesture, but it seemed better than shrieking with disbelief. When she knew her voice wouldn't crack, she said, "The Duke of Thorington is cursed? You must pardon me for not believing you straight away."

"Why do you think he bid so much to win the stone?" Alex retorted. "Thorington is just as cursed as I am. But unlike me, he doesn't want to break it. He wished for great wealth — a wish that has continued to come true for him. And he will do anything to keep it intact. That includes preventing me from breaking the curse. We both suspect that if the curse is broken once, the power disappears for everyone. Thorington can't risk losing his fortune."

Prudence just managed to keep from gasping. If Alex was right, then the marriage Thorington demanded of her would inadvertently give him his money back.

She didn't want to marry Thorington, despite what she had said to the men in Alex's study. Would the curse force her to do it anyway?

"Is that why you don't want me to marry him?" she asked. "Because he is cursed?"

"His curse won't kill you as quickly as mine would. Or I don't think it will. Maybe it would eventually if it thinks Thorington needs to marry an heiress or you spend too much of his income. But I wouldn't want you to marry him even if he wasn't cursed."

There was a quality to the end of that sentence that said he wasn't done, even if his voice dropped off and his eyes shifted away from her to look toward the banked fire in her grate. She waited. When he finally turned back to her, his gaze filtered through the impenetrable darkness of memory.

"I should not ask you this," he said, with a voice that said he was reminding himself rather than apologizing to her. "But...I love you, Prudence. More than is safe. More than I should say. Will you wait for me?"

CHAPTER SIXTEEN

Yes.

The "yes" was on her lips, waiting there for him. It had hovered on her lips for years, waiting for him to ask the only question she'd ever wanted to hear. It leapt to attention, ready to burst forth, ready at last for the moment she'd dreamed of.

Despite it all, she still loved him. Even after weeks spent planning to steal from him, she loved him. She loved his humor, and his strength, and the way he held a conversation with her as an equal. She loved his body, too, and the way it would feel next to hers, even if she tried to confine herself to rational considerations of what might make a man into a good husband.

But her rational mind kept her mouth in check. She covered her lips with her hand, keeping the "yes" pent up until she could force it back from the brink. "How long would you have me wait?" she finally asked.

His shoulders slumped. "That is why I should not have asked you. I may never break the curse. Much as I would like to claim otherwise."

"Can I wish for it to be broken?" she asked.

Alex laughed — a quick, disbelieving sound, as though he had not hoped for humor from her. "I thought of that. But whatever power is behind this curse may decide that the easiest way to break the curse is to kill me. It has too much of a sense of humor to let me live."

"Not the most useful dagger, is it?"

"No."

The thought of a useful dagger distracted her, niggling at some bit of memory that she hadn't unearthed in years. "Does anyone else know of it?"

"Only Thorington. But it must have a long provenance. I've tracked rumors of something similar through ancient stories and correspondence."

"Where did you find it?" she asked.

"It was in a box of Egyptian artifacts that Thorington's father had won playing hazard. Only luck the man had — but it wasn't so lucky, as it turned out. I bought it from Thorington to give him some pocket money, then we tried the dagger one night when we were in our cups."

She considered, but even though it sounded familiar, she couldn't place the reference. "I may have heard of this from someone else, but I cannot for the life of me remember who it might be."

"I shall continue looking regardless of what you choose to do."

She felt she should answer his earlier question. And yet…what answer was there to give? She wanted to tell him she would wait for him. But could she spend an entire lifetime living her shadowed, solitary existence while he tilted at windmills and fought an enemy no one could see?

What if he never found a cure? What if…what if he was mad, and there was no curse, let alone a cure? And what if her whole life passed her by, living in silence with her unfulfilled, aching heart?

That wasn't her only consideration, though. She had tricked him with her forgery. He hated intellectual dishonesty more than anything — witness how he despised Ostringer for selling fake goods. If he discovered what she had done, would he be able to forgive her for it?

In the end, she was a coward. She loved him. She would always love him. But living with that love, and nothing else, while her friends had perfect marriages and left her to crumble into the dust...

It was too great a sacrifice to ask for, when there would be no guarantee of a happy end for either of them.

"I am sorry, Alex," she said quietly. "I wish it were otherwise. But wishes are too dangerous to build a life upon."

His eyes held hers for the longest time — long enough for her to doubt, then reassure herself, then doubt again. But finally he nodded. "I wish you very happy, Prudence. If I had it all to do again, I'd wish for you instead."

She couldn't trust herself to respond. He left without another touch, another word. She stayed perfectly still for the longest time, as though the emotions swirling between them were quicksand she might drown in if she took a single step. In the distance, she heard his study door slam. The reverberation cracked her heart.

She'd broken it herself this time. He'd asked her to wait, and she'd denied them both. A weaker woman — or perhaps a better woman — would have taken what he offered.

Surely she'd made the right decision. Even if this was the moment she would regret for the rest of her life.

But there was no other path she could take.

In the end, there was no one who could care for her but herself. And she would do what she needed to survive — even if she lived only to loathe herself later.

*   *   *

Prudence should have known better than to hope for privacy the next morning. She had hidden herself away in the smallest of Lady Salford's sitting rooms, waiting for an answer to the message she'd sent to Ellie. Her back was to the door as though she could will away anyone who thought to open it.

But her will had been expended the previous night in her vain attempt to forget Alex so that she could sleep. Her sleepless night pressed against her skin, as though her body had turned to porcelain that might crack if she felt any additional strain. Her eyes were gritty and her face felt swollen, even though she had manfully kept her tears at bay.

In short, she was in no state to entertain. She would rather drive sharpened skewers into her tongue than talk about what had happened. When the door behind her opened, she didn't turn around, hoping it was a maid who would come back later to tidy up.

"Why are you hiding here?" Amelia asked, closing the door and coming around Prudence's chair to face her. "I've looked everywhere for you."

Prudence made a show of reading her book, refusing to look up. "Did it not occur to you that I might wish to remain undiscovered?"

Amelia slowly lowered herself into the opposite chair, as obtuse — and concerned — as ever. "Yes, but don't you wish to talk about what happened last night? I vow, I would wring Alex's neck for you if I didn't think he was still a better Earl of Salford than Sebastian would be."

It was a jest, but Prudence didn't smile. "It matters naught."

From over the page she held in front of her face, she saw Amelia frown. "Malcolm told me a story so strange this morning that I could scarcely believe it. Did Alex truly compromise you last night? And did you really release him of his responsibility because you intend to marry Thorington?"

Prudence finally dropped her book. "Your husband was more forthcoming about what happened than I would have wished."

Amelia didn't apologize for him. "He cares for you. We both do. And he would have taken action to make sure Alex did his duty if you hadn't been so adamant that he not."

"I'm sure he would have appreciated paying your brother back for what happened in Scotland," Prudence said. "Please give him my apologies that I denied him that opportunity."

If Amelia saw any humor in the fact that Carnach had essentially jilted Prudence the previous summer and now decided to play her protector, she didn't acknowledge it. "I know Thorington's a higher rank than Alex and has greater wealth besides. But you and Alex have so many common interests."

Prudence shrugged. "Thorington offered for me. Alex did not. There's little point in arguing who would be a better match, is there?"

"I suppose not." Amelia shifted in her chair, too big with her pregnancy to stay comfortable easily. "But I must admit, I had hoped you might one day be my sister."

For once, Prudence found herself without a glib response. She wanted to laugh off Amelia's words, but the image they painted — the feeling they gave her, of a place and a home in which she belonged — was something too precious to sweep aside. Not that she had fallen in love with Alex for his family; on some days, she thought she had fallen in love with him *despite* them. But losing the Stauntons was another loss her heart seemed destined to suffer.

"Thank you," she finally said, with as much sincerity as her usual humor could allow. "Wouldn't that have been lovely?"

Amelia sighed. "I really do wish to wring Alex's neck. I vow that he is interested, even if he may never own up to it. Too late now, though — you cannot jilt a duke, and Thorington isn't a jilt either, despite his blackguard reputation. You're well and truly trapped."

Prudence winced. Amelia was watching her closely enough to catch it. "What haven't you told me, Prue?" she asked.

Prudence looked down at her hands. "The engagement isn't... quite...final."

Amelia gasped. "Did you lie to Malcolm when you said Thorington had offered?"

"No, of course not. Do you think me mad?" She looked up, and saw Amelia looking back at her with an appalled expression. She laughed despite herself. "You *do* think me mad, don't you?"

Amelia tried to compose herself. "No. But what do you mean by not final?"

"Thorington offered. And when Ferguson and Malcolm suddenly turned into overprotective males at the slightest hint of ruined female virtue, I spiked their guns by telling them I had already arranged to marry someone else. You should have seen their faces."

There hadn't been anything funny about it at the time, but Prudence was able to grin just a little bit now. Amelia laughed. "Priceless, I'm sure. But you're playing a dangerous game by involving Thorington in this."

"He doesn't know," Prudence said. "I've said no to him several times already — hopefully he will get the message."

"But Ferguson and Malcolm know. If you don't marry Thorington now, they'll think he jilted you. And then they'll either try to coerce the duke or force Alex to marry you."

Prudence had thought of that. But she had also thought of the fifty thousand pounds that Ellie would soon give her for the stone. There was a third, secret path available to her — one much lonelier, but much freer.

She shrugged. "I'll tell Thorington we don't suit. I'll tell Ferguson I jilted him. Then I'll make it clear that if Ferguson says anything to anyone, I'll divulge Madeleine's former acting career."

Amelia gasped. "Would you really do that?"

Prudence scowled at her. "Of course not. But Ferguson enjoys manipulating everyone else's lives — perhaps he should have a taste of it himself."

"You've become quite ruthless," Amelia said, almost approvingly. "Perhaps you should consider becoming the Duchess of Thorington. Think of how much power you'd have then."

Prudence held up her hands. "I don't want power. I just want a house."

"Well, whatever you do, make sure you contain Ferguson before he ruins your plans. He is the worst."

"Worse than you?" Prudence teased.

Amelia affected a wounded air. "I only ever mean to help. I'm sure I'm not as bad as Ferguson."

Prudence smiled. "You are. But I suppose I love you despite it."

"And I suppose I love you despite the fact that you've given up on the marriage mart," Amelia said. "I wanted you to have a love match, like the rest of us."

Prudence looked away. For a single moment, Amelia's happily-married state, with a husband who adored her and a baby on the way, seemed like something utterly smug and self-satisfied — something that Prudence didn't want to have staring her in the face. All her friends were like that now. One moment, she loved them; the next, she remembered how very different her life was from theirs.

But she could always remember why she loved them, even if it took a moment of wallowing in self-pity before she did. "You never know, Mellie. Perhaps Thorington will turn into a love match in the end. Stranger things have happened."

She must not have sounded very convincing. Amelia looked skeptical. "Thorington's not just an unreformed rake — he's a rake who has no wish to ever be reformed. He'll break your heart if you give it to him."

A footman entered. Prudence took the note he offered her, but even though Ellie's response to her earlier missive was exactly what she wanted, it didn't make her happy. "I should excuse myself," she said to Amelia as the footman left them. "I have to finish packing if I'm to move to Ellie's today."

"Why would you move to Ellie's?" Amelia asked, confused.

She couldn't tell Amelia about what had transpired between her and Alex, not if she wanted to keep her friends from forcing her to marry Alex. "Ellie wanted the company," she lied. "And I told Ferguson I would move in with Ellie because of my engagement to Thorington — better to keep up appearances until I've resolved all of this.

"You should just stay here," Amelia said. "I'm sure, given enough time, that Alex…"

"He won't," Prudence said flatly.

He never would. That was the only fact that mattered. Anything else she did with her life was merely an effort at salvage, not salvation.

*　*　*

The grand ballroom at Rothwell House was one of the largest

private rooms in London. But it struggled to contain all the guests who had accepted the Duke and Duchess of Rothwell's invitation. It was their first major ball since Madeleine had become Ferguson's duchess the previous summer, and the crush filling her rooms had proclaimed her a success.

Prudence had only arrived a few minutes earlier, but she was already on the edge of the crowd, sipping ratafia and willing her stomach to stop somersaulting. Madeleine had greeted her by whispering that Thorington was in the card room. There wasn't time for more than that — the receiving line was too long. But Madeleine's wide-eyed gaze told Prudence all she needed to know.

Ferguson had told Madeleine. Had he told anyone else? No one had treated her any differently than they always did — they were friendly, but not too much so. If they knew Prudence was to be a duchess, surely they would have started fawning already? Or would they all take the same tack as Alex — nod at her curtly, then ignore her completely?

She should have moved to Ellie's that afternoon, as soon as she'd received her note. But her conversation with Amelia had depleted her. She'd laid on her bed all afternoon instead of letting the maid finish packing, staring at the ceiling and imagining the lives in front of her. She could choose between marrying Thorington, rotting as Alex's dependent, or running off to Europe with plenty of money and no friends or connections.

None of them comforted her. But she knew what she would have to choose.

Ellie found her almost immediately, as though she'd been watching the door for her arrival. "Would you prefer congratulations or condolences?" the marchioness asked as they greeted each other.

Prudence shrugged. "Whatever you wish. There's time enough for both."

They could converse just with each other all evening, even if it was unfashionable. Ellie's husband Nick didn't enjoy dancing, and Ellie usually chose not to dance without him. Prudence loved to dance, but there were no partners waiting for her in the wings — unless Thorington chose to claim her.

"I don't know whether to toast you with champagne or hit you over the head with the bottle," Ellie said. "*Thorington?*"

"Shhh," Prudence hissed, handing her half-drunk ratafia to a passing footman and pulling Ellie into the nearest empty alcove. "We cannot discuss this here."

"I would have thought you'd have told me before now. I had to hear it from Madeleine when I came to help her tonight. Is that why you asked for a room? Why didn't you come today?"

Prudence made an apologetic gesture, opening her hands as though an excuse might come out of them. "I still wasn't sure what to do next. But I'll join you tomorrow if your invitation still stands."

"Of course it does. What does Salford say about Thorington?"

It was the only question that mattered. Ellie knew that Prudence wouldn't give a fig what Ferguson or Malcolm thought of her matrimonial concerns. But Prudence didn't want to talk about it. "He cannot offer what Thorington can," she said shortly.

"Did you ask him to?" Ellie asked.

Prudence snorted. "Ask an earl to marry me? Are you mad enough to suggest that?"

Her friend nodded. "Perhaps Salford merely needs a nudge in the right direction."

"If Thorington isn't enough of a nudge, I would have to accept an entire battalion before marrying me crossed Alex's mind."

She couldn't tell Ellie the real reason why Alex wouldn't marry her. It wasn't her secret to tell, and besides, it was still so fantastic-sounding that Prudence wasn't sure she could say the words aloud. Unfortunately, that meant that Ellie still believed that Alex could be reasoned with. "He may turn around once your engagement is announced," Ellie mused. "Nothing like realizing he cannot have you to make him think of you that way."

Prudence smiled despite herself. "You are not a good influence."

Ellie patted her on the arm. "Only to those who wish me to be."

Prudence covered Ellie's hand with her own. "You may influence me any day. But do not concern yourself about Salford. I vow I am not bothered by it."

"That's a lie," Ellie said mildly. "But I shall forgive you."

"How kind of you," Prudence murmured.

"Isn't it?" Ellie pulled away. "I would press, but if Amelia heard of your engagement, I'm sure she's already talked enough about your marital bliss to last you a week."

Prudence laughed. "You know her too well."

"I know you, too. And I know you aren't happy about this, even if you're putting on a brave face."

Her laughter fled. She couldn't look at Ellie's eyes anymore — her friend was too perceptive by half. "I can't wait anymore, Ellie."

Ellie's silence was pensive, not judgmental. And when she spoke, there was a wistful note of memory in her voice. "I made that same vow a dozen times while I waited for Nick. And I broke it a dozen more. But I'm glad you're stronger than I was. I wouldn't wish those years on anyone."

"Truly? Even though you have Nick now?"

"Truly. He was worth the wait, and I wouldn't trade him. Not for anything. But that's hindsight. If he had never come home for me, I would have ruined my life waiting for him."

Prudence sighed. "That's not very romantic."

Ellie grinned, even though she tried to suppress it. "You still crave romance, don't you? This is your chance to find it. Although I must say, I don't think Thorington is the one who will give it to you."

Prudence knew that already. It was all she had thought about that afternoon — that she was leaping out of the pan and directly into the fire if she left Alex for Thorington. "I know," she said. "I don't plan to marry him. I think I would be better off taking my chances in some foreign clime."

Ellie frowned. "Thorington won't accept being jilted."

"He won't be jilted because he doesn't know I accepted," Prudence said. "I said it last night in a fit of pique to keep the men from forcing me to marry Alex. They didn't know that I had just earned fifty thousand pounds, after all. But my real plan is to go to the Continent."

Ellie still frowned. "That's a better plan by far. But it won't work. Ferguson will force the issue."

"I'll take care of Ferguson," Prudence said. "Have you seen him tonight? I need to tell him before he says anything to anyone."

"He won't spread tales — he knows better than that. But you had better put your plan into action at once. If the ton catches wind of your false engagement, you'll be ruined forever if you don't marry him."

A cold touch of foreboding skittered down her spine. "Will you help me find your brother?" Prudence asked. "I would feel better if I find him immediately."

Ellie nodded. But they had left it too late. Thorington intercepted them just as they left the alcove.

"Miss Etchingham," Thorington said, sweeping a grand bow that would have made a lesser lady swoon. "And Lady Folkestone. I knew there must be two great beauties hiding here, what with the glow emanating from the shadows."

Prudence frowned. Ellie, ever graceful even in the worst situations, laughed. "Still a flirt, your grace?" the marchioness teased. "I thought old age would have cured you."

"I'm too far gone for a cure, my lady. But if you will allow me to steal your companion, I shall see if her good behavior may rub off on me."

His voice was warmer than usual. Oddly, it worried her more than his typical sangfroid did. But Prudence took the hand he offered and bid goodbye to Ellie. Ellie left immediately — possibly to seek out Ferguson, although Prudence couldn't tell what her intentions were.

She would have to deny Thorington quietly but firmly. Then she would find Ferguson and Malcolm and tell them she had changed her mind about Thorington's proposal.

But as soon as he had pulled her into a waltz, Thorington destroyed all her plans with a single remark. "Rothwell congratulated me on my good fortune. Do you wish to congratulate me as well?"

Damn Ferguson and his meddling. She took a deep breath and prepared herself for battle. "It was poorly done of me not to discuss this with you first. I am sorry for it, your grace."

He held her gaze. "Then you mean to accept my proposal?"

She took another breath that had nothing to do with the exertion of the dance. "I am very flattered by your proposal," she said. "But I cannot marry you."

Thorington didn't miss a single step of the waltz. His gaze didn't falter, either. If anything, he seemed amused. "You should have taken someone other than the Duke of Rothwell into your confidence, my dear. He won't allow me to jilt you, even if I wish to — which I don't. I'm afraid you're stuck with me."

He was unmoved. Prudence's heart stuttered. "I shall find him straight away and tell him I was mistaken. No one ever need know."

Thorington shrugged. Even his nonchalance in the face of her panic was somehow elegant. "I'm sure you may find him before he tells anyone else. But I'm also sure I shan't let you."

His hand around her waist suddenly felt like an iron band. "Why?" she asked. "You can marry whomever you wish."

"True," he said, with the kind of self-assurance that she'd never felt — the kind of self-assurance that made her hate him just a bit. "But I have set my sights on you, Miss Etchingham. And if I must ruin you tonight to ensure your compliance, I shall."

His mouth twisted mockingly. She suddenly saw he meant it. He had a reputation as the worst sort of blackguard — a reputation that she realized, then, was most likely deserved. "Don't," she whispered.

The duke shrugged again. "It's your choice, Miss Etchingham. Agree to marry me, and everything will be entirely pleasant between us. Or try to break it off, and I'll win you anyway. I truly do not care either way."

"You're mad," she said.

"I'm a duke," he said simply.

"Mad," she said again. "Have you no shame? How dare you force a gentlewoman into marriage?"

Her voice rose a bit on that, but no one looked in their direction. Still, he frowned at her. "You must have intended to accept my proposal when you mentioned it to Rothwell. What changed?"

He had already convinced her that he wouldn't let her go. It seemed that only the most drastic action would save her. "Lord Salford told me of your curse," she said boldly.

"Did he?" Thorington mused. His hand on her shoulder tightened. "I begin to understand your reluctance."

He didn't deny the curse. Her heart had stuttered before, but now it stopped completely. She had thought she'd believed Alex's excuse for not marrying her, but now that it had been confirmed — and confirmed by a man like Thorington — she realized that she had still doubted him.

That doubt was gone, but there was no comfort to replace it. Thorington grinned before she could think through the implications. "I suspected he loved you, but he must have told you of his curse to explain why he couldn't have you. Too bad he wished for something so silly as knowledge. If he'd wished for something else, he might have been able to win you."

"No one may *win* me," she snapped, her patience running thin. "I'm not a prize. And I don't wish to marry you."

"I hope you shall change your mind."

"I shall not."

He waited for her to take back the words. When she did not, he shrugged. "You'll realize that you should marry me instead of him. His curse will kill you. Mine will keep you in books and dresses all your life. You should see my library, Miss Etchingham — if you don't wish to love me, I'm sure you'll find more than enough there to win your favor."

His appeal to her bluestocking nature surprised her. "Wouldn't you rather I do something more ladylike with my time?"

"I require intelligent conversation. Nothing wrong with a duchess who can read Latin. You *can* read Latin, can't you?"

She laughed in spite of herself. "You know I can. But still, surely there are more important qualifications than that to base a marriage on."

Thorington smiled down at her. "You deserve me, Miss Etchingham. You think you want love. But I can give you what you really want."

"What do you think I want?" she asked, sure she didn't want his answer but too curious to let it go.

"Security. You want security, Miss Etchingham, not love. You want someone who won't break your heart. And access to a good library would be an added benefit. I can give you all of that."

It was exactly what she had claimed to want with Alex — why she had decided that she couldn't wait for him. But hearing those words from Thorington's mouth caused her doubts to overwhelm her prudence.

"I'm not ready to settle for it yet," she said. "I cannot marry you."

He paused. Then, he seemed to make a decision. His smile faded. "Very well. But I think you will soon find a reason to change your mind."

It wasn't an offer to let her go, but it seemed to be a temporary truce. "Thank you, your grace."

"You can thank me in a minute, my dear."

Then he tightened his grip around her waist and planted his lips on hers.

CHAPTER SEVENTEEN

Those first moments after Thorington's kiss — if one could call unwanted attention and a bruising press of lips a kiss — were the most awkward moments of Prudence's life. Or so she had thought at the time. The shocked gasps, the speculative looks, Thorington's announcement of their engagement just as Alex and Ellie pushed through the crowd to her side...it was all horrid, and unbelievable, and much too fast to understand.

She had thought the awkwardness would subside. She was wrong.

The carriage ride home was far worse.

She sat next to Lady Salford, who hadn't spoken to Prudence since Thorington's announcement beyond saying that she had a headache and wished to leave. Alex sat across from them, staring out the window — which might have been normal, had the window not been shuttered against the night breeze.

They hadn't run away, precisely — Lady Salford had waited nearly an hour to summon the carriage — but they hadn't stayed to celebrate as long as might have been expected after the announcement that Prudence would marry the duke. And the congratulations Prudence received were just speculative enough that she knew she would be the only *on dit* that anyone would discuss in London's drawing rooms the next day.

It would be the scandal of the Season if she jilted Thorington now. Perhaps the scandal of the decade. It was already a scandal that he had kissed her — but if the ton thought it was a love match, they would forgive a duke his minor indiscretions. They wouldn't forgive an untitled, impoverished spinster for hers. She could either marry Thorington and live the gossip down — or jilt him, and never be received again.

She would have cursed the unfairness of it all, but her reputation was the least of her concerns. It was her heart that drew her attention — her heart, and the heart of the man who seemed unable to look at her.

But she couldn't explain herself in front of Lady Salford. Alex's mother had no doubt expected better behavior when she had taken Prudence as a companion — or perhaps she had expected that Prudence would marry her son. Both of those expectations had been utterly destroyed tonight.

Just as they reached Salford House, Lady Salford turned to her. "Do you think you shall be happy with the duke?" she asked, in a quiet voice that held more concern than condemnation.

"I shall have to be, my lady. At least you'll be free of my care."

The jest fell flat. "I hope you didn't agree to marry him for my sake," Lady Salford said. "His title and estates are a brilliant match, of course. But the man himself..."

She trailed off, too well-bred to continue down the path of questioning the reputation of a duke who would soon be Prudence's husband. Prudence couldn't defend Thorington — no one could, not if they knew that he had forced himself upon her. But she didn't want Lady Salford to worry. "I'm sure he won't harm me. And at least I shall not be a spinster forever."

She couldn't muster up the enthusiasm necessary to sound happy about her changed circumstances. But Lady Salford didn't question her. She just patted Prudence's hand, then waited for Alex to leave the carriage so he could help her down.

He still hadn't looked at her. They had only made eye contact once in the last hour — just as she had pulled away from Thorington. Alex had pushed through the crowd, and his was the first face she had seen when the red haze cleared out of her eyes. She might have done Thorington violence and let her reputation be damned...but it was the look on Alex's face that stopped her.

He was angry — as angry as she'd ever seen him, with his jaw clenched and his fists tight within their gloves. Those lips, the ones that had kissed her with love rather than Thorington's brand of control, were harsh now, as though they knew they could never touch her again.

But it was his eyes that had stopped her. They were angry, yes — but also resolute. He held her gaze long enough for her to know that *she* was his concern, not Thorington.

If he had punched Thorington, as his fists seemed wont to do, he would have ruined her. Instead, he had congratulated her. Even though the look in his eyes said she had killed him.

He had done the noble thing. His words, loud enough for others to hear and pass on, made it seem like he had agreed to her engagement in advance. His tone had been amused, perfectly so, as though Thorington was a man too in love to know better, and not a blackguard of the first order.

He wasn't amused now. Prudence stepped out of the carriage. His hand was reassuring despite it all — solid and ready to catch her.

He was solid, but transitory. As soon as her slippers touched the paving stones, he was gone, escorting his mother into the house and leaving her to trail behind like the companion she was rather than the duchess she would be.

Like the wife she would be, for a man who wasn't Alex.

A night earlier, she had been prepared to leave him. Or she had thought she was. But now she regretted it all.

She had lost him. And there wasn't enough security in the world to replace him.

But that memory of a useful dagger still teased her, making her wonder if some of her endless stacks of correspondence held an answer. He wanted to rescue her, but could she rescue him? If she found the cure, could she win him for herself?

She might not be able to. But she had to try. And if she failed...

Perhaps she could still engrave him in her memory. It was a dangerous, likely immoral thought. But she could still take some pleasure from him, make a memory to warm all the cold nights of the future that stretched before her. Maybe it was better to have him once instead of never.

Or maybe she was a fool.

*   *   *

A better man would have left her alone.

A better man would have respected Thorington's claim, respected the lady's need for security, and respected the closed door between them.

Alex no longer wanted to be a better man.

He should let her go. She had found the security he could never give her. If she didn't accept Thorington, she would continue to live in poverty, dependent on others.

And she would grow to hate Alex for that. He knew she would. And yet his heart was too selfish to care. He needed her, more than he would ever need another. It was a dangerous thought. If he needed her more than his studies, his need would kill her.

But there *had* to be a way to keep her, to love her, without killing her. He just had to convince her to try for him.

He waited for her maid to leave her bedchamber for the night, waited another twenty minutes until the whole house was still, and then slipped through his door and down the hall to hers. He expected to find her in stillness, some pensive contemplation to match the dark thrum of his heart. But when he pushed the door open, he walked into a blaze of light.

"Close the door before someone sees you," she said.

There was paper everywhere — the bed, the floor, her tiny desk, her even smaller dressing table, and both chairs. The only space that was clear was the three feet around the hearth, a small pool of carpet around her feet, and scraps of empty table between her notes and the candelabra she'd set throughout the room.

"It does not matter if someone sees me, you know." He shut the door anyway, not wanting an audience for this. "You're safe from my marital depredations."

He hadn't been able to say it as a jest, and she didn't take it as one. "I don't wish to marry Thorington. I never wished to."

She looked so sad, suddenly, even though she'd seemed full of purpose moments before. He wanted to pull her into his arms, but she wasn't his to comfort.

But Thorington would never comfort her either. He knew it instinctively, not because he was jealous, not because he hated his former friend, but because he knew how marriages in the ton usually worked.

He reached her in three long strides, trying to find safe passage through the paper moat she'd created. "It will come out all right," he said, wrapping her up in his embrace. "We will find a way to make it so."

She let him hold her for a moment, but only for a moment. Then she pushed him away. "You are still cursed, is that right?" she asked.

He nodded. "There is no need to be afraid, though."

Prudence tilted her head. "So your studies still matter more than I do?"

He stepped back, ignoring the rustle of paper under his feet. "I want you to matter more."

"Prevarication," she said briskly. "They either do, or they do not."

"I cannot let you matter more," he said, clenching his jaw to stop himself from saying what was in his heart.

"Then that is a no, which means I am safe."

There was a dangerous light in her eyes. She was in her nightrail, with a robe over it, but she seemed comfortable with him there.

More than comfortable. She started gathering papers up from her bed.

His eyes narrowed. He was supposed to be there to convince her to wait for him, but she already seemed convinced of something else. "What are you doing?"

"I am being brave."

"Prudence," he said, in a voice that was half the warning he meant to give her and half the plea his heart made for her.

She turned. "Do you know, I hate my name?" she said, startling him as she dropped an arm full of papers on the floor. They made a

little cloud around her feet before subsiding, a soft reaction to the violence in her voice. "As though everyone who knows me can constantly
remind me to be rational. When all I want, really, is to *live*."

She said it so fiercely that his heart broke for her. "But you do
live, darling." He called her by the name he wanted to give her, rather
than the name she claimed to hate. "You live like a flame in the darkness. You burn even though the odds are against you. If you knew,
these past years, how jealous I was of your will to live, you would never
doubt yourself again."

He'd never meant to tell her that. But it still irritated him when
she waved his compliment aside, as though she didn't recognize how
serious he was. "I might as well have gone to a convent, for all the
good my bravery did me."

She turned back to the bed to gather more papers, but he reached
around her and swept the rest of them onto the floor himself.

"You do *not* belong in a convent," he said.

Then he wrapped his arm around her waist and pulled them both
onto the bed.

CHAPTER EIGHTEEN

If anyone knew how her heart sped up and her body warmed when he flipped her onto the bed, Prudence would have been forever barred from a cloistered life.

She was already affianced, albeit unwillingly. The man in her bed had told her, more than once, that he couldn't marry her. But for once, her mind, body, and heart were all in agreement.

She would rather share her bed with him than anyone else. And if Alex temporarily felt the same — well, she wouldn't question it.

Not that she *could* question it. His mouth sealed against hers, preventing any protest she might have made. He surely tasted her willingness on her lips, knew that she was melting into him.

But she didn't bother to pretend that she didn't have a choice. She had the entirety of the choice, one he'd ceded to her. He had positioned her atop him, and while his hands roved over her back and kept her anchored to him, she had all the leverage. She could leave him at any moment...

She could never leave him. She kissed him back, nipping at his lips, making love and war with her tongue. It was as though her heart had been set ablaze that night. She ran her fingers through his hair, imagining him as a fallen god she'd captured for her own. In her proper life, with her proper name, she should be penned up, kept safe, stopped from losing herself to passion or letting her emotions rule her decisions.

Her proper life could go to the devil. She was bound to be a duchess, unless she decided being ruined was better than being Thorington's wife. There were any number of nights in the future when she would have to be proper. This night was hers.

And this man was hers, if only for a night. He'd come to her. She knew he wanted her. She even knew, for at least a moment, that he loved her.

It was enough. She sucked him into her mouth, an aggressive move that had his fingers tightening on her shoulder blades. She would devour him, keep him inside her soul, a memory that would light all the nights after this when she could never have him.

"Prudence," he whispered when she paused to take a breath.

"No," she said. "I shan't stop."

She tugged at his cravat, destroying the perfect linen. She wanted to destroy it all. She threw it aside, ignoring the way he winced as the friction burned his neck. She attacked the ties of his shirt next, wanting to bare his throat, to see his Adam's apple jump in time to her strokes.

His hand closed over hers. "Prudence," he said again.

She stared down into his eyes. She saw everything there — love, lust, grief, doubt, need, demand. If his eyes were a mirror of hers, she wasn't surprised to see how deeply he needed her to continue, how deeply he needed her to stop.

"I cannot stop," she whispered. "Give me a night, before I must live my life without you."

Her words broke him. He reared up, tipped her onto her back.

If there was grief in his eyes, it didn't show in his touch, in the way his mouth roved over her skin. The man was an artist with his mouth, letting his hands pull away her clothing so that he could carve a path across her with his lips. She knew what he was after. She'd never thought her breasts particularly remarkable before, but the way he worshipped them painted a new picture for her, of beauty that men would write sonnets for, of soft curves that men would die for.

He worshipped them as he had before, as though they were a dream he still couldn't believe was real. She was content to let him touch her, tease her, because it gave her a moment to watch him. His hair, as he bent to take his prize, was dark against her pale skin. His muscled shoulders bunched up, exerting themselves to keep from crushing her — a crush she might have welcomed, if it meant that she could feel him fully, could engrave this memory into her flesh. She felt him hardening against her thigh and knew, then, that he wasn't just worshipping her — he wanted to claim her, too, merging the pedestal he'd placed her on with the bed she wanted him to take her in.

She dug her fingers into his hair, hard enough that he looked up and met her eyes. "Alex," she murmured, "I want you."

He returned, single-minded, to his task.

She sighed, tugged at his hair, and tried again. "I want you to… deflower me."

She blushed as she stumbled on the word, blushed harder as he looked up at her with an arched brow. "You are very demanding tonight, Miss Etchingham," he said, as though she'd asked for an extra serving of blancmange rather than ruination.

Then he grinned, more devil than doubter. "But I feel rather demanding myself."

His hand slid to her leg, grasped her nightrail and pulled it up.

The slow slide of cloth served as notice of his intentions. His knuckles trailed under the fabric, brushing against her knee, then whispering across her thigh. Her most private place suddenly ached for him, wanting him to hurry himself along and give her what she wanted…

But he was too patient, too devious for that. "You don't want to be deflowered," he said, murmuring against her breast before taking her back into his mouth.

"I do," she said, when she realized he wasn't moving forward. "I vow I do."

"No," he said, breaking away. "You want to be made love to."

He switched to the nipple he had cruelly ignored, and she was satisfied for a few moments — but it wasn't enough. "Ruin me, Alex. Before there's no time left for it."

He paused, just for a moment, and she wished she could take it back. The reality, the hopelessness, of their situation was too close to the surface of what they were doing with each other, and she'd let it bleed into the space between them.

But they both seemed willing to pretend — to pretend that this was what they were made for, that he could love her freely, that she could choose him instead of another. He leaned in and kissed her mouth. But as lovely as that kiss was, it wasn't enough to distract her from the slow stroke of his fingers across her inner thigh. Her skin had never felt so sensitive. His touch was feather light, nearly nothing, and yet everything.

One of his fingers slipped inside her, easing a path into her wetness. She sighed into his kiss, letting her legs spread wider, hoping she could urge him on. His knuckle rubbed against her channel, disconcertingly, deliciously; his thumb stroked around her opening, grazing that sensitive bit of flesh he'd tormented so cleverly with his mouth during his last visit to her bed.

For a moment she could almost pretend that she was an enchant-ed princess, not an impoverished bluestocking — cursed with a dark lover who could only come to her in the dead of night. But tonight, she wanted it all. She lifted her hips, trying to give him more.

His kiss turned possessive, all heat and pressure. He slid a second finger inside her, teasing her, and she knew she was wet for him. It was probably something she should have been ashamed of, how easily he drew her pleasure from her. But she didn't want to be ashamed of anything — not her dresses, not her status, and certainly not her love for him.

The third finger gave her a slight twinge of discomfort — not unpleasant, but just enough to wonder whether this had been the best decision. His strokes were slower, suddenly, and his kiss softened again. "I will not hurt you," he whispered as he paused to take a breath. "No more than I can help it, anyway."

Prudence closed her eyes. She had almost said that she'd rather it be him than Thorington — a true statement in every way, but not one she could share then. Just as she'd rather give Alex her love, she'd rather share her pain with him. Thorington didn't deserve any of her, but he especially didn't deserve this.

But Thorington's name would only defile the moment. She squeezed her eyes shut and vowed to forget him.

Alex mistook the look on her face. He pulled his fingers out, and she immediately missed them. "Perhaps we should wait," he said.

"No," she said, dragging his lips back to her mouth. "No more waiting."

She turned aggressive again, so intent on winning him back that she didn't care what he might think of her. He sighed, but his reluctance didn't last. And he couldn't seem to keep his hands off her, no matter what he said. He nestled into her hidden curls again, then drifted lower, back to the passage that ached for him.

"Are you sure?" he asked a few minutes later, when their kiss had turned hot again, when the slow stroke of his fingers inside and outside combined to drive her mad.

She looked into his eyes, as deep as she could allow herself before the possibility of unleashing her tears became too great to withstand. "I want it to be you, Alex. Please."

She had managed to divest him of his jacket, waistcoat, and shirt during their last kiss, but his breeches still blocked him from her. He made quick work of the buttons, though, freeing himself into his hand. In the bright candlelight, she caught a glimpse of his hardened shaft. She knew that this would work; it was what they were made for, after all. But she also realized exactly why and how it might hurt.

She squeezed her eyes shut and tightened her fingers into the bedsheets. A bit of her desire turned to tension — not enough that she would ever ask him to stop, but enough that he sensed it.

He kissed first one eyelid, then the other. "Don't think about it. Let me make this good for you."

She was expecting pain, but his fingers began teasing her again, greedy with purpose. Soon she was writhing with real need, not just anticipation; her fingers curled into the sheets, now from an excess of pleasure. His hand moved faster, his palm creating friction against her as his fingers pumped in and out. Her breath turned to gasps, little sounds of pleasure that he swallowed as he kissed her again.

There was an unbearably still moment as she hovered just on the edge. She arched up to him, her whole body tensed and ready. He pinned her lips to his, holding her in place with her hair, and she thought for an awful moment that he wasn't going to finish. The kiss left her breathless, stealing whatever air she had left, and her dizziness somehow heightened her agonizing need. She dug her nails into his back, needing him to stop, needing him to keep going...

But then his fingers thrust harder within her. His thumb flicked against her, turning sensitive flesh into the fuse that ignited her. Everything came apart in a rush of sensation, spiraling and unwinding as her whole body shook from it. And still he kept stroking her, kept kissing her. The shaking, the unraveling, the breathlessness — it continued in a long wave, one that tossed her up on some distant shore.

Like a traveler to a beautiful, dangerous land, she wasn't going to be the same after this. Even if the rest of her life was safe, and staid, and perfect, she would dream of this secret adventure. She would crave it. Just as she craved the man who gave it to her.

She felt him waiting at her entrance, the head of his shaft poised to take her. If she tensed, it was minimal; her body was too sated, her thighs too jellied to brace against him. He leaned up over her, one hand left behind to guide himself into her.

"I love you," he said. "Even though I shouldn't."

The words might have stung a week ago, but she accepted them — realized that she'd read his heart correctly all along, despite the lies his mouth had given her. She didn't doubt he loved her. It wasn't enough, and it was too late, but it was exactly what she needed now.

"I love you, Alex," she whispered. "Even though I can't any longer."

His eyes darkened, but he didn't stop. He stroked her breast instead, a gesture she found odd as a response until she realized that he was trying to distract her from the slow slide of his shaft into her waiting channel.

There was a moment of pain that was close to blinding, but she ground her teeth together and willed it away. He was slow, as slow as she guessed it was possible for him to be. She read his mood in the contrast between the glacial pace of his advance and the fast, demanding caresses he gave her breasts.

He was trying hard to make it good for her. Just as he'd tried hard to make her life good, despite her desire to spurn his charity and the curse that kept him from marrying her. He had her best interests at heart, even above his own — so much that he seemed to know that he would hurt her more if he denied her in this moment than he would by risking her life to the curse.

It was a silly thought, one she would renounce later; she didn't want to die. And yet her heart wouldn't have stopped him even if her rational brain had tried to prevail. She would rather risk it all to be Alex's for one night than live safely to become Thorington's.

Alex finally sheathed himself to the hilt within her. He paused there, waiting for something — something she didn't know how to give him. "What should I do?" she asked.

He laughed, but it sounded pained. "Stay still for a moment and learn the feel of me. I am trying to give you time to acclimate."

She privately thought it was a fool's errand. But he kissed her again, touched her again at the place where they were joined, and she realized she had relaxed around him. When he withdrew, she clenched on instinct to keep him there — giving her the first hint of how good he could feel.

She drew a groan from him. "Careful, darling," he said, retreating, then sliding slowly into her again. "If you do that too often, I'll lose myself too soon."

He withdrew again. She closed around him again, liking how

wicked she felt. They settled into a rhythm, conquest and retreat, giving up and taking back. His breath was hot against her neck as he kissed her; her hands were urgent as they roved down his torso to spur him on. He rocked into her again, and again, until she felt a quiet echo of the climax he'd already given her — soft and trembling, a promise of greater pleasure to come.

A promise she hoped to redeem before they had to leave each other forever.

His thrusts turned urgent, his kisses across her collarbone demanding. He drove into her once more, harder than he had before, and shuddered as his seed emptied inside her. She clenched around him again, acting on instinct, wanting to keep every bit of him inside her for as long as she could.

But she couldn't keep him forever. She was already, in her mind, making lists of what she had to do before he recovered enough to roll off of her.

She turned onto her side, curling around him as he lay on his back like a man just barely rescued from drowning. She brushed a piece of hair out of his face. "Thank you, Alex," she said quietly.

He let his head drop to the side so that he could look into her eyes without moving his spent body. "Don't thank me. You'll have me feeling like a man of ill repute."

He grinned as he said this, but the light in his eyes was already fading. They knew what they were destined for. Their faces were inches apart, the love between them was strong enough to bridge across any distance...but his past wish and her current pragmatism had stolen the future they should have had.

"I won't thank you, then," she said. "But you should know it was perfect."

"Really?" he asked. "I haven't ever…"

"You've never taken a lover?" she asked, shocked.

He snorted, then had the grace to flush. "Lovers, yes. Gently bred virgins, no."

"'Gently bred virgins' sound like such a depressing group," she said. "I'm glad I can no longer count myself among their number."

"We should have been more careful," Alex said.

She shrugged. "I can't be too upset for Thorington. He doesn't deserve my virtue."

She wished she hadn't brought it up. Her earlier presentiment that Thorington's name shouldn't be mentioned came true as Alex turned away from her to stare at the ceiling again. "Thorington doesn't deserve a lot of things. But, believe it or not, I would be happy that he had found you if I didn't want you for myself."

"How is that possible?" she asked. "I thought you hated each other."

Alex picked up her hand and twined it in his, a casual gesture of intimacy that tugged at her heart. "His family is difficult, to say the least. The amount of money they go through is staggering. But I'll say this for him — he takes care of his own. And I would wish him happy if he found someone to share that burden with."

If she was sure she was going to marry Thorington, that might have comforted her. But even though she could never go out in polite society again if she jilted him, she felt ill at even the thought of marrying him. "I don't wish to share his burdens," she said.

"I wish I could save you."

She would save herself if she had to — fifty thousand pounds wouldn't buy her friends, but it could buy her safety from Thorington. But after tonight, after this perfect moment, she wasn't quite ready to settle for less.

She tugged at his hand. "We must find a way to break your curse. That is the only plan I wish to pursue."

He dropped her fingers. "There is no cure, Prudence. If there ever was, it was lost centuries ago."

How was he so sure? "I think you are being a trifle too conservative in your assessment," she said.

She had tried to wrap up her condemnation in prettier words, but Alex knew at once what she was saying. "There is no bloody cure. And I've already stayed too long."

He sat up, ready to abandon her. She grabbed his wrist. "I may be able to help. I know I didn't go to Cambridge, but I have read a lot. And I'm sure I've read something about a dagger."

"It was probably a fairy tale," he said dismissively.

The fairy tale she really wanted was currently leaving her bed and searching for its shirt. She sighed. "It doesn't hurt for me to look through my papers."

He pulled his shirt over his head, tucking it in and buttoning it in case he ran into anyone in the hall — not that they wouldn't immediately start speculating where he had been. "Look wherever you like," he said, in the same voice he might use to tell his wife that he liked the pattern of her new dressing gown.

She was being unfair. But she still bristled. "If I find something, shall I bring it to you? Or shall I sell it to the highest bidder?"

It was an unfortunate, inadvertent reference to the auction he had lost — the one he still didn't know she had been responsible for. He scowled. "I must go to my study. I've spent too much time with you already. Perhaps tomorrow night we can discuss this."

"I won't be here tomorrow night." Her voice was suddenly small, not wanting to remind him — or herself — that she had agreed to leave. "I will still come here to help your mother if she needs it, not that she ever seemed to. But it seems…better for me to leave."

"I want to keep you here," he said simply.

She wanted to stay, but that didn't change their circumstances. "It's for the best. But if I find anything in my papers, I will send word."

"Do," he said, in a voice that said he was sure she wouldn't find anything. She seethed just a bit, wanting to prove him wrong — wanting to show him that she was smart enough to correspond about antiquities with him for years without him ever guessing it was her.

But it was silly to waste one of their last moments on seething. So when he came back to the bed and kissed her one last time, she gave herself fully to it.

She would be Miss Prudence Etchingham in the morning. She might someday be the Duchess of Thorington. Or she might be living under an assumed name in some forgotten village in Italy. Or she might be dead because of Alex's curse. But for one last minute, she was Alex's beloved instead. And she wouldn't let herself ruin it without giving them one last chance at happiness.

So when he left, she didn't luxuriate in bed. She began to search instead. She sifted through books, papers, folios, ledgers — a vast and sprawling correspondence that she had carried on, incognito, with nearly every important scholar of the day. Her letters had dropped off in the last few months as she had focused on her forgeries, but surely *someone* in her acquaintance had mentioned the dagger before.

It was almost dawn before she found the letter she was looking for. It shouldn't have surprised her. The handwriting was familiar, the paper the same as he always used. The signature across the bottom was bold and clearly legible, as though he had nothing to hide.

"Ostringer," she whispered.

If only it had been anyone else. How could she convince Alex to ask the antiquities dealer for help?

And what price would Ostringer demand in return?

CHAPTER NINETEEN

She should have left for Ellie's as soon as she'd awoken. But after going to bed at dawn, Prudence had slept until almost ten. Then she had dashed off a note to Ostringer and another to Alex, directing both through the pub at Soho Square. By the time she had eaten and finished packing, it was nearly one — and then she was punished for her tardiness.

"My dear daughter," Lady Harcastle said, rising from the seat in Lady Salford's drawing room where Prudence had kept her waiting longer than she should have. "I am so proud of you."

Prudence returned her mother's kiss, because, really, what else could she do? "I am sorry you heard the news before I was able to tell you myself."

She hadn't thought to try to reach her mother before the gossips did. Her mother waved off her apology. "I know you must have been too stunned to think of me. I confess I was stunned myself. I had never thought that Thorington was a possibility for you. Never in my wildest imaginings."

Unlike Lady Salford, her mother didn't ask if she thought she might be happy with the man. Prudence couldn't help but bristle, already too sensitive after only moments in her mother's company. "I am glad that you are glad, Mother," she said frostily.

"Glad?" Her mother sounded truly confused. "Proud, yes. A duke is nothing to sneeze at. But glad?"

Lady Harcastle trailed off, returning to her seat on the settee as though the question had suddenly made her too tired to stand. Prudence sat in a chair next to her, close enough to look polite without being in danger of an unexpected embrace.

"I expected you to be glad, Mother. You can gloat if you wish," she said. "You have wanted me to marry a title for years. Thorington's is one of the best titles of them all."

"There is something lovely about thinking of you as a duchess," her mother said with a sigh. "And I suppose I am glad to know that you will not have to worry in your old age. I'm sure Thorington will make appropriate provisions so that you do not find yourself relying on the charity of others."

Her mother's hands twisted in her lap as she said this. Prudence felt a twinge of guilt. "It is a brilliant match."

Her mother didn't need to know that Prudence was going to do everything in her power to escape it. She would expect that Prudence would meet her duty head-on, not make a scandal of herself trying to avoid it.

Or so Prudence thought. Her mother surprised her. "Yes, it is a brilliant match. But I worry for you, my dear."

"Why?" Prudence asked, confused.

"It's *Thorington*," Lady Harcastle said, as though the name alone was an explanation. "He is either mad or evil."

Prudence couldn't choke back her laugh fast enough. "But he is mad, evil, and titled."

"True. The same could be said for Emperor Nero."

Her mother's acerbic wit, when turned on someone other than Prudence, was actually refreshing. "Aren't you unkind this morning," she teased. "I'm sure Thorington isn't burning Christians in his gardens."

Lady Harcastle paused. The drawing room door had opened to admit a footman with the tea cart, and whatever she wanted to tell Prudence couldn't be done in front of the servants. So they both waited, in silence, as the man arranged their refreshments. The pause was long enough for Prudence to look at her mother — really look at her, rather than just seeing what her imagination laid over their reality.

Her mother was thinner than she had been. Her hair under her morning bonnet was grey now, not the same brown that Prudence still had.

Her mother was growing old. Older than she should have looked; she was the same age as Lady Salford, after all. But Lady Salford had somehow managed to recover from the death of her husband. Prudence's mother, even though she had loved her husband far less, was still trapped in the shadows of her memories. And it showed in the tight lines of her face, the bitter tinge to her voice.

If Prudence couldn't escape Thorington — still a possibility, even though she didn't want to consider it — could she at least escape the prison of her own mind? Or would she torture herself as her mother did?

The footman left. Lady Harcastle picked up the conversation as though they hadn't been interrupted, not knowing that Prudence was no longer amused. "I'll grant that Thorington isn't the devil himself," she said placidly, pouring heated water into the teapot. "But for all that I wanted you to do your duty, I had hoped you might find more happiness than I did. Thorington does not comfort me."

"Thorington does not comfort me either," Prudence said. "But that choice is gone now."

Her mother fidgeted with the sugar tongs, sending a lump flying across the tray. "There is always a choice, Prudence."

"You know that isn't true." She didn't tell her mother about the fifty thousand pounds, or about the chance she and Alex might have to break his curse. She had to keep up the pretense that she was marrying Thorington — there was no sense in worrying her mother or risking her reputation until she'd escaped.

"It's *always* true." Her mother looked up, determination sweeping away her disillusion. "I'll grant you, I mostly hope you choose to marry him. It's the wisest course of action. You will be safe, protected, and well-fed. You'll have gowns aplenty and invitations to any party you wish to attend. Your children will have the life I could never give you."

Lady Harcastle's hand shook for a moment. She clenched the tongs until it stopped. Then, softer, she said, "But I also hope you are happier than I was."

Prudence had expected that her mother would be happy about Thorington. But hearing that her mother knew the duke wouldn't make her happy but expected her to follow through with the wedding set off her fragile temper. "It is too late for happiness," she said. "I trust you'll forget this advice when Thorington's wealth buys you a house."

Her mother blanched. "Do you believe that matters more to me than you do?"

"Doesn't it?" Prudence stood up. "You would have married me to Malcolm before I'd ever even met him. Marriage is the only thing you've ever asked from me. I wish you very happy with it."

"Prudence," her mother started to say.

"Goodbye, Mother," she said firmly. "I will send word when we've set a date for the wedding."

She walked out — stormed out, if she was being honest. But she couldn't be honest with herself until she had reached her room and slammed the door behind her.

She had been hideously ungrateful. She had been cruel, unnecessarily so.

But the only glimmer of good that she'd found in the idea of marriage to Thorington was that her mother might be pleased. And to have even that cold comfort taken away from her...

If she'd considered Thorington as a possibility before, she couldn't anymore. She'd never wanted him. But there had still been the small, well-bred part of her that couldn't quite contemplate the idea of ruining herself by jilting him.

But now she was ready to embrace her ruin. She threw the last of her papers into a valise, not caring whether they creased each other in her haste. She couldn't bear to look at her bedchamber and remember everything Alex had done to her, everything she'd given him.

Her mother was right, for once. Prudence had a choice. But no one knew how dark it was. Either she would return to Alex's house as his wife...or she would leave England forever.

*   *   *

He missed her. Damn her, he missed her already, even though she had only fled from his house to Ellie's a day earlier. Dinner the previous evening had been worse for it. Amelia had looked at him like he was a prime fool. Malcolm was still cold, unimpressed by Alex's apparent cowardice. His mother just sighed, repeatedly, as though it was her heart that had been broken, not his.

Prudence was better without him. She would stay alive without him. But that rationale was dim and powerless when he wondered whether she was spending the afternoon shopping for her trousseau...

When he reached the pub, Alex slid down from his curricle and handed the reins to a loitering groom, along with a shilling to ensure his horse and carriage were safely conducted to the nearest stables. He was on a fool's errand. But the invitation he'd received the previous day was just tantalizing enough to draw him out of his brooding.

He had corresponded with a scholar named Chandlord for at least four years, but they had never met in person. Chandlord was a recluse, but he seemed to know everyone in the antiquities world through his correspondence. And, oddly, he had chosen to come to London just when Alex wondered whether he should ask Chandlord if he'd heard any rumors about the dagger.

The public house the man had chosen for their meeting was near the Strand and the Society of Antiquaries' chambers at Somerset House. It was quiet, still early enough in the afternoon that there wouldn't be crowds. Alex didn't think the man was any likelier to have an answer than anyone else he'd talked to over the years, but going to the pub was better than stewing in his study alone.

He ducked through the old doorway and stepped inside. An enquiry at the bar turned him in the direction of a private room at the back of the common area. He navigated through the ancient tables and solid chairs, hoping the man proved as charming in person as he was in his letters. The barkeep's smirk had given him just a bit of pause — was the scholar so awkward that Alex wouldn't be able to stand his company?

But he must have entered the wrong room. A woman turned toward him as he pushed the door open, swathed in black, with a heavy veil covering her face.

"I beg your pardon," he said, bowing quickly as he backed out of the room.

She held up a hand. "Come in, Alex."

He recognized her voice immediately. It drew his temper faster than he could control it. "What in the devil are you doing here?" he asked, stepping in and shutting the door before he attracted any attention. "Ladies never come to a place such as this."

Prudence shrugged as she unwound the veil. There wasn't a trace of shame on her face — not that he expected there to be, given how she had changed these last months. "I am not a lady yet, merely a gentlewoman. It would seem a pity not to see this place before my circumstances change. If I can never see the hallowed inner chambers of the Society of Antiquaries, I can at least see where you drink after."

On another day he would have laughed. But he wanted to wrap her in his coat and smuggle her out of there before anything happened to her. His eyes narrowed. "Come with me, before you're seen. I would have brought a closed carriage if I'd known you were here, but I'll find you a hackney to return you to Ellie's where you belong."

Prudence dropped the veil to the floor. "Don't worry about my safety. My maid is waiting in the public room, and one of Ellie's carriages is sitting somewhere outside."

He took a breath. "Why couldn't we meet at Ellie's house? Did you go through my papers to find Chandlord's name and lure me here?"

She sat down at the small table next to the window, overlooking the interior courtyard. The pub had originally been an old coaching inn, and its provenance showed in the cobbled court and the ancient, leaded windows. She pulled the drapes closed over the glass, but there was enough light from the candles in the room to see her without straining.

"Would you care for coffee while you perform your monologue?" she asked, holding up the silver coffeepot. "I would have ordered small beer, but it was difficult enough to convince the man outside that I wasn't a prostitute. Ordering alcohol might have made him refuse me entirely."

"You are going to have to accustom yourself to behaving better when you're a duchess," he said.

He felt nasty and small even as he said it. Somehow, he couldn't stop himself in time. She shot him a look that said she'd rather throw the coffeepot at his head than serve him with it, but she poured two cups anyway. "I do not want to be a duchess. But if you expect me to behave as you'd like me to, you'd best wish for it with that dagger of yours."

Alex sighed and took the seat across from her. The fight he'd wanted evaporated as contrition took its place. "I am sorry. I shouldn't have said that."

"You shouldn't have said many things," she said, adding sugar to her cup and cream to his. But then she grinned, one of those quick, secret grins he'd missed so much over the past two months. "I'll confess I like it when you are just a bit jealous, though."

"Selfish," he chided jokingly, stroking her hand before taking his coffee from it. "Have a care for your safety, Prue. A jealous man could do many things to you in the private room of a public house."

She smiled down into her coffee cup. "I suppose I shall have to risk it, my lord."

Why did he suddenly feel like he'd never loved her more? Her eyes crinkled as she smiled, and her mouth pursed as she blew, inelegantly, across the steaming liquid in her cup. She sipped and closed her eyes, enjoying her coffee for just a moment despite the thorny conversation they were in the midst of. The core of her was resilient, imperturbable, in a way that would have driven a lesser man off in search of a princess to rescue. But her strength only made him love her more.

He wanted that vision across from him at every meal for the rest of his life. He wanted her face to be the last image in his eyes, her voice the last sound in his ears, the soft touch of her skin the last sensation his fingers sought out.

Something in the vicinity of his heart cracked. He'd thought he wanted her more than anything before, but now, in the quiet, when they could be alone together with no one else to disturb them, he knew it. It wasn't just a fantasy. And the knowledge staggered him, left him oddly dizzy, as though the foundation of his world had been ripped away and she was waiting there to catch him.

She looked up and caught him staring. "What is it?" she asked. "Do I have coffee on my nose?"

He almost told her everything he'd just thought. But he couldn't. He kept saying he was going to let her go. Showing her his heart, again, when he couldn't give it to her and she couldn't take it was unfair, even if the weight of his unshared love would eventually crush him.

So he handed her his handkerchief. "Was there something you wished to tell me?" he asked.

She swiped at her nose, then gestured with the handkerchief. "Not if you aren't finished with your monologue. Surely the coffee has fortified you again."

"I have finished for the moment. Please, do continue."

He leaned back in his chair, taking his cup with him and trying to catch his breath. She didn't match his indolent pose; she leaned forward instead, her hands wrapped around her cup as though she'd spent every day of her life arguing arcane points in pubs like this one. "I think I know where we might find a cure for your curse. It took hours of searching through my correspondence, but I should have known it all along."

He didn't know what he had expected — castigation, confession, or something else — but it wasn't this. "What?" he asked.

"Well, there were rather a lot of letters to sort through," she said, as though it was the volume of her correspondence that confused him, not the fact that it existed. "Four years' worth, and my organization is worse than I thought it was. But your reference to a useful dagger reminded me of something someone else had said, years ago. It was just a matter of finding the letter."

"Who have you been writing letters to?"

"Have you not guessed yet?" she asked, tilting her head. Her brown eyes were mischievous, anticipatory, as though she awaited the imminent culmination of a grand prank.

"You are Chandlord, aren't you."

He didn't state it as a question. It was so obvious, now that he thought about her interests and didn't just assume that she had stolen one of his letters. She nodded, smiling wide enough to show her teeth. "At your service."

"How?" he asked. "How did this come about?"

She shrugged. "I was always the scholar, not my brothers. While their books mouldered over summer breaks, I read them all straight through, dreaming of distant lands. And when they finally went to those distant lands and..."

She paused, her voice faltering. But she regained control almost immediately. "I had enough time during those months of mourning to read as much as I liked without Mother thinking I should be trying to win a husband."

"But reading is different than corresponding," he said. "Your mother couldn't have been happy with you sending letters to strange men."

"She didn't know. But I spent nearly all my pin money on postage, although I suspect that Amelia subsidized the expense. The letters went through a pub in Soho Square, and she insisted on having one of your footmen retrieve them so that I wouldn't go there myself. Mother never knew. But if she did, I think she would be more unhappy that I had wasted my money on paper instead of new hair ribbons with which to snare a husband."

She said it lightly, but his heart twisted. "Why would you take the risk? If someone had caught you, it would have been a terrible scandal."

"I couldn't find answers to the questions my books raised without asking other men of learning. I couldn't go to Cambridge as you did. I couldn't darken the door of your bloody club." A deep, yawning well of venom opened up beneath her voice, shocking him. "All I could do was write to those who might have answers, and take learning on paper as a substitute for discussing my opinions with someone who knew my interests."

Chandlord's letters to him had pleased him from the start, even though he hadn't known it was her. Her writing was witty and well-educated, with a dry vein of humor running through it even when discussing the meaning of some shard of pottery or ancient sculpture. And it seemed that he had been receiving those letters for years, from the charming, reclusive historian who claimed to never be able to visit or entertain guests.

The question came out before he could think. "Was I your first?"

She tilted her head. He flushed as he realized how she had taken his question. "Your first correspondent," he amended.

"First everything." Her voice was wistful, more open than he deserved it to be. "I wish we could…try again, you know. I've dreamed of having you in some illicit public house. This room would be perfect for it."

She was blushing slightly. His skin heated as he pictured what she had dreamed of, but he shook his head gently. "I cannot sleep with you again. Much as I would like to. You're in enough danger already."

Prudence was wanton enough to look crushed. "I was afraid you would say that."

He tried to steer the conversation back to safer waters. "So, you wrote to me as Chandlord. Did you ever think to tell me who you were?"

She nodded. "I used to dream of telling you that I was Chandlord, and that you would sponsor me with the Society. You seemed to enjoy my letters enough."

"I would sponsor you if I could."

They both knew he couldn't. While there had been women in some of the artistic societies in London, the Society of Antiquaries was too hidebound to allow her. And even if they did, she would never live down the scandal. An interest in history might be appropriate for some sad, shabby bluestocking, but not for an unmarried lady who had any desire for a more conventional life.

She sipped her coffee and leaned back, deflating just a bit. "I knew I'd never have the opportunity."

He didn't like to see her deflated. "It's come to something good, though, if you think you've found a clue."

"You sound like you're humoring me," she said, examining him over the rim of her cup.

"Do I?" he asked.

He was humoring her. There was no cure. She scowled, knowing him too well to allow him to get away with his subterfuge. "You are. I vow, I should stab you with that dagger."

Alex laughed despite himself. "On another day I might have welcomed it. But tell me what you found."

She looked down into her cup. "You aren't going to like this, I'm afraid."

"You can trust me," he said, trying to sound encouraging. "What did you find?"

She set her cup down on the table and took a breath. Then, at the last minute, she seemed to change her mind.

"Do you think your curse allows you to study how to find the cure for it?" she asked.

He shrugged. "It's never stopped me before. Probably finds some humor in it."

Her slow smile gave him the briefest warning before she asked her next question. "Does it allow you to pay for knowledge?"

"Prudence…" he said.

She held up her reticule. "I have information that would greatly further your studies along. Are you willing to pay me what it's worth?"

CHAPTER TWENTY

She felt wanton, daring…alive. As vibrant and carefree as she'd ever wanted to be, even though her life was so close to crashing around her ears. But Alex was here, and they were alone, and the maid she'd brought with her from Ellie's was too discreet to care what Prudence was doing.

If she had to run away to Europe, she might never have this chance again. And she wanted Alex too much to think about behaving herself.

"How do you want me to pay you?" he asked.

She could tell from the curve of his lips and the tightening of his fists that he had a guess. "It's too crass for a woman to take money. Perhaps…something else?"

He grinned, just for a moment, but his caution overruled him. "I can't, Prue. You know I can't."

"You just said you could pay for knowledge. I have knowledge. I have a payment in mind. And then we can both have what we want."

He tossed his hat on the table and shoved his hand through his hair. "Choose something else."

"This is what I want," she insisted. "You should know I have no intention of marrying Thorington. I'll steal something and get transported to Australia before I let it happen. But if we don't break your curse, I may never have the chance to...to have you again."

She hadn't slept well the previous night, thinking about how he'd taken her, how their lovemaking had felt. She didn't want to lose the opportunity to make love again.

He had other ideas. "Wait until we see whether we can break the curse. If we do, there's time enough after for everything I want to do to you."

"No." Her hands clenched each other tightly in her lap, avoiding the temptation to do more violence to her cup. "If I jilt Thorington — which I will — my reputation will be shredded. After that kiss he forced on me, everyone will assume that he has completely and utterly compromised me."

Alex interrupted her before she finished the thought. "The ton knows you better than that."

She laughed, for once feeling like she had the experience and he was the naive one. "When has the ton ever been logical?" She took a breath, then said what she felt honor-bound to say. "If we break the curse and you choose to marry me, can you live with the whispers?"

"That is a stupid question, Prudence."

His voice was so mild as he said it that she laughed. "It isn't. It is easy to talk ruin when one hasn't been ruined yet..."

He interrupted her, his eyes suddenly dark and intense. "I will love you no matter what anyone thinks of you. Even if it's all true."

It was an unconditional statement, an offering that was everything her heart had ever wanted to hear.

And she knew then that she had been in love with an image before. She had been in love with him from afar, the way a pagan might love a volcano, worshipping it while fearing the moment when it would awaken and destroy her.

Alex was real now, older than he had been when her dreams had started. He was more scarred than she had ever realized. And even though there was love in his voice, a complete conviction that made her heart sing, there was sadness beneath it.

It was as though this was a battle he had seen coming for years, a battle he had never found a way to win. She remembered how he had felt in her bed the other night, the determination in his eyes as he made her feel like the most beautiful, desirable woman in the world. It had been a gift for her, she suddenly realized. A gift that he wouldn't want her to repay. A gift he thought she *shouldn't* repay, for fear it would mean so much to him that it would put her in danger.

She stood up. He rose as she did, temporarily remembering propriety. But she surprised him by coming around the table and pulling him toward her. "Tell your curse that you're paying me for information, nothing more," she said.

Then she came up on her toes to kiss him. It was long, intense, the first inhalation of an opium addict as the sweet drug overwhelmed the senses. His mouth didn't need words to convince her of his need; it was obvious in how he devoured her, in the harsh, almost brutal need they shared as their lips fused together. She pressed her whole body against him, needing to be closer, needing his touch everywhere at once. She felt his erection, sudden and urgent, against her belly. His arms closed around her, ready to keep her there.

But he stopped, even though his body seemed inclined to ignore the ceasefire. "Prudence. I cannot."

She leaned back against the arms he still held her with and removed her gloves, dropping them to the floor as he sucked in a breath. Then she unbuttoned his jacket. "Then you do not want me to do this?"

"No."

"How industrious of you, to want to study instead of indulging yourself," she said, pushing his jacket off his arms. "But you'll accomplish far more today if you pay me like this."

He helped her even as he denied her. "We cannot continue. I've already risked far more…"

She kissed him again. There was something heady about being the aggressor — something sweet about the way he let her take the lead, about the way he couldn't stop himself from surrendering to her touch.

She pushed his braces off his shoulders. He started to loosen his cravat, but she pulled his wrist away. "You can't retie a creased cravat later," she said, sliding her hands down the planes of his torso. "Every servant at Salford House will realize someone ruined you."

Alex laughed. "Let them gossip. If they knew who had stolen my virtue, they wouldn't judge me."

Her thumbs found the indentations of his pelvis. He grabbed her wrist, but he couldn't seem to find the strength to pull her away. She unbuttoned the falls of his breeches, taking her time, sliding her fingers over the erection confined beneath them. He sucked in a breath, and his hand tightened on her wrist. But he made no attempt to stop her.

She sank to her knees. He shuddered. His fingers would bruise her if they pressed any harder against her. "Prudence…you can't."

She ignored him. She'd dreamed of doing this before, when he was just an object for every one of her fantasies. This particular dream had always seemed subservient before, a way to show him how much she worshipped him.

It was also the dream most likely to awaken her, leaving her aching with need.

But this wasn't worship anymore. She wanted to give him something that he had never expected or asked for, to share this moment with him in a way that would give them both pleasure.

She finished the task at hand, sliding the last button out of its hole. The closure of his breeches fell open, and she tugged at his shirt. The tails were long, and he groaned just a bit from the friction as she untucked them.

Then he was free and in her hand. She'd felt him inside her, but she hadn't touched him, explored him, the way she had wanted to. She ran a finger up his sensitive flesh, tracing the vein that ran from the base to the head, and he groaned again.

"You are going to be the death of me," he said.

Her hand closed around his shaft, testing the feel of him, hard flesh covered in velvet. "You are larger than I expected," she said, looking up at him and meeting his intense, need-filled gaze. "Your statue collection didn't prepare me for this."

He laughed, but it turned into a grimace as she stroked her fist up, then down again. "I should hope not," he ground out as she stroked him again. "Most of them were mutilated by pious Crusaders."

She shifted her hand to his testicles, learning their weight, and his words ended in a sharp exhale. "Christ, Prudence."

She stopped. "Am I hurting you?"

This time, his laugh belonged on a gallows. "Not in the way you think. But I warned you about private rooms and jealous men. You are going to find yourself on your back if you don't stop at once."

She kissed the very tip of his shaft before she lost her nerve. "There are worse choices," she whispered against his skin.

Then she took him into her mouth. She had seen enough engravings to know this was possible, and his exploration of her with his own mouth had given her some sense of how it might feel for him. But it was still a surprise when his hand fisted in her hair, when he groaned again.

She slid her tongue around the head, tasting something incontrovertibly male that she wasn't ladylike enough to find unpleasant. She couldn't take all of him, though, and so she wrapped her hand around the base again, holding him steady while she sucked his flesh. She wanted to tease him, stroke him, drive him mad...

She didn't last for long. His warning hadn't been an idle threat. He pulled back suddenly, then pushed her down to the floor. His hand was lightning fast, yanking her skirts up to her waist, plunging a finger into her slick passage. She hadn't realized how wet she was for him, but when she gasped, he laughed.

"You cannot tell me you don't want this," he said, pulling back and circling a teasing finger around the point where all her need was suddenly, achingly focused.

There was no need to respond. She couldn't respond anyway, not as he took his time tormenting her, driving her to the same need she'd forced upon him. When she was near to begging underneath him, he plunged into her, and she felt how tenuous his self-control was.

She arched up to meet him, wanting him deeper, wanting them both to come apart. He sensed what she wanted, hooking an arm around her thigh and pushing her leg back, changing the angle to something that only increased her need. Her hand clawed into his shoulder and he leaned down to kiss her, his tongue and his cock driving into her with the same desperate need. He swallowed her cry as she came apart, then gave it back to her as he spent himself inside her.

She loved him. It was the only choice she'd ever made that really mattered. It wasn't a vow in a church or a signature on a contract, but she was bound to him in a way that made all the rest of it seem superfluous.

She just had to find a way to win him.

She waited until his breath grew less ragged, until he no longer slumped against her like a dead man. "Wake up, Alex," she said, touching him on the shoulder.

"I should punch you for disturbing this dream," he muttered.

She brushed the hair away from him eyes. "Next time. I must tell you what I found."

"Now?" he said. He gestured toward their mutual *dishabille*. "I need an hour to recover, at least."

"We do not have an hour. I must return to Ellie's before her at-home callers arrive."

He gave an exaggerated sigh, then stood and pulled her to her feet. "What did you find?" he asked, rearranging his shirt and beginning to button his breeches.

She shifted her skirt and petticoats around her, then patted the back of her hair to see how badly it was mussed. "I found a letter that references your dagger. I wrote to my correspondent to verify it, and he agreed that he knew all about it."

His hands stopped buttoning. "Who wrote the letter?"

She said it quickly, casually, hoping he wouldn't press for more details. "Mr. Ostringer. He seems to know the provenance of every object to come through London in the last twenty years."

Alex scowled as he finished with his breeches. "You should not have been writing to him. He is utterly without scruples."

"Well, how was I to know that before?" she said. "In any case, his letters were delightful — always full of the most interesting gossip about scholarly circles."

It was why she had gone to him when she first considered selling fake goods. But Alex seemed skeptical. "Ostringer is a gossip? I thought he keeps all his information close to the vest."

She stooped to retrieve her gloves. "Perhaps he thought I was safe to share with, since I said I would never come to London."

"What did he say about the dagger?"

"In the first letter, I had asked him whether he thought there was any truth to the various myths that have been passed down through the ages. He thought there was. He mentioned King Midas and speculated that it was a dagger that had granted the wish and caused the man's woes. He said he had seen such a piece in Egypt years before, but had refrained from acquiring it."

"I very much doubt Ostringer would have refrained," Alex snorted.

She tried not to turn defensive, but she didn't succeed very well. "He said the dagger's power was too dangerous to have it in one's possession. As you and Thorington discovered, if I'm not mistaken."

He shrugged into his jacket, but he seemed to have trouble pulling it over the tension in his shoulders. "True. But just because he saw it doesn't mean he knows the cure."

She walked back to the table and opened her reticule. "I wrote to him yesterday to verify it, and he said that he would be happy to tell me about the cure for the curse." She pulled the letter out of her bag and handed it to him. "Read what he wrote, if you like. If you think it is not important enough to merit a conversation with him, then we shall pretend I never mentioned it."

"If you think I can pretend that today didn't happen, you are sadly mistaken," he said, with a leer that made her laugh. But he unfolded the letter.

The way his eyebrows furrowed, then lifted, gave her the answer before he said anything.

Still, he didn't seem inclined to believe it. "I'll grant this sounds like the dagger in my study," he allowed, folding the letter again. "But his allusion to a cure could be another myth."

Ostringer had said that the cure was readily available, but impossible to execute successfully. She sighed as she took the letter back. "Don't you think it worth the time to talk to him? He is the only clue we have."

Alex clubbed his hair away from his face. A muscle ticked in his jaw. "I have had promising clues before. This will likely turn out as all the others have. And besides, I asked Ostringer about it years ago. He didn't say anything about a cure."

"We must try, though."

"*We* do not have to do anything. I will go talk to the man."

His voice was harsh. She frowned. She hadn't told him how well she knew Ostringer, but she would have to risk Alex finding out if she wanted him to find the cure. "Isn't he more likely to give us the truth if I am the one to visit him? After all, he seems willing to gossip with me but hasn't shared anything of import with you."

"He's willing to gossip with Chandlord," Alex said. "Not you."

She sighed in frustration. Ostringer already knew her identity, but Alex didn't know about their connection. "I'll tell him that I am Chandlord."

"No. I don't want to endanger you. Ostringer is utterly ruthless. And you are already in enough danger without adding him to the mix."

He pulled his gloves on, then rubbed his thumb across his palm. She sighed. "I just want to help."

"You can help by staying out of harm's way. And that includes not trying to seduce me. If something happened to you and it was my fault…"

He trailed off. She didn't know what he was feeling, exactly, but she thought she had some clue because of the way her own heart kept missing beats. "Then you should understand how I would feel if I had the power to break your curse but had to give you up instead."

Alex paused for the longest time, looking down at his hand rather than into her eyes. But when he finally looked up, she saw a mix of resignation and resolve.

"Very well. Send a note to Ostringer and ask for an appointment tomorrow. He won't see you without one. But I will do the interview with him myself."

She nodded, willing to save the rest of the argument for the morning. "Will I see you tonight? I believe Ellie and I are attending Lady Andover's musicale."

"I must work. But send word when you know what time Ostringer wants to see me tomorrow. I will be at home all night."

She reached for her veil, not ready to leave, but knowing she had to. If they couldn't find a cure, at least she would have the memory of this afternoon — not perfect, but perhaps a perfect portrait of who they were together.

Before she could cover herself, Alex suddenly pulled her into his arms. He kissed her again, hard and thorough.

But for all the passion on their lips, the kiss felt like a farewell.

"Never doubt that I loved you, Prudence," he said hoarsely as he pulled away.

Then he was gone, leaving before she could respond. Her hands trembled as she wrapped the veil around her face.

She no longer doubted. But it wasn't lost on her that he made their love sound like the past, not the future.

He didn't think there was a cure. Which meant she would have to prove him wrong…

Or she might die when he was proven right.

CHAPTER TWENTY-ONE

Prudence had barely crossed the threshold of Folkestone House when Ellie's butler handed her a most unwelcome card.

It was the perfect weight, shape, and color. The printing was bold and black, with one word engraved precisely in the center.

She refrained from rolling her eyes, but only barely. "Tell his grace that I will attend to him in twenty minutes," she said to the butler.

He nodded. She wanted to send a note to Ostringer straight away, before she and Alex lost any more time. She also needed to change out of her ridiculous gown. The maid she had taken with her to the public house had already disappeared upstairs to lay out a new dress.

But to reach her room on the third floor, she had to take the stairs past the second floor. And Thorington apparently wasn't of a mind to wait in the drawing room in which he had been placed. He lounged against the wall near the staircase instead, stopping her before she could turn to the next flight of stairs.

"My dear Miss Etchingham," he said, executing a perfect bow. "I am delighted to find you well."

She curtsied on instinct, but her voice couldn't stay polite. "How do you know I am well? Perhaps I have a headache."

His eyes roved over her body, taking in the drab black dress and the hat and veil in her hand. "You look perfectly well, albeit shabby. Are you in mourning? Don't tell me we must put off the wedding."

She thought of lying, but Thorington surely had a copy of *Debrett's* — he would be able to discover if she created a family member only to kill them off. So she tried for an assault instead. "I am mourning my last days of freedom. If you will excuse me, I prefer to spend them in quiet reflection."

She'd overdone it. He laughed instead of heeding her request. "You should spend your last days of freedom visiting the modiste. Ask Lady Folkestone to help you. She dresses well enough, although you won't need as many masquerade costumes as she has."

Prudence frowned. "Does it ever occur to you that the people around you would be happier if you didn't try to order their lives?"

"Ah, you might think that." He took her arm before she could stop him and half-escorted, half-dragged her into the drawing room, where a tea cart waited for them. "But most people do not want a choice. They say they want it. In truth, they are happy enough to have someone decide events for them."

"I am not one of those people," she said, pulling her arm away from him. "And I still am very angry about the way you took advantage of me at the Duchess of Rothwell's ball."

"I am sure you are," he said, leaning against the mantelpiece when she refused to sit. "Which is why, my dear, you are the only wife I want. If you were dazzled by my charm and fortune, I would be bored of you within a fortnight."

"You know nothing about me," she said, her voice fraying. "We haven't exchanged more than a few words beyond your multiple proposals. And what I've seen of your character does not make me eager to wed you."

He crossed one leg over the other. "I know all I need to know. You're intelligent enough to converse with, pretty enough to give me a decent looking heir, and poor enough that you'll eventually be grateful for everything I can give you. And you're pragmatic enough that you'll someday forget Salford. Did I forget any qualifications?"

She eyed the fireplace poker and had a brief, dark daydream of hitting him over the head with it. He saw where her eyes went and laughed. "Ah, and your temper. Strong enough to be entertaining, not murderous enough to harm me."

She wanted to harm him, though. She made a show of sitting next to the tea cart and arranging her skirts around her as though she was a queen on display, not the shabby spinster he knew her to be. Then, acting on some mad impulse, she went for his throat. "I am not actually poor, your grace."

His smirk evaporated. "You are. Everyone knows it."

She shrugged and poured herself a cup of tea. "I recently came into an extravagant sum. Are you prepared to marry an heiress?"

His brows slammed together as he sifted through everyone in the ton who had died that year and tried to guess who might have left her money. "Impossible," he said flatly, once he had considered them all.

"Not impossible," she said, reaching for the lemon slices Ellie's housekeeper had procured for her. "Men do spend silly amounts of money on rare objects. I never expected someone to bid fifty thousand pounds for a mere rock, though."

Thorington reached her in three strides, so fast that she shrank back and dropped a lemon slice on the carpet. "Tell me what you mean," he demanded, leaning over her chair and pinning her with his eyes.

If it were Alex, this might be thrilling. But with Thorington, she was annoyed — and a little scared. "The rock wasn't real. But I suppose it proved to me that the curse exists. Marrying me will restore your fortune, won't it?"

He stepped back from her just as suddenly as he'd approached, as though the very air she breathed had been fouled. "You cannot be telling the truth. Did Salford tell you to say this to me? If you think it will make me release you from our engagement, madam, you are very much mistaken."

He was furious. She should have been smug, but again, the tic in his jaw made her too wary for jubilation. "It is true. And Salford had nothing to do with it. He doesn't know. But if it is any consolation, he may have been more upset than you when he guessed that the Aramaic didn't hold a cure for him."

Thorington eyed her like he'd just cut the head off a hydra and expected her to sprout two more. "The curse always had a sense of humor," he said. "Almost admirable, if it weren't so evil."

"Are you describing the curse or yourself?" she asked, trying to reclaim her stability by lashing out at him.

His grin wasn't evil — it was real, for once, just long enough that she wondered what the duke might have been like if he had lived a normal life rather than a cursed one.

But the grin was gone before she could analyze it. "Call me evil if you wish, my dear. But despite your perfidy about the stone, our wedding date is set. St. George's was only free four days hence, which is unfashionably soon, but it shall have to do. Tell me you have a better dress than that to wear, or I shall drag you to the modiste myself."

Four days. "Impossible, your grace," she said. "I need a month at least."

"We shall marry in four days," he said, utterly unmoved. "But I will be kind and give you time to accustom yourself to me before we consummate our union. A month seems like a fine span — long enough for you to realize that being a duchess is better than being a peasant, and long enough for me to know whether you're carrying Salford's child. I'll claim it, of course — would be too much of a scandal not to, and I will never toss my duchess out on her ear no matter how much she deserves it. Still, it is nice to know if there's a cuckoo in one's nest."

He examined his cuticles as he gave this speech, as though the thought of her bearing his enemy's bastard child was as inconsequential as the possibility of a rain shower in April. But she just barely restrained her gasp. "How are you so cruel?" she asked. "You cannot be this cruel. No one is."

He looked up at her. "I do not enjoy it, if that is what concerns you. But the world runs more smoothly if I am allowed to arrange it. And I find I can arrange it better if I do not allow my emotions to get involved. Too much messiness ensues. I hate a mess."

"This is a mess," she said frankly.

He shrugged. "I will fix it. You will marry me, I will have my fifty thousand pounds back, we will settle into domestic torpor, and this mess will disappear."

Her mouth dropped open. "That isn't a marriage."

"It will be for us," he said. "I think we will like each other tolerably enough. You aren't so different from me, you know."

"That's not true. I would never force someone like you have."

Thorington smirked. "Would you never trick a friend into selling something she shouldn't have?"

"It...that's not the same."

"No? Would you never lie to the man you claim to love? Telling yourself it's for his own good? Arranging everything to give yourself the best possible advantage?"

She would have clapped her hands over her ears if she could do so without giving herself away. Her stomach dropped and breathing didn't seem to help her. "I had a good reason for creating that stone."

"And I have a good reason for marrying you. Several, now that I know you have my money. Admit it, love — we deserve each other."

"I'm not your love. And it's not the same."

He pulled his watch from his pocket, checked it against Ellie's clock on the mantel, and snapped it shut again. "Continue to tell yourself that if it helps. I must be off. I will take care of the marriage contracts — send word if there is something specific you wish to address. And find a dress that isn't quite so horrid with your complexion — green, perhaps. It wouldn't do to shroud your beauty when half the ton will be watching."

He kissed her hand and left before she could stop gaping at him. The man was a menace.

But he was a very intelligent, very perceptive menace.

Ellie poked her head around the door. "I saw Thorington leave. How are you feeling?"

Prudence felt like she'd been hit in the head with a brick. But she tried for levity. "I feel glad that we live in the modern age. If that man could have, I'm sure he would have carted me off and forced me to marry him at swordpoint."

Her friend laughed, but there was sympathy in her eyes. "I can't say I'm sorry that you will be a duchess — you will make an excellent one. But I still find it hard to believe that Thorington pursued you so aggressively. I thought he would stay unmarried forever after the warfare he had with his last wife."

"He seems to think that marrying me will keep anyone else from being able to trick him into matrimony. Ironic that he's done it by tricking *me* into matrimony, but he isn't the sanest man, is he?"

"Ah." Ellie retreated into the hall for a moment, which was odd — until Prudence heard more footsteps coming toward them and had her explanation.

Ellie had called in reinforcements. Madeleine and Amelia entered with her, and Prudence suddenly felt descended upon. Whether they were guardian angels or avenging spirits was still unclear.

"We have come to help you plan," Amelia announced, pulling a piece of paper out of her reticule and asking Ellie for a pen and ink.

Madeleine gave Prudence a quick hug before taking over her duties with the tea cart. "What Amelia means to say, I'm sure, is that we are eager to help you in whatever way you need us to."

"There's no need to help," she protested. "And besides, I'm not sure what I would want help with."

Ellie took the sheet of paper away from Amelia and gave her a pillow for her back instead. "No need for lists until we know what Prudence wants."

Amelia huffed a protest. "What she wants might be a list in its own right."

"I'm not sure that what I want will figure into our calculations," Prudence said. "I am to marry Thorington in four days. That is all he thinks I need to know."

"Four days?" Amelia and Madeleine asked in unison.

Ellie frowned. "That is much too soon. What is the man thinking? You can barely get a single decent dress made in that time, let alone an entire wardrobe fit for your new station. And some will be scandalized by the brevity of your engagement."

"One might almost think this was a love match," Madeleine mused. "But Thorington doesn't seem capable of such a tender emotion."

"He isn't," Prudence said flatly. "The man is a villain."

She hadn't been quite so blunt about her feelings — or lack of feelings — before, and she had stunned them all into silence. When the silence stretched on a few moments too long, she waved a hand, trying to cut through it with a negligent gesture. "He won't beat me, I'm sure. And he does have money and a title. I could have done worse."

They were still silent. Madeleine was the first one who spoke. "It isn't too late, Prue," she said, slowly, as though reconsidering every word as she said it. "You might choose to seek happiness instead."

"I plan to," Prudence said. "But you know I'll be ruined if I jilt him. Even the three of you would have to seriously consider whether to accept me. You could only do it quietly, not at a public occasion. Where could I seek happiness if I could not leave the house?"

"Perhaps that life is still more bearable than a life in Thorington's bed," Ellie said.

Prudence shuddered. "I cannot marry him. But if I don't, I'll have to give up my life to avoid him."

She might never be received, might never see most of her acquaintances again. But she couldn't contemplate marrying Thorington. After seeing him, she was more sure than ever that she would rather hang it all and start again somewhere else.

And surely, someday, she could have Alex. Even if she couldn't tell her friends that she was waiting for him again.

And even if she hadn't told him the truth yet about her involvement in the auction. She would have to tell him if she wanted to take him to Ostringer; the shop owner was too unpredictable to trust that he would keep her secret. She would just have to hope that Alex could forgive her.

If he could not…she would have to go into exile alone. That was still better than becoming someone else's wife.

Ellie seemed to know that she had made up her mind. "If you are going to go, you should leave now. Before Thorington realizes you might run away from him."

It hadn't occurred to her that Thorington would try to stop her. But she couldn't leave quite yet. Not until she made one final attempt to help Alex break his curse.

Still, if she stayed, she might be trapped. Did the slim chance that she could keep Alex outweigh the probability that Thorington would capture her instead?

She'd always claimed that she'd wanted more choices.

Now that she had one, she wished she had kept her mouth shut.

CHAPTER TWENTY-TWO

Lady Andover's musicale wasn't an event that Alex would have wanted to attend even on his loneliest nights. But Prudence's note about meeting Ostringer the following afternoon had been short to the point of terseness.

And the invitation he had received from Thorington that evening — delivered by a footman rather than the mail — gave him a reason for her brevity.

Unless he wanted to go to Ellie's house and wait for Prudence to come home in the wee hours of the morning, he had to seek her out. He arrived at Lady Andover's house just after the first musician had performed. The footman who took his coat seemed a bit miffed that Alex was so tardy, but Lady Andover was quite gracious.

Not gracious enough to provide what he wanted, of course. All he wanted was easy access to Prudence in a place where they could talk. Instead, he spent an hour listening to a reasonably talented contralto, a mostly awful harpist, and a decent string quartet.

As soon as the final strains of the concerto ended, but before the polite clapping had finished, Alex moved toward Prudence's seat. He reached her just as she left the grouping of chairs where she had been seated with Ellie and Nick. "I should offer you felicitations again," he said, bowing over her hand.

"For what?" she asked as she curtsied to him.

"Your wedding," he said. "I expected that you might think to add me to the list for the breakfast, but I didn't expect to attend the nuptials themselves."

Her eyes turned murderous. "Don't say you've received an invitation."

Ellie couldn't stay uninvolved when she heard that. "Thorington already sent out invitations? Lucky, Prudence — I spent days writing the invitations for me and Nick."

Prudence shot Ellie a killing glare. Alex might have laughed if he wanted to prolong the conversation, but he took Prudence's arm instead. "Would you care to stroll about the garden for a moment? You look overwarm."

She didn't look overwarm — she looked like she wanted to find the nearest pistol and call Thorington out. Still, she seemed to remember the rules. "I shouldn't, my lord. But I appreciate…"

"The rules can hang, Miss Etchingham," he said. "You are about to be a duchess. No one will fault you for your sins then."

She hesitated. Ellie gave her a little push. "It's true, dear," Ellie said. "And even if it's not, it's much more entertaining to believe it."

"You truly are the worst influence," Prudence muttered.

But she walked willingly enough as Alex escorted her out the French doors to the balcony beyond. She took a deep breath when they were outside. "The harpist wasn't very good, was she?" she asked.

He didn't bother to respond to her small talk. "When did you plan to tell me that your wedding is in four bloody days?"

His voice was quiet, almost mild. She still flinched. "Thorington didn't tell me until this afternoon."

"Could you not delay him?"

Even in the dark he saw her glare. "Don't say you think this is my fault?"

He sighed and rubbed his fingers against his temple. "No. Of course not."

"I didn't ask for him to marry me sooner," she said. "But he is determined to marry at St. George's. He claimed that it could only happen four days from now."

Alex tried to remind himself that it was Thorington's madness that drove most of their current predicament, not either of their failures. "His first wife insisted on St. Paul's. I don't think she realized that St. George's is more fashionable even if St. Paul's is more grand."

"I don't give a fig for what happened with his first wife," she said.

Alex laughed. "For all that I despise him, I must say that one cannot fault his taste. The woman who tricked him was an abomination, but you would make an excellent duchess."

"How can you make a jest about this?" Prudence asked. Her voice was strained, more than he'd ever heard it. "We only have three days to break your curse."

Three days. He'd had ten years and hadn't done it. But he didn't want her to worry. "If you don't want to marry him, I can help you escape."

"I'm ready to escape. And I'll go wherever I must go. But what are my options? Some town where I know no one? Some manor house where the servants will assume that I've fallen into disgrace?"

"Surely there is something better…"

She shook her head. "I've thought through all the options, Alex. There are none worth considering. There never are for women of our class. It's either marriage, spinsterhood, or death. Unwedded exile isn't something I ever thought I'd need."

"I will support you in whatever you choose, as long as it isn't death," Alex said. "But if you choose exile, I will take care of everything. A carriage, a house, money, whatever you need."

"And what strings come with that? Will I ever see you again? Or is this your curse sending me away forever?"

Her voice sounded so bleak — bleak enough to freeze his certainty into little shards of doubt. "No strings, Prudence. I vow it. You… you don't have to wait for me. If you find another who will love you, take him with my blessings. Just don't marry Thorington. You deserve so much better than what he can offer you."

She sighed again. In the dark, in the cold, she sounded old. "I don't, really. Perhaps he's exactly what I deserve."

"Of course he isn't."

Prudence had been facing out into the gardens, but she turned to him with a motion that almost approached violence. The light coming out from the music room cast eerie shadows on her face. "You don't know me, not really. You're in love with a fantasy. Now let me be proper again and go inside before someone catches us."

He caught her before she could escape, not caring at all whether anyone saw them. He pulled her deeper into the shadows at the corner of the balcony, out of view of the guests still mingling in the music room. "What is wrong? I've never heard you like this before."

"You've never heard a lot of things," she said.

It was like he held a different woman in his arms. She sounded angry, bitter — guilty.

"I don't fault you for thinking you might want to marry Thorington," Alex said, striving to stay rational. "If you have changed your mind and don't want to try to break my curse, I would never fault you for it."

His heart would have broken if she had agreed, but she shook her head. "I will never want to marry Thorington. Ever."

"Then why wouldn't you take my help?"

"I don't want to marry him. But I might deserve him." Her voice dropped. "I can't let you help me unless you know what you're doing."

Alex was totally in the dark. He couldn't even think of a question to ask, beyond a simple, "What?"

"In for a penny, in for a pound," she whispered to herself. He remembered that night in his study, weeks ago. She'd said the same thing then, just before she had drunk his brandy.

Then, she had been so daring, so full of life. Tonight she was falling apart in front of him. But she straightened her shoulders. "Do you remember how you said that the curse had a sense of humor?"

He nodded. But he knew not to say anything — whatever she wanted to say was costing her too much to afford an interruption.

"And do you remember how you thought that whoever Ellie had sold the rock for would regret it when the curse tried to give Thorington his money back?"

His stomach dropped into his boots. "Where did you find the stone?" he asked.

She looked down at her feet. Then, like a hero facing a firing squad, she lifted her eyes to his. "I made it, Alex. I designed it, hired someone to carve it, and sold it."

"What?" he asked again.

He was sure that he had misheard her. An odd roaring had started in his ears when she'd mentioned Thorington getting his money back, and he couldn't quite seem to comprehend her words. But she repeated herself. "I made it. I would take it back if I could."

He shook his head, trying to shake out whatever she was saying. "How could you have done it? Where did you find…"

He trailed off, remembering that he'd left the dagger out when he'd left her in his study that night…knowing in a flash what she'd done. She filled the silence immediately, as though she hoped she could cauterize the wound with a flurry of words. "I'm sorry, Alex. Really. But I was so desperate. You have to know how desperate I was."

"You could have asked me for the money, Prudence," he said.

Oddly, her inability to rely on him wounded him more than her scheming did. She took a step back as if he'd threatened to hit her. "I didn't want your money, Alex. I never did."

"But you would have accepted it if I'd won the auction."

"I…"

She must have thought better of her excuse. "Did you want to hurt me?" he asked. "Or was it just about the money?"

"Do you remember that night in your study?" she asked.

He couldn't forget it. He nodded.

"I realized then that you would never love me. Or at least never enough to do anything about it. But perhaps that's why I deserve Thorington. A better woman would have given up and found a different life. I decided to arrange everything to pay you back."

Her voice cut straight through him. "I have always wanted you, Prudence. I've never lied about that."

"No. But if Thorington hadn't asked, would you have kept me on the shelf forever?"

Alex had every right to be angry. In fact, he was furious. But suddenly he was the one on treacherous ground. "I would have wished you happy with someone else."

"As you did with Malcolm?" she asked.

"That's not the same," he said, his anger turning into defensiveness. "I'm sorry I couldn't offer for you then."

"But you can't offer for me now, can you?"

Alex balled his hands into fists. "I want you to be safe, Prue. That's more important than anything else — our feelings, our guilt, our attraction, all of it is trumped by your safety. I can help you escape Thorington if that's what you want. But I won't see you die just because I've allowed myself to love you."

He was ready to keep fighting. But that pronouncement made her face crumple. She came to him of her own accord and wrapped her arms around his waist. It was an embrace made for comfort, not seduction — as though despite the lies and half-truths and hesitations between them, he was still the only one who could make her feel better.

He sighed. He knew why she'd forged the rock, even if it made him angry to think of the desperate straits he'd driven her to. He kissed the top of her head. "Don't berate yourself for forging the rock. We'll find a way to rescue you from Thorington, even if I can't break the curse."

"Do you really not care that I did it?" she asked, her words muffled by his jacket.

"Not enough to change my mind about you."

It was another half-truth. Later, alone, he would remember that his apparent indifference had pushed her into a dangerous trade, and he would punish himself for it. But the words seemed to give her heart.

"I have to believe we can cure you," she said, looking up into his eyes.

He didn't respond. He couldn't. He kissed her instead, hard and fast, and just long enough that it was difficult to stop.

But the pain of stopping was better than the pain of telling her that her dream would never come true.

CHAPTER TWENTY-THREE

The next day, Prudence sighed as Alex rapped on the door of Mr. Ostringer's shop. He had ordered Prudence to remain in the carriage with Nick and Ellie, who had accompanied them as ineffectual chaperones.

But surely he had known that they wouldn't stay behind. Prudence joined him at his side before he could knock again, while Ellie and Nick stood slightly back, admiring the shop window next door.

"Don't you think you've knocked enough?" she asked.

Alex scowled at her. "You should have stayed in the carriage."

"I know," she said. "That's why Ellie sent the carriage away."

Alex rolled his eyes and knocked again. The interior of the store was mostly dark. Ostringer only accepted clients by appointment, and he made little effort to dress up the front of the store. But Prudence was sure he was in there somewhere. "Mr. Ostringer never misses an appointment," she said mildly as Alex knocked harder. "He might appreciate a few moments to come to the door."

"What do you know of Mr. Ostringer?" he asked.

She colored slightly. She'd told Alex about her forgery, and he'd taken it well — surprisingly well. But she had neglected to mention Ostringer's efforts in her other sales. "I wrote to him when I was corresponding as Mr. Chandlord. And I've had the opportunity to meet him a few times in London."

"You didn't seem to know him when we saw him at Soane's house," Alex said.

Ostringer saved her by opening the door. He blinked, then gave her a very slight scowl before greeting them. "My lords, ladies," he said, bowing just deeply enough to acknowledge them without seeming obsequious. "I am honored by your company, but I cannot take an appointment at this time."

He tried to shut the door, but Alex shoved a booted foot against the frame. "We have an appointment, Ostringer. And we would much prefer to take it in your shop instead of on the street."

Prudence would never look at servants quite the same way again, not after nearly being one herself since her father's death. And so she saw what Alex couldn't after his use of such an imperious tone — the flash of dislike in Ostringer's eyes as his wounded pride turned into something more dangerous.

She intervened before Ostringer forced them to leave. "Mr. Ostringer, I know it's shockingly impolite to have misled you. But I was concerned that you would not take my appointment if you knew that Salford would be with me."

There was a sharp look to his features, as though his nose had been built and trained to sniff out valuable objects and interesting facts. But unless she was deluding herself, his face seemed to soften as he looked at her. "You were correct. Can I convince you to attend to me without Lord Salford's amateur opinions tainting our conversation?"

Prudence laughed. "I assure you, he's quite intelligent for an earl. May we still visit you, or shall we leave you undisturbed? Our friends will examine your collection while we converse, if that is amenable to you."

Ellie smiled, all charm. "How do you do, Mr. Ostringer. I thought that the marquess and I might look for a wedding gift today."

He bowed again, seeming to mean it this time. "You are always welcome. How can I deny one of the best collectors in London?"

Ellie's presence swayed Ostringer in their party's favor. He ushered them into the shop and closed the door behind them, turning the lock to prevent others from intruding.

The shop was splendid. It was what had convinced her that Ostringer was the perfect person to sell her forgeries. He had wide-ranging interests, and it showed in the eras he dealt in. The large main room was neatly divided by tall shelves, creating alcoves dedicated to different time periods and locales. A mummy leaned against one wall. A full suit of armor and a variety of medieval weapons faced it, as though ready to engage in battle. There were Grecian urns, Chinese vases, Persian and Indian metalwork, French furniture, Turkish braziers…and that was just what Prudence could see from the entrance. The room stretched far enough away from the windows that not everything was visible, just the outlines of more treasures obscured by shadows.

"Do you know Ostringer well?" Alex murmured into her ear.

Better than she cared to admit. "I…may have sold more than a stone," she whispered, low enough that Ellie and Nick didn't hear it over their own private conversation.

Alex stared at her. "What in the devil have you been up to?"

She held up her hands. "I'm a badly behaved bluestocking. Now you know it. We can leave if you wish."

"I like badly behaved bluestockings," he said. "Although it would have been more fun if you'd taken me into your confidences so that I may have behaved badly with you."

His teasing warmed her heart a bit, but she tried to concentrate on the business at hand. She turned to Ostringer, focused on finding a cure. "Do you have someplace where we may talk privately, Mr. Ostringer? Lord Salford and I have a question, and I think you may be the only person in London with an answer."

He seemed to size her up again, performing some calculation she wished she could read. Then he nodded. "Please, come into my office. We will be quite undisturbed there."

He called up the stairs that ran along the side of the room, asking one of his servants to come down and attend to Ellie and Nick. Then, he ushered Alex and Prudence toward the back of the shop, leaving the marquess and marchioness to cool their heels among the towering shelves of antiquities. As they approached his inner sanctum, the mustiness grew stronger, adding to the pressing sensation of age and memory.

Ostringer pushed aside a tapestry on the back wall, then opened the small door hidden behind it. His office was more of a parlor, with a large antique desk and an odd assortment of furnishings that he either couldn't sell or had taken a liking to. Against every wall were locked cabinets and chests of various sizes, labeled in a spidery script that Prudence couldn't make out from the doorway.

"Would you care for tea, Miss Etchingham?" Ostringer asked.

"That would be lovely, thank you," she said.

Alex didn't say a word. His opinion hadn't been asked for. She sensed him beginning to seethe beside her.

Ostringer poured water from a pitcher into a kettle and hung the kettle in the small fireplace. "I'll confess I would rather offer you whisky and cakes. But I suppose tea is more proper for the future

Duchess of Thorington."

The gossip had been in the papers for the past two days. "Perhaps whisky would be more appropriate, if you've any knowledge of Thorington," she said.

Ostringer didn't laugh. "You are very perceptive, Miss Etchingham, if perhaps a trifle too loose with your tongue."

She flushed. "I did not mean to insult the duke, Mr. Ostringer."

"It's not the duke I care about," he replied smoothly. "If anything, it's likely that I despise him more than you do. But if you are here, you have taken Lord Salford into your confidence about something related to me. And that is an unfortunate turn of events."

"Let's cut bait, Ostringer," Alex bit out. "Miss Etchingham has only one question. Once you answer it, we can leave you to your hoardings."

"How curious," Ostringer observed, pulling a ring of keys from his waistcoat pocket and rifling through them. His voice was soft, but insinuating, like an assassin's knife rather than a grenadier's assault. "I have never known you to lose your head in a negotiation before, my lord. Have a care, or you will lead me to believe I can name my price for whatever it is you want."

"You know me better than that," Alex said.

But Ostringer knew he had Alex in a bind, even if he didn't know what Alex wanted. He took his time finding the key he needed, then unlocked a box sitting on the mantel. Prudence was disappointed to see that it held tea leaves, not something more exotic. He spooned the leaves into a teapot and gestured Alex and Prudence into a pair of chairs opposite his desk. "If you will wait a few minutes until the water boils, we can be quite comfortable," he said.

They couldn't be comfortable, not with the way he eyed them as though still trying to take their measure. But they sat, mostly because Prudence sat and Alex didn't seem willing to leave her side. She tried to feign disinterest, but it was hard to stay disinterested in a room that held so many secrets. Not only were all the boxes locked, but the window looking out over the interior courtyard was protected by a grid of iron bars. The interior door was reinforced oak with multiple locks and bolts. Despite the fortifications, the room seemed almost cheerful, saved from grimness by bright carpets, lavishly upholstered chairs, and gleaming gold candelabras.

She had never seen Ostringer's office before — they had always done their dealings in the shop. She began to understand why Alex had wanted her to stay away. But it was too late for that. The minutes passed in silence until Ostringer handed around the cups. "No milk, I'm afraid. You'll have to do with sugar."

Alex set his untouched cup on a table. "I suppose I should thank you for showing me your inner sanctum. I never thought I would see it."

"I never saw the need to show it to you before," Ostringer said, taking his seat behind the desk. "I do not care to encourage dilettantes."

She expected Alex to take that as the greatest possible insult, but he surprised her by keeping all trace of a reaction off his face. "I typically do not care to encourage pillaging merchants, but we all have our own standards, don't we?"

"I've never stolen anything," Ostringer said.

Alex scoffed at that. "Every antiquities merchant in London has stolen something. If not with your own hands, then with your money funding activities abroad."

"And your money doesn't fund those same activities? We all have blood on our hands, my lord. Some of us merely have more blood than others. And if the rumors about you are true, you have more blood — or at least dearer blood — than all the rest."

She glanced over at Alex. He had turned perfectly still, but perfectly brutal. He looked like he would happily add to the blood on his hands if he could force Ostringer to give him what he needed.

"What are you insinuating?" Alex asked, his voice remarkably calm given the death in his eyes. "Take care with your choice of words."

Ostringer sipped his tea. "Merely a rumor I heard a decade ago. I'm sure I was mistaken."

He knew about the dagger. From his words, it sounded like he'd known about Alex's curse even before she'd written her vague question to him the day before. Prudence was sure about it. And she was also sure she couldn't waste an entire day watching Alex and Ostringer circle around each other like a pair of jackals.

"If you believe that Lord Salford has the dagger that you and I corresponded about several years ago, you are correct," she said. "Would you be willing to share the cure with us?"

Alex shot her a quelling glare. Ostringer laughed. "Not much of a negotiator, are you, Miss Etchingham?"

He had laughed about it before — she had been completely, eagerly willing to accept his first offer of forty percent of her sales. During that failed negotiation, he had sighed and increased it to sixty.

"You know I'm not a negotiator," she said. "But we aren't here to negotiate. I merely want to hear more about what you said in your letter. Surely you can share what you know in the name of friendship?"

Tonight, he didn't seem willing to extend her the sympathy he'd given her in the past. "Friendship?" Ostringer asked. "I'll grant you, I find you charming. I will help you when I can. But you're in over your head. And the antiquities world isn't a friendly one. Historians, perhaps, would be willing to share for the thrill of discussing what they've learned. Collectors are a different beast. We are all quite cutthroat, aren't we, my lord? The desire to find and possess something no one else has…it's very nearly a disease."

Alex's jaw tightened. "Don't paint us all with the same brush, Ostringer."

The dealer held up his hands. "I am sorry for causing offense," he said, in a voice that wasn't sorry at all. Then he turned to Prudence. "What is it you wish to know? If you are looking for a cure for your upcoming marriage, I'm afraid I can't help you. Unless you'd rather run away with me instead?"

She laughed. "No, but I thank you for the offer. But if Lord Salford can find a cure for the curse the dagger gave him, I might be able to marry him instead of the duke. Do you have any knowledge of how we might break the curse?"

"I might." He paused, looking at the way Alex's hand curled over hers, examining whatever emotions he saw on her face.

"Your letter several years ago said you knew," she reminded him. "As did your letter yesterday."

He seemed chagrined that she had stripped him of that bargaining point. "Very well, I know how to break the curse."

Prudence sighed with relief, already smiling back at him in anticipation. But Alex's hand gripped hers more tightly — not with excitement, but with warning.

She understood, a moment later, why.

Ostringer leaned back in his chair. "The question, Miss Etchingham, is whether you are willing to pay the appropriate price for that knowledge."

CHAPTER TWENTY-FOUR

Alex had known that Ostringer would want something outrageous if he had any knowledge worth sharing. But Prudence hadn't realized it. He should have done more to warn her. Her optimism was quickly turning to dismay.

"You won't help us purely for the sake of helping?" she asked, betrayal layering over her voice.

Ostringer held up his hands. "This is a business, Miss Etchingham. I deal in objects and information. Even my friends do not take anything for free."

"Then it seems unlikely you have friends," Prudence sniped.

"You wound me, Miss Etchingham," the merchant said. "I consider you a friend. Our business has always been such a joy."

Alex wanted to end this quickly, before Prudence's faith in others was utterly dashed. "Name your price, if you have something to sell me," he said. "Be reasonable about it. I have better things to do than haggle with you."

"Better things to do than break this curse you've labored under?" Ostringer asked, taking another sip of his tea.

"What do you know of the curse?" Alex retorted, stifling a fake yawn for good measure.

Ostringer feigned a yawn as well. "This visit is tedious, isn't it? Perhaps you should come back in a few months, when we're both better rested."

Alex couldn't wait months. Thorington wouldn't even give Prudence days. And even if she didn't marry, Alex's love for her grew by the day — the risk that the curse would eliminate her was growing too great to ignore. He managed to keep himself from scowling, but his fist clenched over his scar. "There is no need to trouble you in the future. Give me a price and your information, and we shall be on our way."

"You surely do not think I merely require money?" Ostringer asked.

Alex had known he would want something else. Ostringer usually didn't deal in money, other than when selling decorative objects to society hostesses and theatre owners. All the rest of his business involved trading artifacts, information, or favors. Alex was sure he wouldn't want to give Ostringer anything the man asked him for.

But he tried to look calm. "I wouldn't insult you by attempting to guess your plan," he said.

He succeeded in startling a laugh out of Ostringer. "Good. I doubt you could guess, in any event. I should warn you, though. I require payment in three parts."

Alex stopped himself from rolling his eyes. "Let's get on with it, then. If I must find three things to give you, I want to start immediately."

"Patience, Lord Salford," Ostringer said. "Miss Etchingham, would you care for more tea?"

She hadn't said anything since realizing that Ostringer was not her friend. But her tongue had had enough time to recover. "No more tea, thank you," she said primly. "Just the bill for your services."

He laughed again. "It's a shame you're marrying the duke, Miss Etchingham. If his curse doesn't kill you, I would like to continue our business together."

"I would be more likely to work with you if you will help us now," Prudence said, attempting to throw something into the bargain.

Alex wanted to know exactly how much work she'd done with Ostringer, but he knew better than to ask in the middle of their negotiations. The collector shook his head. "I most sincerely doubt it. Thorington won't want his duchess associating with me. The same holds true if you become Salford's countess instead."

"Then perhaps I shouldn't help either of them break the curse," Prudence mused.

Her attempt to play to Ostringer's atrophied sympathies worked better than Alex's threats had. The man smiled at her — a genuine smile, one that seemed a bit rusty from disuse. "I would rather not help Salford," he said. "I think he deserves to lie in the bed he made."

"He isn't as bad as you think he is," Prudence said.

Ostringer sipped his tea. "I hope your faith isn't misplaced, Miss Etchingham."

"It will only be misplaced if we cannot break his curse."

There was a small silence as they all weighed whatever arguments they might make, whatever prices they were willing to accept. Ostringer was the first to speak. "For your sake, Miss Etchingham, I hope his lordship can break the curse. You should be able to marry someone who might love you. Most desirable thing in the world, marrying for love."

He spoke as one who knew, even though Alex wasn't aware that Ostringer had ever married before. But Alex did not care about what had happened in the man's past. "If you knew this curse existed, and if you suspected that I suffered from it, why haven't you offered to sell me the cure?"

Alex had asked Ostringer about information related to the dagger before. Every time, Ostringer had claimed to know nothing. Today, the man just shrugged. "I never liked aristocrats very much. If you were foolish enough to think you knew what you were doing when you made that wish, why should I help you?"

"But you could have made a lot of money off me or Thorington by selling it," Alex said.

"True. But perhaps I got more value out of knowing that I held the key you were searching for, when you wouldn't give me the time of day if we saw each other on the street."

Alex stiffened. "I…apologize if I have caused you offense, Ostringer."

Ostringer accidentally showed some of his surprise, but he reined it in. "Thank you, my lord. I will help you for Miss Etchingham's sake. But I am afraid you will disappoint her. I very much doubt that you can put the cure into effect."

"Why do you think he cannot be cured?" Prudence asked.

Ostringer's eyebrows furrowed, as though he had given the question serious thought more than once. "The cure requires more self control than most men have. Particularly men who are accustomed to getting what they want. Any man who was foolish enough to wish for something with a cursed dagger is unlikely to be capable of controlling himself long enough to undo the damage."

"Salford can accomplish it," she said. "I'm sure of it."

He didn't think he deserved her blind faith. Nor did Ostringer, apparently. "No one has succeeded with the cure in the three thousand years that the dagger has been in existence."

"How do you know this?" Alex asked.

"The dagger is not what controls the curse — it's merely a vessel. The legends I heard about it in Egypt say that it is a prison for a powerful djinn, one captured by an ancient pharaoh. The djinn refused to grant the pharaoh's wish and was bound to the dagger as punishment."

"A djinn?" Prudence said. "This dagger grows more fantastic by the day."

Alex shot her a sidelong glare — this wasn't a children's tale. She mouthed him an apology before Ostringer continued. "It was an attempt to force the djinn to grant the pharaoh's wish. The priest who did it decreed that when someone who had made a wish successfully cured himself, the djinn would be free. My sources speculated that the priest wanted a way to remove the effects of the djinn's intervention, thinking that it would be easy enough to release the djinn within his own lifetime. Naturally, if the djinn were freed, it would remove the power that fueled any other wishes — so anyone else who had used it would be in for a nasty surprise when their wish stopped coming true. But no one has been successful yet."

"I've never guessed that it contained a djinn," Alex said.

Ostringer nodded. "Every person I spoke to in Egypt in '01 mentioned the djinn first. You should perhaps reconsider trying to break it. A freed djinn might decide to kill you, since it would no longer be bound by your wish."

"I'll risk it," Alex said.

Prudence squeezed his hand. "You can do it, Alex. I'm sure of it."

Ostringer shook his head. "You are very lovely and intelligent, Miss Etchingham, but you shall be disappointed if you do not realize that Salford will not succeed."

"Are your compliments included in your price, or must we pay more for them?" Prudence asked, completely unmoved.

"They are free for you. Compliments for Lord Salford may cost more."

Alex sighed. "Again, name your price so we can get on with it."

"Very well. I want the most important artifact in your personal collection. I want you to sponsor me for membership in the Society of Antiquaries. And I want an introduction to Miss Etchingham's mother."

They both gaped at him. Alex had expected a steep price, but this was...

"You are mad," Prudence declared. "I thought you seemed quite sane before, but you aren't, are you?"

Alex agreed. "That is a ludicrous price for knowledge that I can't even trust exists — for knowledge you claim won't help me in any event. How do I know you are not pulling off the swindle of the decade?"

"Because no one else is clamoring to be introduced to Lady Harcastle," Ostringer responded tartly. "And I should say that it is a reintroduction, not an introduction, if that matters."

"Still," Alex said, "I want proof that the cure exists."

Ostringer sighed. "I cannot prove it without telling it to you. It's quite simple, really, even if it is impossible. But I will tell you that I was in Egypt when the dagger was found in the personal effects Napoleon left behind in his rush to leave. I suspect the emperor himself tried it — one of the soldiers I talked to said that he had wished to be Emperor of France. Lucky for Britain, I suppose; the djinn took him at his word, since all his campaigns seem to fail just as he's on the cusp of conquering the world."

"That's not proof of a cure," Alex said.

"No. But Napoleon's traveling army of historians unearthed all the legends of the dagger there were to find in Egypt. And one of them shared the cure with me while he was in his cups one night."

"If you saw the dagger and had the cure, did you use it yourself?"

The collector held up both hands, palms forward. His skin was smooth. "We cannot have everything we wish for. I knew it then, and you should know now. If you don't…then it's certain you can't break the curse. No matter how much you might wish it otherwise."

CHAPTER TWENTY-FIVE

Alex wanted to accompany her on her visit to her mother. So did Ellie. Nick, however, had no interest in participating in her familial drama.

"Why do the lot of you always insist on interfering with each other?" Nick asked as the carriage carried them away from Ostringer's. "Can you not find enough entertainment in your own lives?"

"It isn't interference. I merely want to help," Ellie said.

Prudence was sitting next to Ellie and couldn't see her face, but Nick's grin gave her a glimpse of what he must have seen in his wife's eyes. "Between your schemes and Ferguson's, it's a wonder the two of you haven't organized half the ton," he said. "If the twins ever stop flirting with music masters and start applying their talents, London will belong to your line."

"The Avenels aren't the only family capable of interference," Prudence interjected. "Alex and Amelia are nearly as skilled."

Alex scowled at her, but Ellie was the one who protested. "Amelia is worse than I am. And Ferguson has never forced anyone to get married."

"Successfully, at least," Alex murmured.

Prudence wanted to kick him, but she refrained. "I do not need company to visit my mother. I'm sure we will more easily converse alone."

Alex frowned. "When have you ever easily conversed?"

The answer tore at her heart. "Perhaps we can make amends."

"What do you have to make amends for?" Ellie asked. "Or do you think it is time to cut ties with her?"

Prudence looked down at her gloved hands. Her gloves were pristine and perfectly cut, bought by her forgeries. Her mother's gloves would either be old or cheaply made.

What was there to make amends for? That her mother had mourned her brothers for too long? That Prudence had felt too lonely, too useless? That there hadn't been enough money, and too much expectation placed on Prudence's marital success?

She wanted to say it all — it was all deserved, after all, a series of wounds that Prudence had never quite forgiven her for.

But it sounded silly and trite, particularly if those excuses were meant to justify never seeing her mother again. That wasn't what she wanted. And she was old enough to know that, if she never saw her mother again, the person who suffered for it longest would be herself. Her mother would pass away eventually, but Prudence would have to live with the guilt of it for years beyond that, without any hope of reconciliation or forgiveness.

"Please, just leave me at her cousin's house," Prudence said. "I shall have her maid accompany me home."

Alex frowned. "If you'll allow it, I will retrieve my carriage and come back to fetch you."

She didn't want to allow it. She didn't know how long she would be, and anyway, Alex should be working to complete the tasks that Ostringer demanded.

But after a few minutes of argument, and another muttered curse from Nick about her friends' meddling, she agreed. Riding home with Alex was better than finding a hackney coach.

And if her mother refused to meet Ostringer, then she could tell Alex immediately that their hopes were destroyed.

*   *   *

Her mother came into the drawing room wearing a new dress. It was a rich dark blue calico, still somber, but so far removed from her old mourning dresses as to be shocking.

"Mother," Prudence said, standing to embrace her. "You look... lovely."

Lady Harcastle returned the hug, holding on a moment longer than she usually did. "Thank you, dear. Your cousin had bought the fabric but no longer wanted it. I don't have the skill of a modiste, but I can be serviceable with a needle when I choose."

It was a choice Prudence never made. She hated sewing more than she hated being out of fashion. So did her mother, if she recalled. "I hope you shan't need to sew your own dresses much longer," she said as they sat down.

Her mother was too proper to shrug, but Prudence heard the ambivalence in her voice. "I would rather tend a garden than sew a dress, but as long as I live here, I have little to do. There is time in my day to make any number of dresses."

She continued on for a few minutes about fabric choices and which colors might be suitable now that she was so far into her widowhood. Prudence gave noncommittal answers, distracted by the alternate path her thoughts had taken. They had both stayed in that house before, during the first year after her father's death when she and her mother had circled through all their relatives. Her mother's cousin was a kind woman, but she had not married particularly well. The husband was a barrister who practiced at Gray's Inn. Their house was comfortable despite its less exalted situation in Bloomsbury, but their social circle was far removed from Lady Harcastle's.

Since the household wasn't invited to higher functions and didn't have the funds to buy seats at the opera or vouchers for Almack's, her mother had likely been lonely. Lonelier now that Prudence was out of the house.

Prudence took a deep breath. It was little wonder her mother usually talked over her. With no one else to listen to her, Prudence was her only audience.

Her mother didn't realize that Prudence was distracted. "I thought I should wear something better than what I might make for your wedding, though, so I had a fitting this morning. The modiste promised to have it done in time. I don't wish to embarrass you. And Thorington would be dismayed if I turned up in rags."

That statement was enough to pull Prudence back into the conversation. "Why do you care what Thorington thinks?"

"He visited yesterday, told me your wedding date, asked whether it was common for females in our family to wear outmoded mourning dresses, told me that he would settle upon you fifty thousand pounds, and left within five minutes of his arrival. He's a beastly man, but fifty thousand pounds is nothing to sneeze at."

Prudence discovered yet another reason to despise him. "The duke is insufferable."

"Indeed," her mother said. "But you can suffer a lot for fifty thousand pounds."

On another day, Prudence would have lashed out at her. But this time she listened — listened to the tone underneath, rather than immediately interpreting the words as an insult.

Her mother wasn't happy. She was making the best of a bad situation.

Just as she had always, unconsciously, taught Prudence to do. Find satisfaction in the moment, because the future was destined to be bleak. Prudence had resisted at first, determined to find her idealized, idolized romantic love. But when Alex had rejected her that night in his study, she had unconsciously taken the lessons her mother had taught her and tried to forge her own path instead.

Would her life have been different if she had never learned that lesson? Alex thought she was brave. But she wasn't, not really. She was simply so certain that the future would be worse that she no longer had any fear about seizing the present.

"What if I told you I don't plan to marry the duke?" she said suddenly.

She hadn't planned to tell her mother. And the look on her mother's face made her regret it. "Why on earth would you say that?" Lady Harcastle asked.

"You know why. How can I condemn myself to a lifetime of having Thorington tell me what to do at every turn?"

"But you'll be ruined. You know this."

Again, she tried to listen to the tone, read the meaning in her mother's eyes rather than reacting on instinct. Her mother's voice was flat — a reminder of a fact she was sure Prudence already knew, not a dire warning. And her eyes were worried — worried, not angry, not judgmental.

"I know," Prudence said, some of the fight going out of her. "I know. But I can live without a reputation. I'm not sure I can live with

Thorington's attempts to control me."

Her mother was silent for a long time. A very long time. She stroked the brooch pinned to her dress. It was an instinctive gesture, the same as Alex's relationship with his scar. But the brooch was different now. For years it had been a cameo surrounded by a braid of Prudence's brothers' co-mingled hair, a macabre reminder of the boys she had lost. But she had replaced it with a locket Prudence hadn't seen in years. It had been her jewel of choice when Prudence was younger — a pretty golden circlet pinned to her dress.

"What happened to your brooch?" Prudence asked.

"It was time," her mother said quietly. "And I hope you do not think that I am trying to force you to marry Thorington, because I am certainly not. He will not be a good husband. Nor, I think, will he be a good father. But he will certainly be a good provider. You may mourn what you could have had with Salford — I would be surprised if you didn't. But please…just make sure you are *sure* you know what you're about before you jilt Thorington. And be sure whatever pain you're experiencing right now doesn't make you ruin everything for yourself later."

"That isn't what is happening," Prudence said, her temper rising. "Why you would bring Alex into this, I don't know. But being a *provider* isn't…"

Her mother cut her off. "I know it feels like your world is ending. I felt that when your brothers died. I felt it the Season I came out, before I married your father. Pain makes you do stupid things, Prudence. If I had been stronger four years ago, and not wallowed in my grief, I might have married again. Or I at least might have been more pleasant company for you. I am sorry I didn't do more."

And just like that, Prudence's temper died.

"It doesn't matter anymore," she said. "Truly. No matter what happens, we will come out all right."

Lady Harcastle had been pretty once, before her grief had hardened her. But somehow, over the past few months, she'd lost some of the bitterness around her mouth. When she smiled, it seemed genuine, not a mask she put on because it was expected of her. "It matters. I want you to be happy where I wasn't. But more, I don't want you to regret your choices. Whatever you do about Thorington, I will support you. Just make sure you won't regret it."

Prudence would only regret it if she hadn't done everything she could to change her situation. She couldn't tell her mother about Alex's curse. Nor could she tell her that there was a chance she might be able to break it and win Alex for herself. But she had to ask the favor she had come for.

"Did you ever know a Mr. Ostringer?" she asked.

The transition was abrupt. Her mother stilled. It was the stillness of a cornered animal, in the instant before it chose to run. "Where did you hear that name?"

"He owns an antiquities shop in Mayfair," Prudence said, trying to sound casual even though her mother's reaction had heightened her curiosity. "I visited there this afternoon."

"You should be visiting modistes, not furniture dealers," her mother said sharply. "I'm sure it's too soon to consider how you might redecorate Thorington's house."

It was an odd reaction, given that moments earlier her mother had claimed a willingness to support her if she jilted the duke. Prudence pressed on. "He said that he would very much like to make your acquaintance. Or your reacquaintance, as it were. Those are his words, of course. I can't think where you might have met him, unless you frequented his shop before I was out."

Her mother stroked her brooch again, staring off into space with some dazed introspection that was utterly out of character.

"Did you know him?" Prudence asked.

Lady Harcastle blushed. It was so rare that Prudence was sure it was a trick of the light until her mother cleared her throat. "I knew him. Before I married your father."

Prudence gasped. "Were you in love with him?"

"No," her mother exclaimed, as though the very thought appalled her.

But then Lady Harcastle sighed. "Perhaps. I don't know any more — it was years ago. I was too young to know any better, and he was so very handsome and learned."

"Did you meet him at his shop?" she asked.

"He didn't have a shop then. He was my father's private secretary."

That told Prudence all she needed to know. Lady Harcastle's father had been relatively wealthy, although not well-off enough to give her a large dowry. But their status had been too high to ever consider a liaison between the daughter of the house and a glorified servant.

"What happened between you?" Prudence asked, too curious to let the subject drop.

"You can guess, I'm sure. He wanted to make his fortune so that he could win me, but my father discovered everything. And then Lord Harcastle offered for me. It was either take his offer, or spurn him and be disowned for it."

She pursed her lips, not sharing how she had felt, only the barest facts. But Prudence wasn't blind. She could fill in all the details from what she'd seen over the years. Her father and mother had not been a love match, even though they had gotten on civilly enough. But Lady Harcastle had rarely received or visited her own father before his death — a fact Prudence hadn't given much thought to until now.

It was odd, how generations repeated themselves.

"Do you wish to see him again?" Prudence asked. "He seemed eager to be introduced."

"Did he really?"

Her mother stared off into space again, as though she could read the story of the life she might have had in the air between them. But she cut herself off after only a few moments of daydreaming. "How silly of him," she said briskly. "Even if we were the same class, it has been over thirty years since we last spoke. The chances that we have more to say to each other than a brief 'how do you do' are miniscule."

"Is class all that matters to you?" Prudence asked.

"I'm too old to be a fool. You know as well as I do that I cannot move in the same circles if I associate with someone from the shop."

"He seems more interested in being a scholar than running a business," Prudence said, choosing to gloss over Ostringer's ruthlessness and remember how charming he had been to her. "And anyway, you can't move in the same circles without money, either. He has more than enough of that."

It was a mercenary argument. But something in her mother's eyes, or the blush beneath them, made her want to see Lady Harcastle and Ostringer come together for their own sake, and not just because it was the price of breaking Alex's curse.

"Very well," her mother finally said. "I shall meet him."

Prudence heaved a sigh of relief, but Lady Harcastle seemed too stunned by the events of the last half hour to have any suspicions about Prudence's motivations. The conversation turned to safer waters after that, both warmer and more pleasant than any conversation they'd had in an age. When Alex finally came to retrieve her, she was almost sad to go.

It wasn't a full reconciliation — she was still too sensitive, and her mother still too abrupt, to make it easy. But it was a start.

And for once, in one aspect of her life, Prudence was sure that the future would definitely be better than the present.

CHAPTER TWENTY-SIX

It took two days to organize everything. Two days Alex didn't have.

Prudence had insisted on staying in London. He had disagreed with her, but she had dug in her heels — and pointed out that she didn't need his help if he didn't want to provide it, since she could afford to make her own escape. The reference to the money she'd swindled from Thorington should have upset him. But he, quite oddly, found himself not caring that she had forged anything.

Those forgeries had given her hope that she might be able to live without a husband. That had, inadvertently, saved her for him. He couldn't be too angry about that.

Still, if Alex failed to implement the cure Ostringer was selling them, Prudence would have little more than twelve hours to escape London before her wedding. "Have you packed your belongings?" he asked as they drove to Ostringer's shop.

They were alone, but neither of them supposed it mattered. In the morning, she would either be his fiancée, Thorington's bride, or the biggest scandal of the decade. Visiting a shop in Mayfair unescorted seemed like the utmost propriety compared to that.

"Yes. But I only intend to take a valise if I must go. Ellie can send the rest of my things along later."

He frowned. "You cannot risk corresponding with her, or anyone else, until Thorington loses interest. He won't be pleased to be left standing at the altar."

"Why are you so certain that is what will happen?" she asked, matching his annoyed tone. "You can break the curse. I'm certain of it."

He wanted to meet her expectations. Despite her frustration, she looked at him like she expected him to be a hero. Like it was obvious that he would win her if he set his mind to it.

He couldn't disappoint her. He couldn't lose her.

But he knew the odds were not in his favor. "Ostringer's warning was clear. You should prepare yourself for the possibility that I will fail. I've already planned for a carriage to take you out of London tonight. The driver will leave at any hour you need him to."

She sighed. "I never have been good at preparing to lose."

"Better to prepare than to be surprised," he said.

They lapsed into silence, a dark silence that matched the twilight gathering around the carriage. Ostringer's was equally dark when they arrived. Alex had sent word ahead, but that didn't mean the antiquities dealer would deign to see them. He pounded on the door, each bang of his fist matching the cruel thump of his heart. He was going to lose her, and she would lose everything because of him...

Ostringer pulled the door open, his eyebrows making his scowl even more impressive. "Manners, my lord," he said. "They will get you so much farther than violence will."

"I have what you asked for," Alex said.

"So soon? You must be in some rush. It isn't Miss Etchingham's wedding that has you hurrying, is it?"

Prudence was supposed to wait in the carriage, but Alex hadn't expected her to follow through. He didn't even bother glaring at her as she joined them. "Please, Mr. Ostringer. If you ever held me in esteem, don't keep Salford waiting. We haven't much time."

Such a direct appeal to the conscience rarely worked with men like Ostringer. But then, if he had some interest in Prudence's mother, he might have some residual affection for Prudence as well. He sighed to show that he wasn't happy about this turn of events, then ushered them inside.

The only lantern was partially obscured by a safety shield designed to keep it from setting Ostringer's collections ablaze. The shadows seemed appropriate for what they were exchanging — for whatever dark deed Alex might have to accomplish to change his fate.

Ostringer shut the door and crossed his arms. "What do you have for me?"

"I found seven members of the Society of Antiquaries to sponsor you for membership. The vote won't take place until the next meeting, but you only asked for sponsorship, not membership. Membership I cannot guarantee — you must pass with a vote of four in favor for every one against, so it shall depend on how many men you've annoyed over the years versus how many you've impressed."

The man looked chagrined, but he didn't argue. He was enough of a gentleman to not blame another when he had made a mistake in setting his terms. "And the object from your collection?"

Alex had carried in a small box under his left arm. He held it out like an offering of tribute. "I thought of giving you the dagger, but you might not appreciate my humor."

"No, that would not do at all," the collector said, taking the box. "What have you offered instead?"

"A necklace, rumored to be Roman. The ruby in it alone is worth a fortune. Even if the provenance of the necklace is more recent than Caesar, it is still a stunning piece."

Ostringer pulled it out of the box. The jewels sparkled even in the dimmest light. Alex's heart gave the tiniest twinge.

"Is this the most valuable object in your collection? I would have thought some of your urns were more impressive."

"Perhaps. I can trade, if you'd like. But this was the first major piece I ever acquired, so it means more to me because of it. And I had intended to give it to my bride someday as a wedding gift."

Prudence touched his back, just briefly — an improper gesture that Ostringer's eyes didn't miss, but that still brought Alex comfort. "I accept it, then. And have you fulfilled my third request?"

"My mother would like to see you again," Prudence said. "She invites you to call on her at any time."

"Will she have more than five words to say to me, or did you have to force her to see me again?"

For the first time in all of Alex's dealings with him, Ostringer sounded uncertain. It was a weakness he normally would have exploited, but Prudence didn't make any attempt to win a better deal. "She doesn't know that you requested an audience as part of a deal with Salford. And she seemed…pleased. Perhaps too experienced to be truly swept away by the thought, but certainly able to consider the possibilities."

That statement unlocked the last of Ostringer's reserve. "Very well. Salford, I didn't expect you to get this far — perhaps there is hope for you after all."

"What is the cure?" Alex asked.

"The paper that was given to me had a few lines in an ancient dialect of Greek. The dagger itself is obviously from a far older Egyptian line, but I suspect the Ptolemy dynasty had it for a time — they must have written down what they had heard about its origins. The paper, of course, was a copy of a copy of a copy, so it's possible some of it was lost through the centuries."

If this was any other object, any other night, Alex could have discussed its provenance for hours. But he was out of time. "What did the paper say?"

Ostringer gestured toward his office. "I can retrieve it for you in a moment, but it sounds so simple as to be unbelievable. Translated, it says that he who wishes to break the djinn's power must relinquish his original wish with all his heart, all his body, and all his soul. He who is no longer tempted by the power of the djinn is freed of its influence — and frees the djinn to return to its own plane of existence."

"That cannot be the cure," Alex said flatly. "There has to be more to it than that."

Ostringer shook his head. "I vow that is what the paper said. It also said this was part of the djinn's punishment — for denying the pharaoh's power, it was imprisoned until it found the person who would deny its power instead. I doubt the priest expected that it would take three thousand years, but then, ancient pagans weren't the most merciful people to walk the earth."

Prudence touched Alex's back again. "You can do this."

He could. He wanted her more than anything, more than his studies, more than life itself. If it was a matter of relinquishing his original wish, he should have no trouble.

But if that was true, why hadn't the curse already broken itself?

*   *   *

Prudence's heart swelled as Alex took her back to Ellie's house. He had done it. They had done it. The cure to the curse didn't require some object they would never find, as he had suspected. He wouldn't have to make any of the evil sacrifices she had imagined. Alex's heart was noble enough, and his love for her strong enough, that the solution to their problems was within their grasp.

He sat next to her in the carriage, not across from her, with an arm wrapped around her shoulders. It was an easy, comfortable gesture, fitting for the life they might have together. She stroked his knee, already daydreaming. The *yes* she had always wanted to give him was waiting in her mouth, confident, eager, ready.

He kissed her hair. But he didn't say anything.

The silence stretched until the carriage reached Ellie's house. Her enthusiasm was undimmed; he seemed unsure, but she was sure enough for both of them. And even if he was concerned, it wasn't stopping him. "Shall I escort you upstairs?" he asked.

It was a bold, shameless proposition. She nodded her agreement. In any other house, even his own house, she would have had to deny him. But Ellie's staff was entirely discreet. The marchioness was no longer particularly scandalous, but she demanded servants who wouldn't spread rumors about her. They wouldn't say anything about Prudence's guest. And if Ellie caught them together, she would ask a hundred questions in the morning, but she wouldn't force them to marry.

Not that it would matter — by morning, they would be ready to be married anyway.

Alex helped her out of the carriage, then murmured an order to his coachman to return to Salford House without him. It was still bold of him. Folkestone House overlooked Portman Square, one of the most exclusive addresses in London. Any number of Ellie's neighbors might have seen them.

Again, Prudence didn't care for appearances. They made no attempt to find their hostess, no request of the servants to send up tea or refreshments or anything else. She guided him straight to her bedchamber as though it was theirs — as though they already belonged to each other in name as well as deed.

He was on her as soon as the door closed. Her skill at kissing had grown, and she was better able to breathe as their kiss deepened, but this one was something else — like all the other kisses until now had been restrained in a way she'd never realized. He was fully with her, fully entwined with her, with his hands unraveling her hair and his mouth unraveling her control.

She wanted him. More, she wanted him to know it. She ran her fingers down his chest and began unbuttoning his waistcoat. Their kiss went shallow again, turning into fast, stolen sips as their hands made quick work of each other's clothes. Her pelisse, then her dress, pooled around her feet. His cravat and coat joined them, along with two pairs of gloves, a hat, a cap, a petticoat, a shirt, her slippers…

He had to stop to pull off his boots, a task he had some difficulty doing for himself, but he was too impatient to try for elegance in the attempt. And then he was kissing her again, roving his hands over her body, unhooking her stays, taking a moment to tease the cleft of her derriere, to skim over the curve of her backside before tracing back up her spine.

She wanted to do the same to him, tease him the way he was teasing her, but there was time enough for that. There was time enough for everything. She focused on their kiss instead, the way he tasted, how her head had turned light and her heart had begun to beat too fast. She stroked her thumb across his cheekbone, loving the contrast of stubbled evening beard and smooth skin.

He pushed her chemise off her shoulders. His eyes, when she looked up, were dark and intense with need...and something else, that look she'd always thought was love. "Let me give you everything," he said as the linen slid slowly down her body. "Let me prove you're mine. Let me break the curse for you."

Yes. She didn't say it, though — she dropped her hands to his waist instead, attacking the buttons that were the only barrier remaining between them. When he was free, she slid her hands around his waist, pushing his trousers down, feeling the indentations above his buttocks, then his firm, muscled flesh.

He kissed her again, and it was different again — different when all she felt was skin and heat, when his need for her pressed insistently against her belly and her need for him turned her breasts into hardened peaks. She tilted her head back, wanting him to keep kissing her, wanting him to keep up the delicious torment of his large hands running over her.

He picked her up, suddenly, and carried her to the bed. He didn't bother to pull the covers back. As he laid her on the coverlet, the embroidery teased her. But it was nothing compared to his mouth.

"I could worship your breasts," he whispered against her skin. "I could spend hours just looking at them, imagining what I would do to them. And yet more hours touching them..."

His hands caressed her. His touch was light at first, as though still in his dream, but it soon turned insistent, conquering. He found just the right pressure, enough to have her arching against him, but not enough to turn her need into a frenzy.

"And then I would take them into my mouth," he said. "Until

you begged for more and I knew you wanted me."

"I want you," she said, looking into his eyes. "You know that."

"It's not enough. Not until you think you'll die from it. Then you'll know how I felt, these years when I've dreamed of you."

He sucked her into his mouth. His tongue swirled around her nipple. His fingers kept teasing the other breast, kept stroking, while his mouth took its time turning pleasure into torture. She dug into his hair, pressing him against her, wanting more…but he grabbed her wrist and pulled her away.

"This is my dream," he said, pinning her hand to the mattress. "Stay still and let me worship you."

The idea of it, of not moving, of not acting, of letting him touch her however he wished, suddenly made her tremble. She wasn't sure she could do it. She wanted him so badly already.

"I don't need you to worship me," she said. "Please, let me…"

"No."

He was always saying no to her, but this time she didn't mind. He stopped talking, giving all his attention to her skin, making her shudder as she realized that he wasn't going to stop. He was taking his time, indulging himself — indulging her. His touches were slow, sure, heavy enough to erase her doubts but paced in a way that kept her far from sated.

But it wasn't until his hand dipped down to the juncture of her thighs that she knew he would eventually be able to make her beg. She squirmed under him, trying to get him to move faster, trying to urge him on, but he kept the speed he wanted — slow, stubborn torment.

His fingers traced a path through the thatch of curls that covered her sex, then down to the channel that ached to be filled by him. He didn't stop kissing her breasts, didn't stop his worship, but it was secondary for her now, an assault that was meant to keep her off balance, unable to resist his real intentions. One of his fingers dipped into her, then slid back out, tracing her own moisture up to the small, hidden peak that would soon drive her wild.

He stroked her, slowly, relentlessly, until the worship turned to torture, until her need turned into something mindless, ravenous. Her whole body was hot. Her mouth felt empty, unloved, wanting to say *yes* to a question he hadn't asked, wanting even more to kiss him again, to take him into her. Her sheath was even emptier, clenching on air. And still he stroked, no urgency, just focus.

"Alex," she whispered. "Please."

He didn't stop, but he didn't give her what she wanted. "Tell me what you need."

She didn't understand what he was after. But for once in her life, she didn't care to analyze it. "I need you inside of me. I'll die if you leave me now."

He stopped. Just for a moment, but it was enough to make her moan, as though her whole world had crumbled away. "You won't die," he said, moving up her body to kiss her again.

It was a vow-sealing kiss, the kiss she would have wanted at their wedding but wouldn't be able to have in public. "You won't die," he murmured again as he broke away from her. He was covering her fully now, his cock already at her entrance, his hands planted on either side of her shoulders, his eyes looking down into hers with the kind of promise she'd always wanted from him. "I love you, Prudence. I love you more than anything. And I renounce everything else — with all my heart, all my body, and all my soul."

Yes. "I love you, too," she said. "Above everything else."

He plunged into her, hard enough to rock her back into the bed, hard enough to tell her that his control had finally slipped. She dug her fingers into his shoulders. He was far gone enough that he didn't try to keep her still. He pulled back and she met his next thrust, no longer able to stay still beneath him. They pulled apart and came together, again, and again, until she couldn't wait any longer, until she buried her face in his neck to muffle the cries she couldn't swallow.

When she finally came apart, he was only moments behind her. She couldn't breathe, couldn't think beyond knowing that he had come with her, that he had spent himself inside her.

Yes.

He slumped against her. His breath was hot and ragged, still mindless. She kissed his shoulder, stroked his back, and waited.

And waited.

He finally moved, flipping onto his back next to her. She came up onto an elbow, curling around him. "We did it," she said, trailing her fingers over the planes of his chest.

Alex opened his eyes, but he looked up at the ceiling, not at her. "I wish I could be as sure as you."

"Why do you say that?"

His arm came around her shoulder, but he still didn't look at her. "How do we know I broke it? I don't feel any different than I did this morning."

Her dream, so close to being a reality, began to shatter. It was a slow shattering, like a flaw that had been hidden in crystal, only later turning into a crack, then a spiderweb of cracks, then a disintegration.

"You said you wanted me," she said, grasping onto the words that had seemed to buy their life together. "You said you love me."

"I do. I do love you. I do want you."

"But you're doubting." Her voice turned flat, hollowed out because the only emotion she could have filled it with was anger, and she was trying so hard to stay calm. "Why are you doubting?"

"I don't doubt *you*," he said. He finally looked at her. The intensity in his eyes was more chilling than reassuring. "I doubt Ostringer. The cure couldn't be this easy, or it would have already happened. I was ready to renounce everything but you months ago. Years ago."

"Were you?" She pulled away from him, rolling out of bed and grabbing her chemise from the floor. She covered her breasts with it, too upset to bother putting it on. "I know I would give up everything for you."

"Really?" he asked. Somehow it didn't seem like a question.

"You know it's true," she said. "I'm the one of us whose feelings aren't in doubt."

Alex snorted as he pulled on his trousers. "Remind me again what you said when I asked you to wait for me."

She pressed her hand against her mouth. Whatever *yes* that waited for him had fled, leaving a bitter taste that was a precursor to tears. "That was different," she said.

He looked up from his buttons. "It didn't feel different. In fact, it felt like you didn't love me very much at all."

She hadn't realized that she'd hurt him then, just as he didn't seem to realize how much he'd hurt her now. "I was trying to be pragmatic. It isn't easy to give up everything for a dream, Alex."

"Perhaps that's why I didn't feel the curse break," he said quietly. "Are we just a dream?"

He hadn't said it, but she guessed, then, where his doubt came from. His life had been easy with the curse. Yes, he had to deal with the guilt of his father's death…but otherwise, his estates were profitable and his days were as he ordered them.

Could he give up all of that for her? Could she expect him to, when she had almost traded him for her own freedom?

She pulled her chemise over her head. As it fell down to cover her, she felt like she was donning armor — but whether it was to fight for him or to protect herself, she no longer knew.

"We aren't a dream. But we can't break the curse until you know that."

His eyes were haunted. "I don't know how I could love you more than I already do."

They were words that should have made her heart sing. They turned it to stone instead. He loved her, as much as he was capable of — but it wasn't enough.

She straightened her shoulders. "I will wait for you, Alex. But I cannot wait here. I must leave London by dawn. Ellie will know where to find me — come to me when you are ready."

CHAPTER TWENTY-SEVEN

He had failed her. It was a litany in his head, matching the drumbeat of his heart. He had failed her, and he would lose her.

He walked down Ellie's staircase like a man going to the gallows. There was nowhere he wanted to go. Perhaps killing Thorington would help his mood, but it wasn't the duke's fault that Alex had failed to break the curse. The fault lay in Alex's heart, buried so deep that he hadn't sensed the danger it presented.

What if he could never love her enough? He had been so sure that he did — so sure that she was all that mattered to him. Oddly, he was still sure. But the cure rested on his heart, not the strength of his intellect or his will. Perhaps he'd ignored his heart for so long that it had atrophied, no longer able to perform as it should.

He wanted to smash his fist into Ellie's perfectly plastered walls. But he kept walking, staring straight ahead, leashing the temper that threatened to overwhelm him. If this was an enemy he could fight with swords or guns, he would go in for the kill. If this was a rumored menace that he could stave off with clever words, he would give the performance of his life.

The heart was another matter. How could he fight for something he couldn't see, with only his love for her as a weapon?

Alex was so focused on reaching the door that he nearly ran headlong into Nick. "Easy, Salford," Nick said, avoiding the collision. "Didn't know you were visiting tonight."

"I'm not," Alex said, his voice clipped.

He tried to step around Nick, but Nick clapped him on the shoulder. "You seem to be in a mood. Come out with me — I could use your temper as a buffer between me and Ferguson."

"If you don't like the man, why do you associate with him?"

"Who said I don't like him?" Nick asked. "He's a bit of an acquired taste, but I find him entertaining when he isn't antagonizing me."

Alex suspected he would feel the same if he had the chance to spend more than a few minutes at a time with the duke, but it wasn't meant to be. He had failed Prudence. But he had also failed himself, failed the life he might have had, the one in which he could socialize with someone other than a set of dead historians in his moth-eaten books.

"I thank you for the invitation, but I must return to my house," Alex said, stepping around Nick.

But just as he reached the front door, the footman opened it — not to let him exit, but to admit Ferguson and Malcolm. "Ah, my second-least-favorite Staunton," Ferguson exclaimed, as though delighted. "What a pleasant surprise."

"Come to give us a second chance to drink you under the table?" Malcolm asked.

"Shouldn't you be home with your wives?" Alex retorted.

Ferguson nodded. "But the ladies ousted us — said they had to prepare for Miss Etchingham's wedding." The look he gave Alex was slyly observant. "I would think you would want a drink tonight of all nights."

He did. He wanted a vat of the stuff, if only it could make a difference for him.

It wouldn't. But suddenly he didn't want to go home. He couldn't go back upstairs — couldn't face Prudence's eyes again as he wondered why all his love wasn't enough. Still, what was waiting for him at home? Sitting alone in his study, staring at dead languages he no longer cared for, reading texts that ultimately gave him no pleasure?

"One drink," he said.

*   *   *

As it happened, Prudence didn't cry as many tears as she thought she would after Alex left.

Instead, she opened her traveling writing desk, retrieved a sheet of paper and a bottle of ink, and considered her choices. She had choices, after all. Alex's departure a few minutes earlier wasn't the end of her life, just an unwelcome event.

She had thought to make a list of what she could do next. But as she sat there, she realized she was asking the wrong question.

The real question was whether Alex loved her enough to break the curse.

She didn't have to write down the evidence. Her heart knew the answer, with more certainty than she had ever dreamed she would have with him. Alex loved her, as much as she loved him. It had been unfair of her to say that his love was in doubt. His love had come to be the only thing she *didn't* doubt.

But was it enough?

They had made love only a half hour previously, and while the feel of him had faded from her skin, his scent hadn't. It was as though a bit of him had remained behind, comforting her when he could not.

And then, she realized a final choice that she had never considered making. It was possible that Alex had broken the curse without realizing it. Ostringer hadn't said how they would know if he had succeeded, only what he needed to do to make it so.

But if he hadn't succeeded yet, she didn't have to give him up. She just had to accept that his love for her, and her love for him, might kill her.

It was ludicrous to even think it. She'd read her tragic romances. She had always thought that Juliet was too stupid for words. But she understood now. She didn't want to die, had to trust that it wouldn't happen. But if this was her destiny, if this was the choice in front of her…she would rather die with him than live without him.

She pushed her desk aside and grabbed her pelisse from the floor. She'd already dressed, although her hair was likely still a mess, so she found her largest hat and shoved it on her head. Then she went downstairs, summoned a footman, and commandeered one of Ellie's carriages.

Alex loved her enough to break the curse. She was sure of it. She just had to convince him to stop worrying about her safety and embrace their destiny.

*   *   *

It wasn't until his second drink that Alex noticed something odd.

Ferguson had made him laugh. More than once. And Alex didn't even have to be polite and remember to laugh — it had happened on its own, drawn out by the conversation.

Alex frowned into his glass. He felt warm, warmer than he should have in a room with no fire. Nick's study didn't have anything burning in the fireplace. It was a warm enough night to do without one. Alex would have liked a fire. The crackle of burning wood was often the only thing he'd found comfort in in his own study, on all those endless winter nights when he'd dreamed of Prudence and tried to lose himself in a book instead.

He couldn't let himself think of her.

He drained his brandy. Nick had good taste in spirits. This one was expensive enough that even his curse hadn't been able to turn it to swill. He wanted a fire to savor his next glass with. He should make one despite the heat...

But when he tried to stand, he fell back into his chair.

Ferguson, Malcolm, and Nick all paused to stare at him. "How are you in your cups already?" Malcolm asked. "We've barely begun."

"Impossible," Alex said.

He had been about to do something. He couldn't remember what it was. He was suddenly bone tired, though. He dropped his head against the chair. The back was too low to support him, so he slouched into the cushions, letting his body slide as though this were his own study, not his host's.

"Unsporting of you not to tell us of your weakness for brandy the other night," Ferguson said, reaching over to refill Alex's glass. "I think I still have a headache from all that claret."

Alex shook his head, but it made everything spin a bit, so he stopped. "I cannot get foxed," he said. "Constitutionally incapable."

"I thought you were constitutionally incapable of lying before this week, but you keep surprising me," his cousin-in-law said. "First you say you cannot marry Miss Etchingham, when it seems to be all you want to do. And then you say you cannot get foxed, when you are clearly near to unconsciousness after only two glasses."

What they were saying finally lined up opposite what he was feeling. Alex realized, then, that they were a perfect match. "Good God," he whispered. "I'm drunk."

Nick laughed. "Malcolm and Ferguson warned me your intellect was too prodigious to trifle with."

He tried to stand again. This time he made it to his feet, with only a bit of weaving. "I must find Prudence."

Malcolm stood up and put a hand on his shoulder. "I don't think this is a good time to seek her out," he warned. "Her wedding is to-morrow…"

Alex shrugged off his hand and his words. "She wants me. I want her. I have to tell her."

Ferguson sighed. "Must you have waited until now to realize this? Malcolm and I tried to help you with her earlier and you didn't take it. Thorington won't like this."

"Thorington can go to the devil," Alex said succinctly.

He made it to the door without tripping, which he was quite proud of. He hadn't been drunk in a decade, but he wondered if it was like sea legs. Being able to walk whilst unsteady seemed to come back to him easily enough.

Nick caught up to him. "Can I help you up the stairs? Wouldn't want you to break your neck in my house."

"I thought you didn't like that we involve ourselves in each other's dramas," Alex said.

Nick looked chagrined — or, at least, Alex thought he did. Mostly he just looked blurry.

"Better to involve myself in your dramas than to explain to the magistrate how an earl broke his neck on my staircase after only two brandies," the marquess said.

Ferguson and Malcolm came along as well, letting Alex lead them up the stairs. He had the dim thought that Prudence might not appreciate an audience — particularly this audience — but the need to find her, tell her, was too great. He was drunk, which meant the curse was over.

Which meant his love for her was great enough to earn them both a better life.

He knocked on her door. She didn't answer. He thought for one moment about leaving her be, but that thought was beaten to death by the mob of thoughts that told him to tell her immediately.

But when he opened the door, there was no one there to tell. Prudence was gone.

CHAPTER TWENTY-EIGHT

Prudence expected to find Alex in his study at Salford House. But when she pushed the door open, she found something entirely different.

"Why are you here?" Ellie asked. "Shouldn't you be on your way out of London?"

Ellie sat behind Alex's desk like she belonged there. She appeared to be drawing something with his pencil and drinking his whiskey like she was a man, not a lady. Amelia lounged on the settee, a book balanced on her still-growing belly. Madeleine sat next to her in one of the chairs, also holding a book. There was a half-eaten tray of sandwiches sitting between them, as though they had brought provisions for a siege and already exhausted most of them.

"Why are *you* here?" Prudence retorted. "Where is Alex?"

"Why are you wearing that hat with that dress?" Madeleine asked.

Amelia looked her over. "Did you run here in a wind storm?"

Prudence looked down at her dress. She'd done up the buttons wrong. The dress was blue muslin, but the hat was yellow straw with red cherries on the brim. Enough hair stuck out from underneath it to look completely wild.

It didn't matter. "I was in a rush. Shall you tell me where Alex is, or must I find him myself?"

Ellie put her pencil aside. "We haven't seen him."

"He must be at his club, then."

She turned to go, but Madeleine rushed up to catch her before she made it more than three steps down the hall. "You cannot go to White's," she hissed.

Prudence turned around. "I know that. But I have to find him. Tonight. Before everything goes wrong."

Madeleine pulled her back into the study and shut the door against any servants who might overhear them. "What changed?" she asked. "I thought you were leaving town tonight, but we've heard nothing to say the wedding has been called off. You aren't going to jilt Thorington at the altar, are you?"

"Please say you aren't," Amelia added. "Because I would dearly love to see it, and I shan't be able to attend in my condition."

Prudence would have laughed, but there wasn't time. "I cannot tell Thorington in advance that I won't marry him. The dreadful man would likely abduct me and force the issue if I tried to turn him down. He will have to find out at the altar when I don't arrive."

"You cannot stay in London another minute," Ellie warned. "Thorington will kill you if you embarrass him like that. You should have left when we discussed this days ago."

Prudence hadn't told them why she had waited — it was too absurd, to say she was waiting to see if Alex could break an ancient curse. "I want to leave tonight. But I must find Alex first."

"Why must you find Alex?" Amelia asked.

Madeleine and Ellie exchanged a look.

Amelia narrowed her eyes at them. "What was that look for?"

Prudence tried to stave off the revelation. "Salford merely offered me the use of a carriage. I must find him so that I can leave London."

"Don't lie," Amelia said cheerfully. Then she frowned at Ellie and Madeleine. "I'm not completely addle-brained by my pregnancy. I've known for months that Prudence is in love with my brother. But the two of you should have told me if you thought so too."

"You didn't tell me," Madeleine complained. "I had to realize it myself."

Prudence wanted to scream. "This discussion is neither here nor there. I need a carriage. Which means I must find Alex."

"Why don't you wait here with us?" Amelia suggested, returning to the current scheme. "We can send footmen to canvas White's, the Society of Antiquaries, and anywhere else he might be hiding. You may as well wait here in comfort."

Prudence considered her options. Her friends were right. She couldn't search London for him herself. She could either stay with them or return to Ellie's. Alex would have to come home eventually, though. He never stayed out beyond the midnight hour, and that was only an hour away. Going to Ellie's meant she might miss him.

She couldn't afford to miss him. She was sure he had broken the curse. But if she didn't find him by dawn, she would have to leave London and hope he someday found her. At that point, her fear of Thorington would overrule whatever tender sentiments she wanted to share with Alex.

There would be time enough for tender sentiments later, as long as she didn't find herself married to Thorington first.

"I shall wait with you," she said, taking off her ridiculous hat. "Let's send out the footmen."

*　*　*

Alex never came home. It was as though he had gone to ground when he had left her at Ellie's earlier. The footmen searched the entire city for him, from the highest reaches of White's to the lowest gaming hell they'd ever known of him to go to.

They didn't find a trace of him. Prudence was just the slightest bit annoyed.

That wasn't true. She was just the slightest bit furious.

Ellie yawned. "This has grown tedious. Why did Salford pick tonight, of all nights, to be unpredictable?"

Amelia jerked awake when Ellie spoke. "Is he here?" she asked.

"No," Madeleine and Ellie said in unison.

Amelia scowled. "I shall kill him. Send someone to the docks with a message for the next ship for Bermuda — Sebastian must return so that he can inherit."

Prudence stood up. "I must go back to Folkestone House. The wedding is in seven hours."

"Are you leaving London?" Ellie asked.

"As soon as I retrieve my valise. Alex told me I could use one of his carriages, but I shall have to find another way to leave if I cannot find him."

"You should take his carriage anyway," Amelia said. "I shall tell the coachman to take you wherever you wish to go."

Amelia was considering practicalities, but Madeleine was still examining Prudence's face in the firelight. "Tell me — why would Alex discuss how you would escape from Thorington?" she asked.

Prudence tried to keep her face unreadable. "He merely wished to help me. I'm sure he guessed that I wasn't happy to marry the duke."

Ellie toyed with her pencil, drawing spirals around the edge of the paper. "Now, why would Salford interfere if he didn't intend to marry you himself?"

Prudence shrugged.

"And why are you so intent on finding him, rather than just taking his carriage and leaving?" Madeleine asked.

"To thank him for his hospitality?"

It didn't sound anything like sincerity. Ellie laughed. "All right, no more questions. You should leave now. But we will wait here for Salford. It might do him good to hear our opinion on the matter."

"I very much doubt that he will appreciate it," Prudence said.

Amelia waved a hand. "Sometimes men need to be told what to do. In case Alex is still too much of a fool to see what he could have with you, we will make sure to explain it to him. Slowly, and with short words, so we don't confuse the poor thing."

Prudence did laugh then. They had no idea just how much Alex knew what he and she could have together — what they already had together. But now was not the time to educate them.

"Thank you for your company," she said, gathering up her hat. Her dress looked slightly better, since she'd surreptitiously redone the buttons, but there was nothing to be done for her hair. "I shall send word when I've safely settled elsewhere."

"Make sure you move frequently at first," Ellie warned. "And never give your own name. Pretending to be a widow would be a wise course."

Ellie had offered to go with her, but Prudence had declined. Ellie's red hair was too distinctive to hide, and the marchioness couldn't help but attract notice. Prudence nodded her thanks. "I shall be quite safe."

It was madness to think she could run away on her own. But if Boudicca had led the Celts into battle and Joan of Arc had fought the

English, Prudence could get herself to a country inn without incident. She picked up her reticule, went to the front hall, found the sleepy footman who had been waiting to see the women home, and sent for Alex's carriage.

She ordered the carriage to take her to Ellie's, but warned the driver that she would need him to take her out of London immediately after. The look he gave her said what he thought of that, but Alex had told her that he'd held the driver in readiness — the man wasn't surprised by the order, just disapproving.

She would retrieve her valise first. Then she would ask the carriage to take her west. Thorington might expect her to go to the Continent, despite the war, so Dover wasn't safe. He also might expect her to go north, toward Lancashire and Alex's country seat. So she would try Cornwall, and hope that the wilds there would dissuade the duke before he searched for her too intently.

But she planned to send Alex's carriage home from the first inn — the coat of arms emblazoned on the doors was too easy to find for anyone who searched for it. So perhaps she should take the coach north, to the first major carriage inn on the Great North Road. There, she could send the coach home, and then hire a new conveyance to double back and take her west.

It was a good plan. When the carriage stopped ten minutes later, she was still considering it, mulling over options and whether to use some of Thorington's money to hire outriders as well as a carriage. It was unlikely that she would be attacked by highwaymen, but...

The door finally opened. She turned, expecting the driver to help her down.

Instead, Thorington stepped up and pulled the door closed behind him. "Good evening, my dear," he said, taking the seat across from her and tossing a valise on the floor. "Where are we off to?"

CHAPTER TWENTY-NINE

Alex awoke with a blinding headache. He turned onto his back, but the movement made everything spin. He waited out the spinning sensation, waited until everything cleared. The headache still sawed viciously behind his eyeballs, but at least he could see when he opened his eyelids.

He was no longer drunk. He wished he was. Or perhaps he wished he was dead.

"I think he's awake," Nick said from leagues away.

"He should have stayed asleep," Ferguson said. There might have been a note of sympathy there, but it sounded mostly like laughter. "He cannot feel well."

Alex pushed himself up into a sitting position, then paused as everything spun again. When the world righted itself, he scowled. They were back in Nick's study, but he couldn't quite remember getting there after his heroic attempt to reach Prudence had been thwarted earlier. "What time is it?"

"Just past two," Ferguson said. "Really, Salford, you shouldn't drink if you react like that. I haven't seen someone lose consciousness after two glasses of brandy since Malcolm smuggled a bottle into Eton."

"In my defense, I was twelve," Malcolm said. "I can hold my brandy now."

"At least Salford hasn't puked all over his bed like you did," Ferguson observed.

Alex wanted to drop back to the couch and cover his eyes until they all left and his head stopped hurting. But it was two in the morning — far too late an hour for what he needed to do.

He was going to do it anyway. "I must go up to Miss Etchingham," he said.

He stood. The room spun, but it wasn't as bad this time...until Nick spoke. "She still isn't here. Nor is my wife. Do you think they met each other?"

Prudence shouldn't be out of the house this late. Had she already left London?

"Did she take your carriage?" he asked Nick.

"Only to your house. She sent it back. That was hours ago, though."

Alex wanted to punch the man. "Could you not have told me this hours ago?"

Nick held up his hands. "I didn't know until we found Miss Etchingham missing. By the time I questioned the stable staff, you were already incapacitated."

That just made Alex want to punch himself. "I need to find her."

"Do you want us to come with you?" Ferguson asked.

"No."

He walked away. They followed him like a party of peasants following a tumbrel to the guillotine.

"Leave me be," he said.

"My wife is at your house," Malcolm pointed out. "So is Nick's wife, if the stable staff is to be believed."

Ferguson sighed theatrically. "Which means my wife is likely there too. A shame, given Amelia's influence, but I tolerate it."

"I shall have to call you out for that eventually," Malcolm said. "Not now, though. We should take Alex home before he faints again."

"Or before he leaves you here," Nick observed. "I don't think he appreciates your meddling."

"I don't," Alex said over his shoulder.

But they didn't listen. They never did. He didn't have cause to be grateful for it until they reached Salford House, found three of the four women they sought in Alex's study, and learned that Prudence had departed twenty minutes earlier.

"How did you miss her?" Ellie asked, as though it was Alex's fault. "She should have been there within ten minutes."

His blood ran cold. "Thorington."

"Do you really think he would be able to find her in the middle of the night?" Ferguson asked.

He didn't answer them. He ran for the stables instead.

*   *   *

"I shall tell you again, even though you don't seem capable of comprehending," Prudence said, growing desperate. "I have absolutely no desire to marry you."

"You are boring me with your refusals," Thorington said, leaning back into the cushions and crossing his arms. "But I commend you for not crying. I would have to gag you then, and that would be unpleasant."

"You're mad," Prudence said. "How does no one know you're

mad?"

"I'm not mad. I'm powerful. There is an important difference."

The carriage was moving too fast for her to jump from it, although she'd already considered it twice. But she didn't know where they were. If she broke her leg in the jump, Thorington would probably take her to a priest before he took her to a bonesetter. And if she somehow managed to escape, it was still the dead of night — she could walk into a far worse situation than this one.

Although as she met Thorington's mocking gaze, she wasn't sure how many situations were worse.

"Why are you so determined to keep me?" she asked. It had bewildered her since the moment of his proposal. If she was trapped with him, she might as well get an answer.

"You have my fifty thousand pounds. I find that I need it back immediately."

She threw her reticule at him. "You can have everything on my person. We can go to the bank tomorrow to draw the rest of the funds. I haven't spent any of it."

He actually opened her bag to see how much money was inside, but the sum didn't impress him. He tossed it back to her. "Spend it at the modiste I shall take you to tomorrow. That hat is an abomination."

She was going to scream. She was still too angry to be scared — angry enough that she had completely lost control of her tongue. "If you force me to marry you, I shall wear sackcloth every day. I shall tell the entire ton that you are a wretched blackguard, and…and impotent, besides. I shall put arsenic in your soup and ants in your bed."

That last threat started off well and ended poorly. She stopped, flustered. Thorington laughed. "You sound positively pleasant compared to my last wife. We'll get along quite well after the second or third year, I'm sure."

"She was probably unpleasant because you were so horrid," Prudence spat out. "Did you beat her?"

Whatever humor had played around Thorington's mouth fled into the shadows. "I am many things, Miss Etchingham. But I have never beat a woman. You are tempting me, though."

She had crossed some line that she didn't realize the duke had — he was too outrageous for lines. She felt the oddest compulsion to apologize, but she bit it back. "Can you please return me to Lady Folkestone's? That is where I was going before you waylaid me."

"Do you wish for me to take you up the Great North Road as well? Or were you planning to go to Dover?"

She thought about brazening it out, but it was clear he planned to force her whether she had thought of escape or not. "How did you know I planned to leave?"

"You have been a trifle less grateful for this match than I had expected," Thorington said. "Not that it bothers me. But I plan for all eventualities."

"Were you following me?" she asked. "How did you know I was in this carriage?"

"I bribed servants in Alex's house to keep track of you. You should have used Lady Folkestone's carriage instead — I wasn't able to pay off any of them."

It was the only time she'd heard of him being thwarted, but it didn't give her much comfort. "Alex will find me, you know."

"He won't." Thorington leaned back, as calm as ever. "We'll be married before Alex even gets his boots on."

She sucked in a breath. She still wasn't scared. But her anger was giving way to an ugly, trapped feeling — as though all those choices she'd debated endlessly over had suddenly evaporated, leaving her only with this. "Where are you taking me?"

"St. George's. The priest is a friend of mine from childhood, and I gave a very large donation to the parish recently. I had so wanted to be married there — my mother is buried there, after all. The wedding will just have to be a few hours earlier than I had planned."

Her mouth tasted like ashes. "You're mad," she whispered.

He shrugged. "You'll recover. Wait until someone calls you 'your grace' for the first time. You shall forget Salford ever existed."

CHAPTER THIRTY

On horseback, Alex reached Thorington's house within three minutes. But even though he banged on the door, awoke the butler, and demanded to know where Thorington was, he didn't receive any satisfaction.

The duke had vanished. And Prudence had vanished along with him. The only information he received worth noting was that Thorington had left the residence in a carriage that wasn't his.

Alex was in a killing mood. His headache still raged, but it was nothing compared to the wild, desperate beat of his heart. He had to find Prudence before she came to harm. Even if he hadn't broken the curse, he would have felt that way. But he loved her more than anything — far too much to lose her now.

He wanted to betray the footman who occasionally spied on Thorington for him and demand to see the man, but it was unlikely that he knew where Thorington was going. Before he could do it anyway, Nick pulled him away from Thorington's door and nodded at the butler. The servant took the opportunity to shut Alex out and slam the bolts against him.

"No sense murdering a servant," Nick said as Alex pushed away his hand. "Save your wrath for the one who deserves it."

"I shall. If I can find them in time," Alex said, striding back to his horse.

Ferguson and Malcolm were waiting on the street, holding the horses and, seemingly, betting on the outcome of Alex's search. "Where next?" Malcolm asked. "Ferguson put ten pounds on Scotland, but I wager that Thorington has a special license. He won't need an anvil wedding at Gretna Green."

"Easier in Scotland," Ferguson said.

"But he would have to get Miss Etchingham there. Too much risk she would knee him in the bollocks and escape at the first coaching inn," Malcolm pointed out.

"I agree," Alex said. "She would have to be willing. And she most certainly isn't."

He looked across Grosvenor Square as though it could give him an answer. The grand houses were all mostly dark, its inhabitants either in bed or still out at their clubs. The streets were quiet enough that a carriage should be relatively easy to find, but Thorington had at least fifteen minutes on them. He had likely gone too far for them to catch without knowing his direction.

"What would you do if you were Thorington?" he asked them all.

Ferguson yawned. "Marry someone who appreciated me more."

Alex turned to the other, marginally saner, members of their group. "Carnach, what would you do?"

Malcolm shrugged. "Wait for you to force me to marry her — worked for me before."

He was going to murder them all. "If you cannot help, leave me to find her myself. I do not have time for your humor."

"We will find her together," Ferguson said, his tone suddenly serious. "Depend upon it."

Alex sighed. "Folkestone, do you have an idea that is more help-ful than the others?"

"I would take her to the closest priest and pay him to ignore her protests," Nick said, showing a bit of the ruthlessness that had earned him his fortune. "Thorington has the blunt to bribe anyone. No need to go to Scotland to do it — he could do it in London for the right price."

Thorington would never spend three days in a carriage with a crying woman — not that Prudence would spend three days crying. She would spend three days trying to kill him.

But the duke would want to stay close to London anyway. Alex knew the pressures on him well enough to know he wouldn't waste his time on an extended jaunt to Gretna Green. Thorington would want to end this quickly, with minimal fuss, in a place of his choosing.

And then, suddenly, he had his answer.

*   *   *

She wasn't going to be saved in time. She sensed the seconds tick-ing forward. Time was passing at the same rate it always did, but it was much too fast for her preference. They had reached St. George's within ten minutes of leaving Thorington's — almost as soon as he had told her where they were going. The priest was not entirely pleased to see them, but he wouldn't deny Thorington's presence.

He also wouldn't listen to her refusal. She had started to tell him that she would never, ever marry Thorington, but he had just told her to settle her nerves while he arranged for witnesses.

"I am going to kill you, your grace," she said mutinously. She was sitting in the priest's parlor, but only because Thorington had pushed her into a chair and told her, quite politely, that he would tie her to it if she tried to run.

"I look forward to the attempt," the duke said. "Now, will you put on the dress, or do you need me to play lady's maid for you?"

The valise he'd brought wasn't for him — it was for her, with a lovely dress of green silk that would be perfect for her coloring. She loved it on sight, and hated him for it.

"I am not wearing it," she said, trying to stall.

"I wanted to marry in St. George's, but I shall not marry a lady dressed as an urchin," he said. "Put on the dress, my dear."

"No."

He stood up. "I suppose I shall have to help you."

She had begun to despair. She didn't want him to touch her. She didn't want this night to draw to what seemed to be its inevitable conclusion. She didn't want...

She heard voices in the chapel. Raised voices. Masculine voice. *Angry* masculine voices.

"Alex," she breathed.

"Damn it all to bloody hell," Thorington said. "Stay here."

He left her. He should have tied her up if he'd meant for her to obey — there was no way she was staying there otherwise. She dashed after him, sliding into the chapel just in time to see Alex striding up the aisle. He had her friends' husbands with him, but he was the only one she could watch. She'd always seen him as scholarly before — handsome, but more at home with a pen than a weapon.

But tonight, he looked like a knight coming forward to defend his lady's honor. There was a dark menace in his eyes, along with a clarity of purpose that made her heart sing.

He had come for her. He would protect her, pull her into his arms and kiss her…

He didn't come for her yet, though. He walked directly to Thorington and punched him in the mouth.

"You bloody arse," Alex swore. Thorington raised his fists, but Alex swung again before he could shield himself properly, striking him just below the eye.

Thorington retreated, but only far enough to avoid Alex's next punch. He came back with a swing aimed precisely at Alex's jaw, snapping Alex's head back.

Prudence shrieked, but she clasped her hands over her mouth to avoid distracting Alex. He didn't even seem to feel the blow. "The lady doesn't wish to marry you," he said savagely, punching Thorington again. "Take your revenge on me if you must, but leave her out of it."

The priest came up and tried to pull them apart, but Malcolm strong-armed the priest back into the periphery. Prudence thought of interrupting…

But then she thought better of it. It wasn't a very proper thought, but she hated Thorington. And Alex, after all, was winning.

He hit Thorington again. Ferguson and Nick were critiquing his stance, mostly admiringly. But Alex and Thorington didn't seem to hear any of it. "Promise me you will stay away from her," Alex demanded, holding his fists up but not striking again. "Vow it on your mother, or I will kill you."

Thorington, oddly, dropped his fists away from his face. "Don't bring her into this," he said.

Prudence was utterly confused. Alex wasn't, though. He dropped his fists as well. "She's what you've done everything for, though — isn't that right? Vow it on her grave and I'll believe you. I might even help you."

She couldn't see Thorington's face, but she saw him bow his head. "You did it, Salford. You won."

"What happened with his mother?" Nick whispered, not quietly enough, to Ferguson.

Ferguson shrugged. "Don't know. Family's a mess, though — would have been smart for Thorington to marry someone as steady as Miss Etchingham."

Other women would have taken umbrage at being deemed merely steady, but Prudence was too focused on Alex and Thorington to react. Alex's face, despite the swelling that had already begun around his jaw, seemed oddly sympathetic to the man he had just tried to kill.

"Did my…winning affect you?" he asked quietly.

Thorington was silent for several moments. Finally, he said, "Four days ago I thought I was having heart palpitations. Then I went to Wattier's and lost a thousand pounds on a single turn of hazard."

Four days earlier was when she and Alex had made love at the pub. They had made love…

Had Alex broken the curse then, not even knowing how it was done?

But after, when she had gone home, Thorington had come to her and told her they were marrying immediately. If what he said was true, he knew then, even though they did not, that the curse was broken. And he would have forced her to marry him anyway.

She went up behind him and clouted him on the head with her reticule. "You are a vile, vile man," she said.

"And you are a thief with fifty thousand pounds I am in desperate need of," he shot back, pulling her reticule out of her hands.

The conversation had gotten far too deep for the other men, who all gaped at their trio as though they were a poorly written, but still fascinating, theatrical production. But Alex seemed to have pieced together exactly the same puzzle that she had. He came up to her, finally, and put his arm around her.

"We will give you the money, Thorington," he said. "Consider it a peace offering between old friends."

"You were never so magnanimous when you were losing," Thorington said bitterly.

"And you were never so friendly when you were winning," Alex said. "Take it, or not. But either way, I am marrying Miss Etchingham, and you can go to the devil."

As proposals went, it wasn't much of one — in fact, it wasn't one. But the *yes* that had waited in her heart came to life, burning with urgency now that its time was at hand.

Alex seemed to realize, an instant later, what he had said. He turned to her, pulling her slightly away from their audience. His jaw was turning purple and she was sure he smelled of brandy, but the light in his eyes could only be described as radiant. "I forgot to let you have your say. Miss Prudence Etchingham, will you do me the incredible honor of marrying me?"

"*Yes*," she said. "Yes."

He wrapped his arms around her and kissed her, as thoroughly as he liked and much more thoroughly than he should have. Their audience was better about it than she might have expected, but her ears were stopped up to their comments anyway.

"I love you, Prue," he murmured as they broke away. "More than anything."

"I know," she said.

He grinned. "Don't get too cocky, love."

It was an idle threat. She stroked her hand over his heart. "I love you too, Alex. I thought I loved you before. But now...I love you more than I'd ever dreamed was possible."

"I know," he said.

She laughed as he kissed her again. They had said yes. They would say yes again in the morning, in front of a priest and a crowd of people who wondered if they had misread the invitation to Miss Etchingham's wedding. They would say yes again in bed, and at the breakfast table, and in his study, and as they grew old together.

They would always say yes. And it was the best word in the world.

CHAPTER THIRTY-ONE

"I cannot believe we are doing this," Prudence whispered to Alex as they waited to greet their guests.

Alex had wrapped his arm very improperly around her waist. "Smile, darling. No need to add to the gossip by looking annoyed with me."

She glared up at him, but she couldn't feign anger when they were both so happy. She laughed instead. "I never thought I'd manage to escape Thorington and still celebrate my wedding in his house."

Alex had commandeered all of Thorington's plans, from the priest to the church to the breakfast after. The wedding itself had been delayed by a few minutes — the bishop didn't like being dragged from his bed at six in the morning to give Alex a marriage license — but the guests had all arrived on time.

And they were all supremely confused about what had happened.

"When were you going to tell me that you were marrying Salford instead of Thorington?" her mother asked. She had somehow edged her way to the front of the crowd so that she could greet Prudence first. "I didn't realize it until I saw Salford standing at the front of the church."

Prudence kissed her on the cheek. "It was all rather…sudden. I hope you approve?"

Lady Harcastle smiled. "A happy countess is better than a down-trodden duchess."

On another day Prudence might have taken offense, but today she only felt like teasing her mother back. "Surely the title doesn't matter all that much," she said.

"I hope not," Lady Harcastle said. "It would be a shame if you refused to associate with me because my title is less than yours."

She was smiling about something that Prudence didn't understand. But then Ostringer reached Lady Harcastle's side. "I offer you many felicitations, Lord and Lady Salford," he said. "As I said, it's the best thing in the world, marrying for love."

Then he offered Lady Harcastle his arm. She smiled up at him. It was like all the years and all her grief had melted away.

Prudence gasped.

"Oh, don't be so scandalized," Lady Harcastle grumbled. "You act like you've never seen a love match before."

They strolled away before Prudence could close her mouth. Alex cleared his throat. "That was…strange."

Prudence didn't respond. There wasn't time; their guests were on them in earnest. Everyone had the same questions, although none of them were so uncouth as to ask them. They danced around the issue of Prudence's broken engagement to Thorington, even though they surely all wondered why he had disappeared and why Alex was standing in his place.

"Where is our esteemed host?" one of the bolder ones asked.

Alex shrugged. "Indisposed."

They hadn't seen Thorington since he'd told them to take the church and the breakfast so the food wouldn't go to waste. He was surely somewhere in London, but while he had finally agreed to let Prudence go, it didn't mean he was eager to watch her marry Alex instead.

The next guest looked at Alex's jaw. "Did you hit your head on something, my lord?"

Prudence smiled as though nothing was amiss. "Poor man ran into a door. Dreadful luck."

"A door?" Alex whispered in her ear as the guest walked away. "Am I that much of an idiot?"

"Do you want me to say I punched you?" she suggested. "Because we can't say that Thorington did it or the rumors will really fly."

He grinned. "Carry on, darling."

The guests wouldn't get any answers that satisfied them. But as long as Prudence was safely married and none of her friends or family seemed particularly upset by it, the rest of the ton would probably still accept her.

It helped that her friends occupied the highest rungs of the social ladder — and that they all seemed eager to take credit for her marriage. "I am thrilled we convinced you to stop being stupid, brother," Amelia said as she came up and kissed Alex on the cheek.

"I would have married Prudence without your interference," Alex said.

Amelia patted him indulgently on the arm. Then she embraced Prudence. "Welcome to the family, sister," she said. Then she leaned in to Prudence's ear. "If he is always so slow to realize what he must do, hit him over the head until he learns to behave," she whispered.

"I heard that," Alex muttered.

Malcolm clapped him on the back. "Glad to see you came to your senses. I will guard your house while you go on your honeymoon."

"What if you and Amelia took our honeymoon for us and I guarded my house instead?" Alex suggested.

"No need," Malcolm said, some unholy humor brightening his grey eyes. "We like your house. We might have to stay the rest of the summer to enjoy it to its fullest."

Prudence laughed as her new sister-in-law and brother-in-law made way for the next guests. "I should have thought about your family before I agreed to marry you, my lord."

"Thank the gods you forgot about them," Alex said. "Would that I could be so lucky."

His cousin Madeleine found them next, with Ferguson, Ellie, and Nick close behind. "I must admit there was a part of me that had hoped you would be a duchess," Madeleine said to Prudence. "Then we could have lorded it over Amelia together."

"Amelia doesn't give a fig for titles," Prudence said. "Can you forgive me for settling for an earl?"

Madeleine eyed Alex skeptically, then gave Prudence a sympathetic grin. "You could have done better. But I'm glad you're part of the family now."

"I thank you for your judgment," Alex said drily. "You could have done better, too, but I still love you."

Ferguson tapped his walking stick on the floor. "Careful, Salford. You might become my least favorite Staunton with words like those."

"I am a Staunton now," Prudence said. "Where do I rank?"

Ferguson took her hand and kissed it as though he was just as rakish as he'd been in the past. "Above all the others, my dear. I wish you very happy with this Puritan you've captured."

Ellie interrupted them. "Salford's no more of a Puritan than you are, brother. Now let me congratulate them for taking my excellent advice."

"Your excellent advice?" Ferguson asked. "Do you think it was *your* actions that brought this about?"

"Of course," Ellie said, winking conspiratorially at Prudence. "I told her to tell Salford how she felt."

Ferguson sniffed. "I was instrumental in helping Salford rescue her. She could have been Thorington's bride this morning if it weren't for me."

Nick sighed. "I am sorry, Lord and Lady Salford. You deserve better than to have this joyous occasion marred by the lot of us."

Prudence and Alex looked at each other. She saw in his eyes exactly what she felt — love, amusement, slow-burning lust, and mild exasperation.

She grinned at him. He grinned back, a bit lopsided, as though he was thinking of something far removed from whatever their friends were still bantering about. She felt his arm tighten around her waist.

"Shall we leave our friends to their debate?" Alex asked.

Prudence nodded. "Perhaps they can send word of their conclusions so that we know who to thank for our marriage."

He pulled her through their circle, not stopping to acknowledge their laughter. They didn't stop for the remaining guests, or for the footmen who scrambled to gather their outer garments, or for the small crowd outside hoping to catch a glimpse of them. Carriages lined the street, and Alex stole the closest one, not willing to wait for his own carriage to be brought from the stables.

Prudence caught a glimpse of the coat of arms on the door as he gave the driver the extravagant sum of three guineas to drive to Salford House. "Ferguson won't be happy to lose his carriage," she said as Alex handed her up through the door.

"Will he not?" he said, leaping up after her. "I should give the driver an extra three guineas to crash it into the Serpentine after."

"Evil man," she said. Then she nestled herself beside him as the carriage lurched into motion. "We are never going to hear the end of it from them, are we?"

He kissed the top of her head. "They'll all find someone else's life to meddle in soon enough. Thorington had better stay away from his house until they're gone or he might find himself at their mercy."

"It would almost be enough to make me feel sorry for him," Prudence said.

"You should feel sorry for him." His lips moved closer to her ear, and she shivered as his voice turned lower. "I pity all the men who will never have you."

She arched her head away from him, letting him trail kisses down her neck. "I'd wager you don't pity them that much."

Alex laughed. "You know me too well."

He kissed her then. They had time for everything they wanted to do to each other, every pleasure they had ever dreamed of.

Still, they reached Salford House far too soon. She was breathless by the time they arrived, somehow both eager for a bed and desperate not to stop. "Do we have to go in?" she asked.

They would have to explain to the butler that Prudence had returned as their new countess. Then they would have to let the servants cheer for the marriage. Alex should give them ale and porter, and possibly the afternoon off. By the time all of that was accomplished, Malcolm and Amelia would be home from the breakfast and looking to give suggestions about their honeymoon.

Alex's darkening eyes showed that he'd just had the same realization. "No," he said, kissing her again. "Ferguson was so eager to help.

Let's see how far his carriage can take us."

He called up to the driver and ordered the man to take them as far north as he could go before the horses needed rest. Then he returned his attentions to Prudence, kissing her collarbone while she laughed at his audacity.

"I knew marrying you would put me in danger," she said. "Do you plan to make a criminal of me?"

He stroked his hand up her back, then began attacking the pins holding her hair in place. "Between forgeries and horse thieving, we make quite the pair."

"Should we become highwaymen next?" she asked, wrapping her arms around his neck. "I've always thought it might be rather thrilling."

"You might have to live in a tent," Alex warned her. "Criminals on the road don't always have access to houses."

"How sad," she said. "I would have made an excellent highwayman."

"I don't doubt you would. But I find that I prefer badly behaved bluestockings. Especially *my* badly behaved bluestocking."

Prudence smiled, a slow, secret smile that made Alex's eyes light up. "Be careful what you wish for, my lord. I can be *very* badly behaved."

He kissed her, not particularly well behaved himself. "I would wish for that every day of my life, my lady."

She leaned up to kiss him back. "Then I think we shall be very happy together. Until Ferguson has us transported to Australia for stealing his carriage."

"That would be an adventure," Alex said. "But I plan to keep you safe here in England, where you will be much more comfortable while

I ravish you."

She laughed. "How dastardly of you, taking advantage of my virtue like this."

His hand skimmed down her shoulder and palmed one of her breasts. "We're only getting started, Prudence. There's a whole world for us to explore together. And I, for one, don't want to wait a moment longer to begin."

She stroked her fingers across his jaw. "You were worth the wait, Alex. But we don't have to wait anymore."

And so they didn't. If the driver heard just how badly they behaved, he was too smart to mention it.

THE END

Books by Sara Ramsey

<u>Muses of Mayfair</u>

Heiress Without a Cause
Scotsmen Prefer Blondes
The Marquess Who Loved Me
The Earl Who Played With Fire

<u>The Heiress Games</u>

Duke of Thorns - coming Spring 2014

What's next?

Thanks so much for your support for the Muses of Mayfair! I still have more stories to tell with this group, so there will be more Muses stories in the future. But the next book starts a spinoff series about a group of female cousins from a scandalous, dying line - one of whom is on a collision course with the Duke of Thorington. Thorington is in for the shock of his life, and I can't wait to share it with you.

You can find out more when *Duke of Thorns* comes out in early 2014. If you want to be the first to hear about launch dates, special sneak peeks, and giveaways, please make sure to visit www.sararamsey. com and sign up for my newsletter. You can also get all the latest news on Twitter (@sara_ramsey) or Facebook (www.facebook.com/ sara.ramsey).

I really appreciate the time you've spent with the Muses of Mayfair. If you feel so inclined, please consider leaving a review (positive, negative, or otherwise) on your favorite bookseller's site. Happy reading!

Best wishes,

Sara Ramsey
San Francisco, California

About the author

Sara Ramsey writes fun, feisty Regency historical romances. She won the prestigious 2009 Romance Writers of America® Golden Heart® award with her second book, *Scotsmen Prefer Blondes*. Her first book, *Heiress Without A Cause*, was a 2011 Golden Heart finalist.

Sara grew up in a small town in Iowa, and her obsession with fashion, shoes, and all things British is clearly a rebellion against her hopelessly uncool youth. She graduated from Stanford University in 2003 with a degree in Symbolic Systems (also known as cognitive science) and a minor in history. She is currently living the hip romance writer life in San Francisco, California. Read all about her Regency obsessions and upcoming works at www.sararamsey.com.

www.ingramcontent.com/pod-product-compliance
Lightning Source LLC
Chambersburg PA
CBHW032150190626
46814CB00005BA/1929